HEARTLESS DARK

J. P. BUXTON

First published in Great Britain in 2011
by Hodder Children's Books

1

A Catalogue record for this book is available from the British Library

ISBN 978 0 340 97006 5

Typeset in Adobe Garamond by Avon DataSet Ltd,
Bidford on Avon, Warwickshire

Printed and bound in Great Britain by
CPI Bookmarque Ltd, Croydon, Surrey

The paper and board used in this paperback by Hodder Children's Books
are natural recyclable products made from wood grown in
sustainable forests. The manufacturing processes conform to the
environmental regulations of the country of origin.

Hodder Children's Books
a division of Hachette Children's Books
338 Euston Road, London NW1 3BH
An Hachette UK company
www.hachette.co.uk

For Angharad

Loss is nothing else but change and change is nature's delight.

Marcus Aurelius, *Meditations VIII*, 5, 168 CE

Promise to watch, death to use, strong and warm with the moon at the top.

Pictish nonsense verse, 52 CE

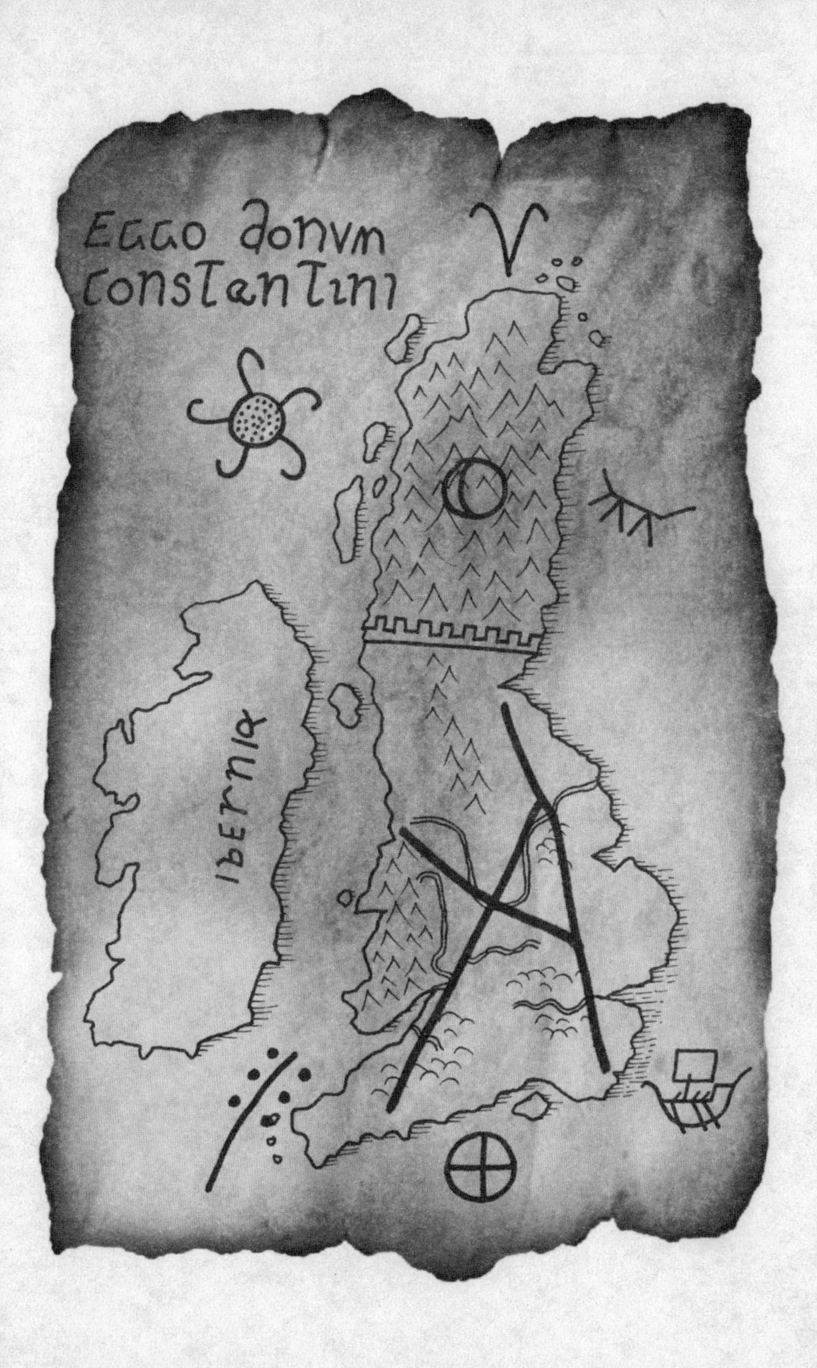

Eggo donum
constantini
IBERNIA

1

Sun: rising or setting, beginning or ending

First to Jenna, Queen Jenna, leaning on the warm, stone windowsill, staring at the lake.

Deep in thought, she didn't see the children skimming across the water in their little rafts, nor the bee fly right past her nose with its butter-coloured leggings of pollen. She was deaf to monks chanting in the little chapel and to the hoarse, manly noises of the king's bodyguard as they practised their swordplay.

All she heard were her own doomy thoughts and all she saw was trouble ahead.

The problem is this, she said to herself: on the one hand, it's hard to be honest because the truth is so awful. On the other hand, I can't carry on pretending things are fine. I'm the high queen, I'm fifteen and I should be up to dealing with whatever's put in front me. But oh, it's horrible.

Of course, the weather didn't help. It was the hottest summer anyone could remember. Cattle groaned. Birds panted. The big inland lake around the island had shrunk so the lake people's houses stood high on their stilts, freakish and spidery. Strange creatures had been spotted: man-sized owls in the Polden hills; singing sea creatures in the River Baridos; fairies that bit the heads off chickens . . .

Everything was ominous and of course people were blaming it on the high king, her husband, Artognu. Jenna's problem was that she could not really blame them for blaming him.

The thing was this: having been brought up a princess in the bracing, northern kingdom of Prydhain, she actually knew that ruling boiled down to two basic rules. One, it was impossible to be right all the time, and two, you accepted help whenever it looked useful.

Now, there are ways of sharing these insights with your husband. You might take him to one side, tell him he's wonderful, so wonderful that he's in danger of exhausting people with his brilliance and might he not be exhausting himself? Or you might sit him down and point out that if it took a blacksmith ten years to learn his craft, how could the proverbial boy from nowhere expect to know everything about ruling in three months?

Had she done either of these things? Well, not exactly.

Instead she had pretty much told the king that he was wrong about everything and needed all the help he could get. Not surprisingly he had lost his temper, something he had been doing a lot recently. That temper had meant he had already lost the services of Melanius, his trusted adviser, and Jenna suspected that he would have sacked her if he had known how. Not knowing how, he had stormed out, making this the most depressing morning since she had become queen. Tog's mother, notable Cornish royalty, was an alcoholic and Jenna was beginning to understand why.

I just want my past back, Jenna thought. I just want to be the brave, vicious girl who thought she could take on the world with her wits and a selection of deadly hardware.

Then she slapped her hand down on the windowsill and said out loud, 'But I'm not, so get a grip. Either I stick with Tog and try and make him a better a king, or I . . . what? Betray him? Replace him? Impossible. Why? Because I love him.'

That was it. Love had made things so simple at first; now it was making life so much more complicated. She loved the way Tog was trying to be a good king and she admired the fact he plodded on against all the odds. She loved the way he smiled when he finally grasped he had a problem, then the way a little crease would appear between his eyebrows as he tried to work out how to solve it. But, she realized with a tight little skip of the heart, what she wanted most of all was to love him because he won through.

'So do something about it,' she said. 'And get a move on.'

A loud shout came from outside. Vinny, her personal servant, bustled into the bedroom, looking sweaty and swearing.

'Bloody kids! I hate them.'

Happy to be distracted, Jenna asked, 'Goats in the flowers again?'

Vinny blinked. 'No. A *kid*. Sneaking and spying.'

'Oh, that sort of kid. How old?'

'It was small. Well, little younger than you, your – er – gracious highness. Little monster.'

'Have you seen it before?' Jenna asked.

'Not this one. Anyway, talking of monsters . . .'

Jenna rolled her eyes and said, 'I blame the parents.'

Vinny, rolling her eyes in return, replied, 'No, monsters. The lakers have found a real one out at Fenny Castle. It's got horrible eyes, teeth like a pike and claws like an eagle. About this long.' She held her big red hands out wide.

'Seriously?'

'I have it on the best authority,' Vinny said pompously.

Jenna had never trusted authority. 'We should go and see. Have fun. Make a picnic,' she said.

'There was another thing.' Vinny frowned. 'This man, said he was a bard, wanted to see you. Ugly great thing. I sent him packing but he's still hanging around.'

'A bard? I'm not having a bard ruin my picnic by singing. I'll deal with it later.'

Her mind moved on. In fact, she could kill two birds with one stone, she thought, forcing herself to form the phrase in British. She could invite Kai and Allanza, Tog's two best friends, and they could work out how to help him together.

After all, when it came down to it, she owed him. They all did. They all owed him everything.

2

Next, to Kai and Allanza who spent the night on top of the Tor, trying to catch what little breeze there was.

The Tor was the highest point of the island and dawn found them marooned in mist, everything dreamy, and the distant hills showing like dolphins in a golden sea.

Allanza was huge, talked softly and was a good person to have on your side in a fight. Wiry and red haired, Kai was a complete liability but ruthlessly honest. He liked to deal with what he called the matter in the hand and if anyone objected, he'd look irritated and say they should just crack on.

Right now he was making a point. Or rather, a great many points.

'I'm not superstitious but the truth is that it all began

to go wrong when he threw the sacred sword away. Forget the fact that we all risked our lives carrying it back here. Forget it being the most famous sword in the whole country, if not the world—'

Allanza interrupted. 'Be fair. He threw the old sword away because it had been used for blood sacrifice and he wanted a fresh start. And keep your voice down, please. One of the guards might hear.'

There were four guards on the Tor, facing east, west, south and north. They worked four shifts and watched the country all day and all night as part of their training.

Kai flapped his hand at Allanza's objection and snapped, 'The sword should be bigger than his feelings. People expect him to have it and, let's face it, he hasn't got much else going for him.'

Allanza stripped a grass stem and sucked its sweet white base. 'I just wish Melanius hadn't taken off. Tog needs—'

'Melanius didn't *take off.* Tog fired him.'

'No.'

'Yup. I just found out. They had an argument, and that was that. He's been banished. It'll be one of us next.'

Melanius was a Greek merchant/imperial Byzantine spy who had rescued Tog, Jenna and Allanza from freezing to death on the Cornish moors just three months ago. Along with his brutally efficient English mercenary called

Borthweald, he'd been a fixture at Court, always encouraging Tog to look beyond what people told him and examine instead what they wanted from him.

Allanza shifted uneasily. 'We still should remember what he did for us. You'd have starved to death and I'd be a slave. If he needs our help now—'

'That's exactly the point I'm trying to make. We need to help him but first we need to be honest with each other. He's out of his depth. He ran out of money and had to sack half the army, then sent his best general off to guard the northern approaches when he should be keeping an eye on him here. I mean, have you seen Jenna's face in those council meetings? She winces when Tog tries to make a decision. She'll end up despising him, you mark my words.'

'Shh,' Allanza said sharply. 'It's her.' He nodded to the brow of the Tor where Jenna had just appeared, waving and out of breath after the climb.

'I need to see you both!' she called.

Kai shut up but the damage had been done. The guards had overheard him and, as soon as they went off duty, started spreading the news: the queen despised the king and, what was more, she had climbed all the way to the top of the Tor to arrange a secret rendezvous with his two best friends somewhere out on the lake — and well away from the island. Who knew what they were up to?

When the new shift of guards took over, they lay down on the grass, played dice or just dozed. After all, why should they stay loyal to a king whose wife and two best friends were scheming behind his back?

3

And now to Artognu, High King of Britain, sitting on top of his too-big throne and trying to radiate a haughty calm – without much success, it has to be said.

He was the youngest person in the narrow, thatched hall and would have swapped places gladly with any one of his guests, courtiers or servants. Or slaves for that matter.

His hands gripped the carved ends of the arm rests and sweat stuck them to the smooth wood. His newfangled crown – all the rage on the continent, he had been assured – was too big and threatened to slide down over his eyes. He fought with acid in his mouth and sickness in his stomach. Some days he threw up before these audiences. Still, at least he didn't have to worry about anyone stabbing him in the back when they could just turn up and watch him die a little, day after day.

The hall was packed and stuffy – small hall rather than big crowd – and, even with the main doors open and the shutters taken down, people were restless as the summer heat built up. Not that there was much to keep them inside at the best of times: no hangings on the wall, no gold on the woodwork and precious little intrigue or gossip. In other words, a small, poor Court for a small, poor king.

Mornings were given over to ambassadors from various kingdoms, tribal leaders and assorted chancers. The work was almost over, just an introduction to someone claiming to be a bard and an ambassador from the north.

The ambassador was small and clever-looking, with cropped, businesslike white hair and a beautiful cloak of sky-blue wool. 'I'll be blunt, my lord: we are concerned about any challenges to your authority,' he said. 'Your security affects all the kingdoms, all the tribes and all the people of Britain. My question is: have you heard the rumours of an attack and what steps have you taken to protect your position?'

An awkward silence fell. Tog's advisers, General Kradok and the Abbot Hyacinth, had told him to be distant and give nothing away but it was hard when someone asked such a direct question. These things never had happened when Melanius was here and Tog was only beginning to understand the work his former adviser had done behind the scenes. But Tog had argued with him, just as he argued with everyone else, shouting that he was sick of being told what to do and he never wanted to see him again. Mistake. When a king says something like that, people make it happen and within the hour Melanius and his bodyguard, Borth, had been thrown off the island. No one had heard of them since.

Tog felt his mask slipping. The ambassador had clever eyes and needed a good answer. He couldn't think of one and now the crowd of courtiers were staring at him, whispering behind their hands, sniggering . . .

'Umm,' he said. 'Yes. Steps are having to be taken and . . . I mean, er . . .'

Kradok cleared his throat fussily. 'The king is saying that we have taken all necessary steps,' while Hyancith followed with, 'Merely to have *heard* of *rumours* of an attack in no way presupposes that such an attack will occur, thus rendering redundant the second half of your question.'

The ambassador tried again but the Court had lost interest. His words were drowned out by a growing hubbub and all Tog could hear were a few disjointed words: 'If . . . do not know . . . Perhaps help . . . people . . . saying . . . queen is the . . .'

The queen is the . . . ? It sounded like 'key', Tog thought. A memory stirred like a vole in grass but his head was so crammed with caution and diplomacy that there was no room for anything else. Anyway, Hyacinth had replaced the ambassador with a shambling, long-limbed, round-shouldered figure whose thin hair was smeared over a large bald patch and whose face looked like cracked pastry. 'This is the bard we were talking about,' he whispered. 'He has travelled the world. He has been to Rome, my lord. He will add lustre to your court but be sure to find out what his rates are.'

The bard's dark, rather wet eyes widened and sent an intense blast of interest at Tog, but he could only think of the ambassador. He nodded and pushed past, blushing as the crowd parted in front of him.

'The king is leaving,' a courtier called. 'Clear the way!'

He was the son of a wealthy warlord who laughed at Tog's jokes and crucially had never offered him any advice whatsoever. Tog thanked him, noticing that the courtier wore rather more gold than he did.

'The king is dining?'

'I'm sorry?'

'As part of the queen's party?'

Too slow to recognize a trap, Tog walked straight into it. 'What party?'

'You didn't know? I beg your pardon, my lord. She's on a picnic with my lords Kai and Allanza, but I imagine it's all quite above board. They have taken a boat to Fenny Castle where a fabulous creature has been discovered. But what entertainment has the king planned while his wife and friends are . . . enjoying themselves together?'

He smirked; Tog floundered then suddenly realized that the ambassador had slipped out the hall. He pushed his way out after him and looked around. There was the monks' main dormitory, there were the royal quarters up the hill, there was the little church that the Christman himself was supposed to have built. A sheep wandered across the grass, followed by a line of adopted ducklings. Had the man rowed off across the lake already?

Kradok bustled out of the hall, relentless and fussy. 'My lord?' His ash-blond hair was dark with sweat and he looked flustered.

Tog held a hand up. 'Not now, General. That ambassador—'

'Exactly what I wanted to talk about, my lord. Exactly that. A troublemaker, if you want my opinion.'

'He said something about the queen.'

'The queen? What about the queen?'

Tog looked at him suspiciously. 'I suppose you know all

about her picnic with Kai and Allanza on Fenny Castle?'

'On Fenny Castle? But she can't—'

'But she what?' Tog snapped. 'Isn't she free to do what she likes? Am I meant to keep her on a lead?'

Kradok's eyes went dead and Tog suddenly remembered that his general had been having wife trouble of his own recently – some nonsense about her going off with the fairies, which always meant something rather different. Tragic Kradok: that was what people were calling him. 'I'm sorry,' Tog said. 'I shouldn't have . . . I mean I . . .'

'My lord wishes for a boat to find his queen. My lord shall have a boat,' Tragic Kradok said coldly and walked quickly away.

Tog looked around for the ambassador one last time, then followed Kradok to find a boat.

4

Now Jenna, to Vinny, Kai and Allanza, punting off to see the monster.

Allanza enjoyed the easy rhythm of lifting the pole, letting it drop through his hands, pushing down into the shallow water of the lake and using it to steer the craft through the network of water-alleys. Jenna was trailing her fingers in the water and looked relaxed for the first time in weeks. Kai lay on his back, stared at a hovering hawk and, above all, was silent. Vinny fanned herself and hummed a new song about winnowing.

Life should be like this all the time, Allanza thought, as the strange lopsided mound of Fenny Castle rose above the reed tops. He slid the punt up to a rotting jetty and they disembarked, all apart from Vinny who flapped and clucked until he offered to carry her so she could swoon in his arms.

Half a dozen lake people were gathered at the end of a spit of black soil, looking at the monster that was crouched in an eel trap. The trap was made of bent willow; the monster seemed to be made of slime, teeth and gristle.

'Move back, move back for the queen.' Kai liked this sort of thing. The lake people turned their attention to the royal party and nodded politely.

Allanza knelt and put his head close to the basket.

'It's hideous,' he said.

The moaning rose quickly to a crescendo and he jumped back as the creature spat explosively. It was covered in muddy scales, and had a small flat head with evil-looking blue eyes, a lithe body and a long, thin tail. It seemed to be starting the moan/spit cycle again.

'It's just a skinny otter,' Kai laughed. He broke off a reed and poked it through the bars of the cage. This time there was an explosion of movement. The reed end was shredded.

'Some otter,' Allanza said. 'Anyway, its tail's far too thin. I think it's a sort of weasel. What do we do?'

'Too big for a weasel. Kill it and take it to the Lady of the Lake. She might be able to do something with its bones,' Kai suggested.

'Ask the lakers to tell us what they know,' Jenna said.

Kai drew himself up and addressed the crowd. 'You people. Approach the queen. Come on. Don't be scared.'

A mud-coloured man with a lopsided head approached and was joined by a younger man with a beard. Neither was scared; both looked polite and curious.

'Well,' Kai said. 'What do you make of this . . . monster?'

'Him be smallish for a monster,' the mud-coloured man said. 'Angry though.'

'Angry is often the way of monsters, my tadpole,' the younger one corrected him gently. ' 'Tis very angry though. And as ugly as you. Every bit.'

'Who caught him?' Kai demanded.

'The eel trap, he caught him,' the second laker suggested, looking at the first. 'He's a cunning little trap, though not so cunning as not to trap a monster rather than an eel. So only cunning-ish, he be. The trap, I mean.'

'I don't care about the trap's intelligence,' Kai snapped. 'I mean, who does the trap belong to?'

The lakers, who cultivated vagueness when it came to matters of ownership, looked at each other again. 'The liddle monster?' the first one said slowly. 'That's why he went in. Mebbe.'

Jenna could see the conversation was going nowhere.

'And why do you think the monster went into the trap?' she asked politely.

'Mebbe for mortal love of the trap, mebbe for the wriggly ol' eel who was in it. I'd lifted him and left him and were planning to come back and look at him, but when I did so, who was there? The liddle monster.'

'So the trap was on land when the monster went in?' Jenna said.

'Mostly.'

'It's hungry,' she said decisively. She approached the cage very slowly and waved a pigeon wing over it. The monster's eyes followed the meat. Jenna put a finger through the mesh. The monster didn't attack; it sneezed.

'It's cold,' Jenna said. 'I want it. Unleash it, then I desire to remove it with me to mine picnicking place.' When she was nervous, she muddled up talking-British with poetry-British. Now she turned to Kai and Allanza. 'But of all the most, of Tog talk I must.'

5

Tog waved at a group of lake people before following the trail of flattened grass that wound up the hill towards the fortifications.

The castle was protected by two earth rings with a ditch between them, just too wide for an armed man to jump. Ideally, you would defend the first wall and kill the enemy as they tried to climb it, but if they got over that, they would be in the ditch and you could kill them there as well. These days the ramparts were broken by tree roots and the slopes blurred by wild flowers. An old soldier with no teeth had told Tog that there were a dozen abandoned forts within a day's walk from the island and each one had once had its own king and each king had since been forgotten.

He shook his head. Forget about it. Today you are

going to have a picnic. He heard voices from inside the ramparts – Kai sounding off by the sound of it – and laughed. That was so like Kai, Tog thought fondly.

The further he was from Court, the lighter his mood became. The Court was poisoning him, he realized with blinding clarity. Of course things were better away from Hyacinth, Kradok, ambassadors and weird bards. Why shouldn't Jenna go off with Allanza and Kai? They were her friends too. And as for that row this morning, he knew what she had meant but had been too proud to admit it. Right now, all he wanted was to sit on the grass with his back against a tree, eat good food, talk with his friends and try and remember that life was, more or less, fine.

He reached the outer ramparts and, instead of walking straight in through the entrance, thought he would follow the ditch round, climb up the rampart and surprise them by calling out something like: 'As High King of Britain I command you to give me some pie.' There would be a moment of shocked surprise and then they'd all laugh and things would get back to normal again. He felt happier than he had for months.

Out of the eel pot, the monster was transformed. It shook, sneezed, then followed them up the hill, making a strange wailing sound, and trying to steal the food from Vinny's basket. Now it was stretched out in the sunlight, cleaning a back leg. Almost dry, it was elegant and dangerous and made Jenna profoundly uncomfortable. When a small blue butterfly danced in front of it, it shot out a paw and trapped the insect on the ground. The monster watched it twitch, sniffed it, let it go, hit it again and ate it. Where had it come from? What was it doing? Along with the fairies and giant owls, it felt like another omen. She made a mental note to go and see the Lady of the Lake that evening and ask for her expert opinion, then tried to listen to Kai, who was still airing his views on Tog. Jenna was heartily regretting she had ever suggested the outing and envied Vinny, who was asleep under ramparts, invisible yet audible.

'So let's face it,' Kai said loudly. 'He's sacked his best adviser, refuses help from you, Jenna, and won't talk to us. No one respects him and he's used up pretty much all the goodwill that came when he took over from his father. It's sad but it's got to be said: you can take the king out of a Cornish hovel but you can't take the Cornish hovel out of a king. He just isn't up to it. Admit it.'

'All right. I admit that . . .' Jenna began, then looked up to see Tog on top of the ramparts, looking twisted, frozen and sick. She swallowed the word in her mouth, desperately hoping he hadn't heard Kai or her. Some hope. She tried to turn away, then turned back, as if her face were dragged by hooks. She dropped her eyes. She couldn't bear the look he gave her.

'We thought you were supposed to be . . . somewhere else.' Kai managed to sound hard done by.

Tog allowed himself a bitter smile. Grasshoppers sprayed from his legs as he walked towards them through the long grass. Butterflies danced around his head. He felt as if a very large ladle had suddenly scooped everything out of him.

'Sorry to disappoint,' he said. 'Some kind people told me my wife and best friends had gone off without me. Eaten, have you? I'm starving.' He squatted down. The others stayed standing. 'Sit down,' he said, and they sat. He tried to control his breathing, picked up a roll and then saw the monster.

'What's this?' he asked.

'A monster,' Allanza said. 'We were checking it out. Tog—'

'My lord—' Jenna interrupted.

'I've got an idea: let's not talk,' Tog said. 'Now that I know what you think of me, I don't see what more needs to be said.'

Jenna tried again. 'My lord . . .'

'Please don't call me that unless you really mean it,' Tog

said with worrying smoothness. 'I know you're dying to tell me what to do. The only trouble is—'

Jenna clenched her fists and stamped her foot. 'MY LORD!' she shouted.

'We were trying to work out how to help you,' Allanza said.

'That's exactly what it sounded like,' Tog said.

'But it's true,' Kai said stubbornly. 'You do need our help and, you know, considering your upbringing, it's not surprising.'

Tog gave a damaged smile. 'Of course. By the way, your monster is nothing but a cat. Quite common on the continent, I believe.'

Suddenly he felt old and sad. Terribly, terribly sad. His throat ached. No one spoke. The silence grew heavier until it was broken by Vinny's sudden, high-pitched scream from the far side of the clearing. She was sitting bolt upright, her mouth wide open and pointing at the entrance to the fort where sunlight dappled the ramparts in shadow.

Movement. Something or someone was coming. A laker staggered lopsidedly into the sunlight, blood on his face, holding his side with one hand and a tiny fishing knife in the other.

He subsided as they ran over to him. Blood was pumping out between his fingers as he tried to hold on to the curling edges of a hole in his side. He looked sick and bewildered, then his lips jumped.

'Attack,' he said. 'Attack.' And fell back.

Jenna touched him on the forehead then unclamped his fingers from the knife. Vinny screamed again and pointed to the ramparts that were suddenly spiked with soldiers. They were all big, all armed with short stabbing swords and all armoured with shaped leather breastplates. A proper army with a proper uniform.

'Not my men,' Tog thought. 'Not my men at all.' And for a second he could not take it in. This was supposed to be impossible. His army to the north were meant to be protecting them from invasion, and the lake was a natural defence.

The enemy moved down the ramparts like dark water draining.

'Vinny! Come here!' Jenna called.

Vinny bounded across the grass, holding her skirt up. 'No hair! No hair!' she moaned, and collapsed on the ground with her skirt over her head.

It was true. The attackers had no beards, no eyebrows and no hair escaped from under their helmets. Not one of them made a sound.

'Fight our way to the entrance?' Jenna asked softly, but when Tog looked over his shoulder he saw more attackers at the gate. He tried to swallow but his mouth was too dry. The little earth castle had become a trap.

The first attack was cautious. Six men came in and worked in pairs. When one jabbed and forced a parry, the other slid the blade in under the guard, just to test them. After Allanza managed to wound one of them on the forearm they retreated, but only to reform a ring.

'This is never going to work,' Tog said.

'Oh, Tog,' Jenna said. 'I'm so sorry.'

'Me too. It all seems . . . you know.'

'I know. Yes.'

'The walls are broken over there,' Tog said, nodding to the south. 'It's our best chance.'

'There are a lot of them.'

'We're more mobile.'

'Not Vinny.'

'We'll carry her.'

'I'd like to see you try, my lord.' She gave him a quick smile and touched his cheek. 'We attack.'

She struck, slashing the little knife across a soldier's eyes. He gave a shocked cry and dropped his sword, allowing Tog to lunge. The soldier fell backwards, blocking the man next to him and then they were through the ring, running across the long grass. Two more soldiers rushed in from the sides to cut them off: another blocked their way ahead. Allanza used his momentum to shoulder-charge him and Tog slashed at the man coming in from the side. He felt his sword jar on something, saw the man drop away, then they were over the first wall and into the ditch between them.

Straight ahead, the bank was too steep to climb; to their right a fallen tree had torn a gap in the ramparts but as they ran towards it Vinny slipped, and Jenna stopped to help her.

'Let Allanza do that!' Tog shouted, but Allanza and Kai were parrying the slashing cuts from above them, so he had to help lift Vinny, who was twice his age and almost twice his weight.

'Run on!' he panted to Jenna. 'Lead us out! Kai! Allanza! WATCH JENNA!'

It was too late. A soldier jumped down into the gap between them, and more and more followed. Jenna screamed. Tog saw her being lifted and carried away, writhing, fighting but completely overwhelmed. He redoubled his efforts to get to her but there were too many men now between them and he suddenly realized: this was planned. Jenna was being wrestled away by a snatch squad while the rest formed a protective wall.

'They've come for Jenna! They must be taking her to the lake!' Tog shouted.

The soldiers in front of him were giving way but not letting him past. He fought his way out from the ditch and into the main body of the castle with Kai and Allanza. Jenna was out of sight. 'We've got help,' Kai panted. 'Reinforcements. Look.' Tog felt a lessening of pressure from the line in front of him. He heard shouting. Yes, soldiers – his soldiers – were forcing their way into castle from the outside, so that half the attackers had to turn.

Stab. Hack. Parry. Parry. Hack. Stab. Now he seemed to be part of a group of his own soldiers. Another swirl in the action and now Tog was exposed again. He raised his sword, tried to roar. Parry, hack, stab. Parry, hack, stab. But what about Jenna?

The main fight swirled off. Chest heaving, mouth bitter, his arm as weak as straw, he took stock. If he could get to the entrance now . . .

'I'm going after Jenna,' he panted to Kai, who was standing by him, leaning on his sword.

'You can't!' Kai gasped. 'If the men see you leave they'll lose heart. We're outnumbered. It's touch and go as it is. It'll be a massacre!'

'But Jenna!'

'You're the king! Those soldiers have come to rescue you! You have to fight!'

The battle re-formed and now Tog was in the front

line again. All around a press of men trying to kill each other. You were on the outer slopes of the castle now, struggling to keep your footing in the long grass. You bared your teeth, you grunted, you shouted, your ears were full of other people's shouts and the dull smack of metal on metal.

Hack, parry, stab. You were advancing. You were retreating. Your lungs were smoking. Your throat was sore. Your mouth was bitter. Your arm was tired beyond tired. Men fell. Others took their place and died instead of you. The long grass was so greased with blood you slipped on it.

There was the lake. You were supposed to be thinking about getting to the lake. Jenna . . .

Stab, hack, parry. You had been walking backwards for hours, it seemed. Or forwards. Who could tell? The sun was in your eyes and red.

Parry, hack, stab.

It was quieter. Where was everyone? Someone was shouting for you. Allanza. He was fighting in the water and you joined him. You were up to your shins in a sort of black, peaty soup and suddenly there was no one in front of you. They had melted away. You couldn't follow. You were too tired. You fell to your knees. The sun was low and orange. Then you remembered. Where was Jenna?

6

The earth groaned, the sky bled. Every other person was wounded, some walking, some not. Everyone moved slowly, as if underwater. There was Vinny, going from body to body, shaking her head if they were past help, comforting them if they weren't, somehow finding words.

Men came to Tog to check he was alive, to be touched by him, to kiss his hand, to find out what to do. All he could say was, 'Did you see the queen? Did you see the queen?' They had seen her carried away from the battle. They had seen her bundled into a boat. But my lord was safe; that was the main thing.

'Boat!' Tog shouted. 'BOAT! Vinny! We're going after the queen!' His throat was rough as stone, his voice tiny.

'The queen went hours ago,' Vinny called back.

'You don't understand!'

Vinny just shook her head and bent over another wounded man.

Lake people appeared in their small dug-out canoes, almost invisible in the dusk. They seemed unresentful, Tog thought, of the trouble he had brought down on them. Most of them had escaped, hiding out in the reed beds. The monks, it seemed, had not been so lucky. The monastery had been ransacked and burned and they were lying there, dead. They hadn't flown up to heaven after all, the lakers said. So sad. The old ways were best.

'And the queen?' The lake people shook their heads. No one had seen her, but at least the foreign army was gone. Rowed to the north shore and headed off for the Big Straight Way.

'We've got to follow them,' Tog shouted. 'We've got to!'

It was Allanza who talked him down. 'We can't fight them. We have to be clever. You have to think like the king. We need to get to the Refuge. I'll find a guide and a boat.'

Just in case some of the enemy had stayed behind, they lay flat in the punt and paddled away from Fenny Castle with their hands. Stars glittered in the black water. A thin moon rose and followed them for a while. Tog could smell the island burning.

Once ashore, the guide led them south-west. Reeds pressed in on both sides. When the guide stopped to think, they sank into the soft earth. When they moved, their path quivered like a fat pig's back. No one spoke. The memory of the fight ate up all other thoughts, then exhaustion ate the memory.

By dawn the island was behind them. The sun rose and for a while the track grew firmer, with trees on either side, then suddenly disappeared underwater. Ahead was a featureless expanse of reeds, the monotony broken only by hills in the distance and a strange rounded hump a mile or so away. 'We're going to be on an old wooden track but we keep this part of the marsh flooded so it's underwater,' the guide said. 'Find your way with your feet.'

A heron took off, wide wings slowly clapping the quiet.

The black water never came higher than halfway up Tog's shins and he felt the old wood through the soles of his shoes. The bog crinkled on either side of them. They turned a sharp corner and were faced by a section of track that reared up like a standing stone, held in place by ropes. From the rushes on their right a long, flat boat nosed out from behind a clump of bulrushes, dark shapes with bent bows humped in the back.

A tired voice asked, 'What do you want?'
'Men want treasure,' the guide replied.
'What kind of treasure?'
'The true kind of treasure.'
'Pass, friend. We've been waiting for you.'
It was midday, and the weather hot and clear.

7

The Refuge was a place of last resort: a few turf huts on a long, embarrassed shrug of land.

Two retired soldiers called Lug and Sug and a small company of loyal eel fishers made the place their home. It was fortified but not so strongly that attackers would single it out, and stocked with emergency rations, a bit of gold and a small cache of weapons. At the eastern end it rose to the mump – the rounded mound Tog had seen – which made a good lookout over the surrounding water meadows and marsh.

A few soldiers had made it, mad-haired and smelling of smoke. Tog found the strange bard, who bowed humbly, and General Kradok, who started then fell on his face and grabbed him round his knees.

'I thought you were dead, my lord. We all did.'

'What happened?'

'It was a well-planned attack.' Something behind Kradok's face seemed to squirm. 'The lake was crawling with boats.'

'And the guards, the ones I said should stand on the Tor and watch the lake, all day and all night and all year?'

'Playing jacks and drinking cider, I'm afraid, my lord. And dead.'

'And the main army? That was supposed to be guarding us from an attack from the north?'

'The attack came down the River Axe on fast boats and through the gap in the hills. Anyone trying to warn us would have been overtaken.'

'I've got to find Jenna,' Tog said automatically.

'We must wait, my lord. This is the gathering point. People will meet here and there will be news.'

The wounded were laid down in a roundhouse and the king went round, touching them because it was considered lucky, clinging to the thought that his fingertips might recognize Jenna. They didn't. He crashed out.

Tog woke in the dark. While he slept, a nightmare lay down on the mattress next to him but when he twitched the blanket back, nothing was there, just swollen emptiness.

And he woke to the real nightmare: no Jenna.

Losing the island, losing the battle, meant nothing to him. He felt sick and dizzy.

Outside, the air was warm and clammy. A dark shape rose against the dense mist of stars.

'Who's there?' Tog called out.

'Ordan the bard, my lord. I—'

'I've no time for a bard now!' Tog felt his voice rise and he blundered away in the darkness, following the dull ribbon of land north-west to the high mound. The ground rose suddenly and he scrabbled up a steep hill belted with sheep tracks. All around the marsh glittered and crinkled. Peace failed to arrive even when he closed his eyes and tried to breathe himself calm.

When he opened his eyes, someone was sitting next to him.

'Whoa!' He leapt to his feet, lit up by fear, feeling for his sword.

'I could have gralloched you by now, if I wanted.' The voice belonged to the local witch, or Lady of the Lake, depending on your spiritual orientation.

'How did you get up here?' Tog asked.

'Woodcraft not witchcraft, plus no one has bothered to

set guards. Anyway, you were distracted.'

'I lost Jenna. I lost the battle. I lost the kingdom. I lost everything,' Tog said sonorously.

'Remorse doesn't make you a better person.'

'I . . .'

'That was uncalled for. I'm sorry. I came to tell you that this mess is not entirely your fault. You were betrayed by a traitor in your court and I suspect that plans were laid a long time ago.'

'How do you know? How long . . . ?' Tog thought of the bard turning up on the day his world collapsed.

'Just by getting lucky – I happened to go out of my front door and saw that the lake was covered with boats. Managed to jump into my coracle and hide in the rushes. One of their boats was nosing around, looking for survivors, I suppose, and I heard a soldier say, "*So is she here or isn't she?*" Well, I thought they were looking for me but then another answered, "*Latest news she's on an outlying island with friends. Still, we've been told to pick up anyone with tattoos.*" '

The witch paused as Tog grappled with this new revelation.

'But going to Fenny Castle wasn't planned.'

'Exactly, which means someone told them *on the day*.'

'They could have tortured somebody as soon

as they landed.'

'Granted, but there's one other thing. They started talking about a map.'

'A what?'

'The point is they wanted it.'

'But what is it?'

'Something the queen had.'

'I don't understand.'

'Can you remember the dowry she brought with her?'

'Of course I can,' Tog said. 'It was gold and robes.'

'And a map.'

'How do you know this?'

'Promise you won't lose your temper?'

'Yes.'

'Melanius told me about it.'

'You know that was an accident. I never meant . . .'

'Of course. Even you're not that stupid. Apologies again. What I wanted to say was that Melanius found this thing called a map, and was studying it when he happened to be exiled. That, oddly, was a stroke of luck because it means he managed to get it to me just before he was kicked off the island – as opposed to it being in the treasury. Anyway, here it is. Trouble is, he didn't tell me how it works.'

She reached inside her robes and produced a thin leather

tube, as long as a man's foot, which came apart in the middle when she twisted it. Sticking out of the shorter half was a roll of parchment.

From somewhere close by a bird sang. Then another. Then they all started. In the east, the sky was lighter. Tog unrolled the parchment but could make no sense of it. On one side there was an irregular shape drawn in ink and some writing; on the other a collection of marks that looked like some of Jenna's tattoos: a dog, a boat, a ram . . . The thought of her skin made a fist-sized hollow in his chest.

'What on earth is making that noise?' the witch said.

Someone rather heavy, clumsy and unfit was trying to climb the mump. Then a voice called out, 'My lord? Are you there?'

'That bloody bard's found me,' Tog said between gritted teeth. 'I can't talk to anyone now. Get away down the other side.'

All through the day, survivors arrived in ones and twos, on foot and in boats, wounded and healthy.

Each was asked the same questions: Have you heard news of the queen? What news of the army? Do you know who the enemy is?

And all day long the answers came back the same. No

news of the queen; the army scattered: the enemy melted away.

All information was picked over, analysed, discussed.

Tog's army to the north had deserted. The shores of the lake were littered with abandoned boats where the attackers had dumped them before marching towards the Big Straight Way, the old Roman road that headed north and east. Who was the enemy? A complete mystery. Were there any wounded enemy soldiers to question? No one had seen one. Where did the road end? No one knew.

More questions. No answers. A madman started telling everyone who would listen that the fairies were taking all the women away, down the river and into the sea. They dunked him in the marsh until he stopped talking, tied him up and gagged him.

Then, midway through the afternoon, two rumours started swirling around the Refuge, passed from the well to the wounded, gaining intensity among depressed, frustrated men.

The first was that the boy king was going back to Cornwall where Mummy would find him a boat and whisk him off to Brittany. The second concerned the witch who had arrived in the night on a giant frog, or a giant bat, and had brought with her a magic weapon. Everyone knew it was small and powerful, as indeed she was, but opinion was divided as to what it really was: Queen Mab, with her teeth like raspberry pips and a bite like an adder; a special poison that only killed foreigners; the sacred sword . . .

All would be revealed at a council of war, one hour after sunset.

8

They were inside, standing round a trestle table. The air smelled of tallow candles.

Kai held the floor and spoke. 'Let the record show that the Great War Council of Artognu the High King comprises the Witch of Avalon, also known as the Lady of the Lake; Kai, son of Ecta, that's me; Allanza of Brittany; General Kradok, son of Kradok; Lug of the Refuge; and Sug of the Refuge. All right, everyone? Let's see what we've got.'

The witch opened the leather tube and unrolled the parchment. Four small smoking lanterns were placed on the corners.

'I don't get it. This is the secret weapon?' Kai seemed to speak for everyone. Disappointment sharpened the smell of breath, smoke and sweat. 'It looks like a blob.'

'I think I see a fish,' Tog said. Allanza suggested an arrowhead, Lug a spruce tree. It all depended on where you were standing.

'My lord. Can you read that writing?' the witch said.

The woodcutter, Tog's guardian, had taught him to read and write but had written on a slate in capitals. These letters, as far as Tog could see, were the small kind and the monks had only just started tutoring him in them. Small *A*, did not look like a ladder but an *O* with a tail on the side. *B* lost its top loop. *E* . . . surely the one that looked like a bent spoon was a little *E*.

So *E*, or rather *e*, was the first letter. Next came *c*, two of them. Well, that was easy enough. And *o*. Good.

'This little bit at the top is Latin and, because it's above all the other writing, it's the most important,' Tog said. He looked around the ring of faces, shadowed in the weak light. Now they looked alert and expectant. Allanza met his eyes and smiled. For the first time since he had become king Tog felt needed.

'This first word is *ecco*. It means "Here is" or "Behold". Next we have a *d*, then another *o*, then an *n*, a *u* and finally an *m*. *Donum*. Gift.' He frowned. The next word was beginning to form in his head and was already causing him problems. *Constantini*?

'Well?' Kai pushed him. 'Behold the gift of . . . what?'

'Of Constantine,' Tog said, and frowned. 'There was a Roman emperor called Constantine.'

'Is that his seal at the top?' Kradok said.

The roll had once been secured with wax. It was cracked but there was an impression of what might be a head on it.

'It could be,' Kai said.

Allanza said hesitantly, 'I was talking with Borth, before he . . .'

'Before I exiled him,' Tog said. 'It's all right.'

'And he mentioned that Melanius was really interested in this Roman . . . thing . . . that told you where to go and what the ground was like and how far it was between towns, even if you didn't know.'

'Magic?' Kai asked.

They all looked at the witch, who snapped, 'What? I'm meant to be the expert, am I? The Romans were a superstitious lot from what I've heard so I wouldn't rule it out. You could burn it, I suppose, and see if the ashes told you anything.'

'No.' Kradok surprised then all by speaking sharply. 'I mean, isn't that a bit final? We could risk losing its true value.'

'Good point,' Tog said. 'Burning is a last resort, then.

Could someone get more light on to it?'

Allanza lifted a lamp so Tog could peer at the surface of the parchment without shadowing it. On one edge, where it might have been torn, the surface was discoloured by a dark stain, but underneath he thought he saw more writing. He turned his head. He was looking at it upside down. '. . . ernia,' he read. 'No, ibernia. Hibernia. That's another name for Ireland, isn't it?'

'What's that got to do with anything?' Kai asked. 'We're looking for spells, aren't we?'

Tog turned his attention to the shape drawn in the middle of the parchment – the fish on its side. It had a narrow head, a wide tail and irregular fins at the top and bottom. It seemed so random, not like anything really and yet those lines seemed to have significance – the straight ones slashing their way across the shape, the other ones wavering. And what about the little triangles – a lot at the narrow end of the triangle, then a row down the middle? Could they be scales?

'Can I speak again?' Allanza asked. He sounded nervous.

'Of course,' Tog said.

'There was this man who stopped in our village once – a stranger who had a sort of sickness that meant he couldn't sleep in one place more than one night, and who liked to walk. He told us that in the mountains far to the east of our village were shepherds who left messages scratched on to the walls of caves. It wasn't writing or anything as clever as that; they were like pictures of the land. A wiggly line would mean a river; a triangle might mean a mountain; and a whole lot of triangles with a line running through the middle might mean a valley with a river or a road running down it. That way you tell people that you'd taken your sheep two valleys along and over a river. I was thinking: you know the way writing stores the message until someone wakes it up? Suppose this is a stored message about . . . somewhere.'

The same idea came to all of them at the same time. 'Britain?'

'But how could you do it?' Kai said. 'How could you make a picture of a whole country?'

'If you marched all over it and knew whether you were going east or west or south or north, you could.' Tog was excited. 'You could say: mountains for two days to the west. Well, if you marched forty miles in two days, then you could say the line of mountains was forty miles long.'

They looked at the parchment, stunned into silence by the thought that all of Britain could be contained within those lines. Tentatively, Tog swivelled it round so the word Hibernia was on the left-hand side of the parchment.

'That's it,' he said. 'Look, Ireland's to the west of Britain and if we stand here, east would be to the right, north to the top and south below. All the little triangles must be mountains and I suppose the wiggling lines are rivers, and the straight lines roads. No wonder the Romans had the beating of everyone if they knew in advance where the mountains, rivers and roads were.'

'To sum up so far,' Kai said, 'we have this thing, this map, of a Roman emperor and it may or may not have magical properties. What do we do with it?'

The question started a long silence that was only broken by the Lady of the Lake. 'Is it just me or is it getting rather stuffy in here? May I suggest we all take a turn outside? Clear our heads and come back refreshed?'

'Good idea,' Tog said. He overrode Kai's protest. 'Let's take a breather and come back with some ideas. Remember,' he added. 'This came from Jenna. It was her treasure, and the attackers who took her were looking for this. Maybe it'll tell us where she was taken.'

'That's it? What's going on?' Kai stood close to Tog so only he could hear. They were outside, the door to the roundhouse shut, and Kradok standing guard. It was dark – the moon had not yet risen.

Tog swallowed. This was the bit he was dreading.

'Interesting, isn't it?' he said.

'You didn't know about this map thing?'

'Not before today,' Tog said, relieved to be telling the truth.

'You and the witch were alone together this morning really early, before anyone else was up.'

'Maybe we were,' Tog said. 'But how did you know?'

'Glamour-boy Ordan. The bard?'

'He's been following me around.'

Kai let the silence grow, then said, 'I still want to know what you and the witch were talking about.'

Allanza joined them. 'Perhaps he doesn't want to say,' he remarked.

'Is that it?' Kai asked. 'You don't want to say? Or maybe it's more that you don't feel you can. I thought we were past all that.'

'When did I have the chance to get past it?'

'When? When we were fighting together. Look, I was wrong. We shouldn't have gone behind your back but we tried to talk to you and you kept brushing us aside. And now you're going to Brittany? We've heard the rumours. Why can't you tell us?'

'I want to, it's just that—'

Then they heard the shouts from the far side of the Refuge.

* * *

By the time they arrived, the witch was there, holding up a small oil light that barely illuminated two men wrestling in the mud by one of the eel fishers' boats. When they got closer they could see that Ordan was kneeling on someone's back, pinning one of his arms behind his back and pressing his face into the mud. Sug had his arm round Ordan's neck and a knife pressed into his Adam's apple.

'What's going on?' Tog asked. 'Report, Sug.'

'I was on watch down by the boats, like you ordered,' Sug said. 'Heard a fight and found this. It's General Kradok under the bard.'

'Let him up,' Tog ordered. 'Now, both of you. What's going on?'

Kradok spat mud. 'He broke into the roundhouse to steal the map. I stopped him and he attacked.'

Tog looked at Ordan, who shook his head. 'The same, my lord,' he said regretfully. His sparse hair had fallen over his face and he patted it tenderly back on his head before he continued. 'I admit I went into the roundhouse to see this wondrous weapon and found this man trying to steal it.'

'And you just happened to beat the general in a fight?' Tog said.

'On the road we have to protect ourselves.'—

'Right,' Tog said. 'Ordan, stand back from Kradok. Kradok, stand up straight.'

'You're not trusting him over me, are you?' Kradok sounded outraged. 'My lord, I—'

'I am doing what my father said; trusting no one,' Tog replied. 'It's fairer that way.'

Lug stood by him, an arrow notched in his bow. He wouldn't look at the general but Tog was relieved to see that the bow, though lowered, was aimed right between the men.

The flickering lantern picked up something half buried in the mud at their feet. Tog knelt and retrieved the map's leather tube, wiped the mud off it and checked that the parchment was inside. He glanced at the witch, tapped it in his hand and said, 'Care to check it?'

The witch pored over it. 'Seems undamaged,' she said.

'He dropped it.' Ordan and Kradok spoke together, trying to hold Tog's attention.

'Ordan, why were you interested in the map?' Tog asked.

'I am a scholar. A learned man. I travel. I observe. I thirst after knowledge. I have heard of maps. I wanted to see one.'

'Kradok?'

'I am a simple soldier, the king's dog. I was simply

guarding his property.'

Tog said lightly, 'Well, I hope you got a good look at it. I may as well come clean now. There's a traitor close to me and we were only using the map to get him to show his hand. It's done its job, then. May as well get rid of it.' And he pulled his arm back and threw it.

Kradok lunged towards the lake, his cry of despair cut off as Lug raised the bow and shouted, 'Stay!'

He stopped dead. When he looked at Tog, his face was both baffled and contemptuous.

'Have you any idea what you have just done? Idiot!'

He gasped as Sug grabbed his arm from behind and bent it upwards. He fell to his knees and spat out, 'You deserve all that comes to you, you Cornish brat.'

Tog bowed to Ordan. 'I'm sorry,' he said. 'I had to be sure.'

Ordan bowed and said, 'Your wisdom exceeds your years. Indeed it rivals Solomon the Great.'

'Who's Solomon?' Kai asked.

'An ancient king from a faraway land,' Ordan said. 'When two women were claiming the same baby, he ordered his guard to split the child down the middle so each woman got half. The woman who screamed that she'd rather give the baby up than see it killed was deemed to be the true mother. Kradok believes he is the real owner of the map and so cried out when the king threw it away. It therefore followed he would be the likelier one to steal it.'

'Brilliant,' Kai said, 'but for a small detail. We've lost the map.'

The witch produced the leather tube from behind her back. 'I switched it. The king threw a stick into the lake.'

She looked at Kradok. 'I don't do this often, you know, but I'm cursing you for betraying your master. You wanted to chase the stick into the lake; so a dog you will become.'

'Kill him,' Kai said. 'He betrayed you.'

'Worse than that,' Tog said, 'he betrayed the queen.' Anger, sudden and choking, rose in him like a hot cloud. He took a step towards Kradok and was stayed only by a soft hand gripping his arm.

'Forgive me, my lord, but we must think,' the witch said. 'The map, my lord, we must concentrate on the map.'

Tog forced himself to step back. He took a breath. 'All right. All right. Why Jenna? Why not me?'

Kradok's smile grew more fixed and ghastly. 'You were only ever king because Dragon let you rule. Now you are just a child with no army and no friends. Dragon is everywhere. You are nothing.'

'Who, or what is the dragon? the witch asked.

'The more you talk, the more dull you seem. All of you.

Dragon lives in no man's land. He will rise when the sun is highest and the seeking will be no more when the truth is revealed. On midsummer's eve, Dragon will eat the world and we will be reborn!'

'But Dragon's another name for the high king,' Allanza said. 'And that's Tog. Isn't it?'

Kradok threw back his head as if to laugh, but suddenly went limp as if something inside him had snapped.

Sug was taken by surprise and staggered forward. Kradok shrugged off his jerkin and darted to the water. A flock of ducks exploded into terrified flight. Lug let off an arrow, and then another, but the night was dark and Kradok was out of sight before anyone thought to follow him. By the time they launched a dug-out canoe and found that Tog had removed the paddle to stop anyone escaping, all was quiet again. Kradok was gone.

Lug broke the silence. 'That general were never the same after the fairies stole his wife. Tragic bloody Kradok.'

'Thank you for that,' Kai said sarcastically.

'I only tell it,' Lug said, 'because perhaps it sent him mad.'

'But that's nonsense,' Kai protested. 'Everyone knows it's what people say when a man's wife runs off.'

'Kradok was different,' Lug said. 'All the soldiers talked about it. Why Tragic Kradok and not Kradok the Fool or

Kradok the Cuckoo? I'll tell you. People saw the fairies. They were little but not so little, bold as brass, vicious. Came to the village where he had his farm in broad daylight, went into the house, and took her.'

'And no one could do anything?'

'The neighbours, they were scared and she was blind. That's the tragedy. Who'd want a blind wife? No one unless they loved her.'

'And it sent him mad so now he thinks there's a dragon about to eat the world?'

'Could be.'

The black cloud in Tog's mind was suddenly pierced by a pinprick of light.

'What about that madman who turned up here and started talking about fairies? Lug? Sug?'

'He stopped talking in the end but only when they gagged him.'

'Fetch him.'

The man proved not to be mad at all, though wet and cold and annoyed. Tog apologized, ordered apple brandy for him and asked him to tell them what he had seen.

'I was fishing on a high bank when a boatload of fairies came past. I could look right down into the boat,' the man said.

'And how did you know they were fairies?' Kai asked.

'They weren't human,' the man said. 'They were half sized and the one that looked up at me had fangs, not teeth, and he hissed.'

'And this was where?'

'On the River Baridos. Heading west, to the sea.'

'And you said they were capturing all the women in Britain?'

'I said they had a captive. In the bottom of the boat. Trussed up, she was, sack over head, ropes all round her.'

'Why do you say "her"?' Tog asked.

'Are you really the high king?' the man asked.

'I am.'

'It was a girl's foot. Begging your pardon, a young woman's foot.'

Tog felt there was more. 'And?' he said.

'Well, it was bare. And tattooed. Like they say the queen is. One other thing. They had an animal in there. Colour of an otter but leggier.'

9

Rising bird: hope, escape, flight

After she was captured at Fenny Castle, Jenna had been hooded, tied at the wrists and ankles and placed in the bottom of a boat. That was when things got strange.

She felt as if she were at the centre of action but there was an eerie sense of calm around her. When she tried to smash a hole in the boat's side with her hard, Pictish skull she felt hands close round her head, cradling it.

Small hands.

She went very still. Being taken away by creatures with small hands could mean only one thing: fairies.

The monster that Tog had called cat seemed to be in the boat with them and curled up on her stomach. It was dense and warm and not at all comforting. Dimly, through the loose weave of the hood, Jenna saw the day turn to night.

She was wet from the bilge water. All she could hear was the slap-slap-slap of wavelets against the bows and the creaking push of the oars.

Still the fairies rowed. And rowed. And rowed. As relentless as insects.

To Jenna, fear was a shambly, vicious old dog with dark-brown teeth that she had been running from all her life.

When she was six years old, her father had noticed that she was scared of horses so he hoicked her on to a little shaggy pony, slapped its rump and laughed like a maniac when it galloped her across the glen with the fear dog lurching along behind her. It nearly caught her when the pony dumped her on the heather, but she jumped back on to her mount and rode it straight at the dog, who yipped and staggered out of the way.

When her father finally found her a day later, her lips blue with bilberries, he could not believe how easily she took her punishment but she was happy, because she had discovered that it was possible to beat the stinking beast. From that day on, courage became a sort of habit.

Following the pony incident, the bravest things she had done were: crossing the field after the midsummer feast to the boys' corner and asking the biggest and handsomest one to dance aged nine;

slicing through the bull's neck at midwinter and drinking its hot, livery blood aged eleven;

killing her first adult, a stringy, warty old cattle thief, roughly the same age as her father, who had made the mistake of murdering her favourite cousin.

She was twelve then, and thirteen when it was first mooted that the King of Pictland should send a daughter south to marry the High King of Britain. Jenna was the natural choice and all the local princes heaved sighs of relief that they wouldn't be hitched to a skinny little harridan like her, and might even end up with one of her sisters: plump Argol or sexy Mila, girls who could sew, make cheese and also promised unimaginable pleasures of the flesh.

Well, enough said. On each occasion, the old dog had wandered towards her on its stiff old legs, and on each occasion she had faced it down.

Until now. Her courage had gone and the fear dog's brown teeth were hooked in her belly and it was shaking her so hard she cried.

A fairy hand reached down.

Light fairy fingers touched the hood over her eyes, rose to a blurred fairy face and fluttered under a blunt fairy nose.

* * *

She jerked herself awake. It was night – no light coming through the hood. Her arm had gone to sleep and felt heavy, like a club. Her neck was cricked. What had woken her?

Fairy voices? Choppy and hoarse.

'You think we'll make it?'

'What? The plan, Fra Trouble Trouble?'

'Yeah, the plan, Toothache.'

'If we make it to Stop-off One on schedule we'll hit Stop-off Two no probs then it's a straight run to the Centre.'

'Even with the baggage?'

'Even with the baggage.'

'Yeah. I think we'll make it, right? Think Dragon'll be pleased?'

'Yeah, Dragon'll be licking his gob.'

'Dribbling.'

'Thinking about the baggage.'

A tiny change in their voices told Jenna that they had turned to her when they were talking about the baggage. She was the baggage.

Panic flooded her. She jackknifed – lifted into the air, touched something with her legs and kicked out. The cat yowled. A shout, the boat lurched, tilted.

'Hey, Log, hey, mate! Watch the sandbank!'

The boat bumped, staggered, rolled like a whale and Jenna was tipped down the ribs. Shouts, another sudden lurch and suddenly she was tumbling over and over then there was cold and wet all around her.

All too sudden for her to take breath.

The water was freezing and everywhere, inside her and out. She writhed, twisted and sank. When she coughed she sucked in solid cold and collapsed around the wetness in her lungs. When she broke the surface, the air loosened the sack on her head but when she whooped in air, she just sucked in sackcloth and went down again, screaming silently.

Then she was cartwheeled in space, dumped down on the grass, thumped in the back and the river poured out of her lungs. When the hood was ripped off, she lay gasping and rasping on the ground, her throat and chest hurting more than anything had hurt before. Surrounded by fairies.

There were six of them: a tall one with bad spots, black eyes and a mouse-fur moustache on his upper lip; a girl with short hair and a blunt snotty nose; a thin one like a ghost, whose mouth never stopped moving; a big redhead with spiky hair; a skinny one with a shrivelled face, and a young one so beautiful Jenna could not tell if it were a boy or a girl. The cat was draped over his shoulders like a scarf.

Fairies? Really?

The tall one with spots was swearing at everything but mostly at Jenna. Because she had sunk the boat they had a day-and-a-half forced march to make Stop-Off One if they were going to hit the schedule. The moonlight showed the long reaches of a broad estuary: glistening mud flats and distant water on her left, dunes on her right.

'What are you?' she heard herself ask.

Silence.

'What are you doing?'

Silence.

'You'll never get away with it. The king will hunt you down.'

The girl hawked and spat. They untied her wrists and legs, knotted the rope around her waist and yanked her to her feet.

At first she was relieved not be hooded or tied but she soon forgot this as the fairies, or whatever the vile creatures were called, kept up an unvarying, grinding jog. Months of southern living had made her soft, while the fairies were fit and hard. Mile after mile they kept up their shambling, jogging walk, first one, then the other taking the lead as they followed the endless estuary shore. Jenna's lungs were on fire before the river was out of sight, her feet were raw and aching a short while later, and her legs felt like wet straw not long after that.

On and on they went. The moon dropped and the sun rose. The heat got up. When they came to a stream, the fairies dropped their heads into it and drank like dogs. When they came to a creek, they swarmed across like rats. The sun climbed higher. They slowed but did not stop. Jenna was so tired that a fuzzy grey veil dropped over her eyes. They were all slower now. Another creek. She thought of drowning herself in it but was pulled across. The sun started to drop. They rested. Jenna watched her feet bleed. Another creek, which she seemed to float through, then realized the others were carrying her. The sun set. The red sky roared in her lungs.

When she caught a glimpse of the big square building looming high against the evening sky, she was too tired to see its significance. She was hooded again, and took the opportunity to collapse. Her captors were talking to a man with a rough voice.

'She for us?'

The tall one answered, 'Touch her, you die.'

'Down boy, down.'

'Word is that you're not hitting targets. Dragon thinks you're dipping your hand in.'

'It's just that no one drops by any more, see? People talk.

We've developed a bit of a reputation.'

'Do something about it or you'll get a visit from you-know-who.'

'Believe it when I see it. You're cutting it fine, aren't you?'

'We made it. That's what counts. Lost the boat. Need another.'

'That's a big ask.'

'It's not an ask. It's an order. Do it. Now we want to eat. And I want ropes and a blanket for her.'

They pulled her to her feet, dumped her on a bench and pulled the hood back from her mouth to feed her. Jenna didn't mind the blanket as she was shivering. She didn't mind the food either, even though it was disgusting. She even managed to get down a few swallows of thin, bitter beer before they tied her up again, wrapped her in the blanket and dropped her in a side room.

10

She woke up under a pile of smelly, grunting young bodies, her mind oddly clear. Two of the fairies and the cat were using her as a cushion. The tall one's head was on her belly while the one with the shrivelled face was nestling his in the hollow of her shoulder. He was blowing foul air at her through sharp, sand-coloured fangs.

She looked around. Across the stone floor, a doorway glowed firelight red. She worked her shoulder and tried to slither free. The tall fairy groaned and muttered. Jenna stopped to let him settle back into deep sleep, then began again. It was hard – the red-haired creature was digging into her back but he seemed to be in a deep sleep as well. She pushed against him, and felt the two heads slide off her on to the floor. The cat stretched and walked away to watch.

Jenna's heart started to thump. All she had to do was get her leg from under the girl . . .

The tall one rolled on to his side, threw an arm around her waist and smacked his lips like a baby.

She could have wept. She wriggled herself into an upright position. It was like the game she had played with her sisters when she was little – you tried to pick sharpened sticks out of a pile without moving the others. She always lost – too impatient.

'It's all right,' a voice said in the darkness. 'You could pick 'em up and drop 'em and they wouldn't wake, and if they do, you can tell 'em they're asleep and they'll believe you. They took a lot of sleep, you see. There's a liddle box of it and we mixes it in with the beer. Go on. Lift his head.'

A girl was standing in the doorway, lit by glow of the fire somewhere behind her.

'I can't,' Jenna whispered. 'I'm tied up.'

'Here, I'll show you.' The girl lifted a fairy head by a hank of filthy hair then let it thunk back on to on the floor. She smelled of grease and smoke. Knotted hair fell over her face.

'I want to get away.'

'Eh? You a Little Sword or not?'

'Little Sword?'

'What they're called on account of their having little swords specially made for 'em. You don't talk to 'em, you don't look at 'em, and then you hope they go away.'

Jenna thought back to the conversation she had heard when they had first come in. 'They said your lot were dipping their hands in.' She watched the girl carefully.

'Waddayouknow? So what if they don't hand all the stuff over?' the girl hissed. 'We send what we can upriver to the Centre. Now, you keep your blabbing mouth shut.'

Jenna shrugged and looked away. 'I don't want to upset you. Look at me. I can't do anything. I don't know anything. What do you do here?'

'You do your job, you keep your head down. That's what you do, girl.'

Jenna was not sure if she talking about herself or giving advice.

'I never keep my head down,' she said.

The girl laughed shortly. 'And look where it's got you. And you talk funny. You from off?'

'The north. We have our own language. How do I get away?'

'You don't, not from here. Only one way in, only one way out. If you get away, they'd kill me.'

So she wasn't going to escape. She crawled away from

the sleeping bodies and collapsed against the far wall. The girl followed her.

'They kidnapped me. Stole me.'

'Lucky that's all they did. I heard them talking – said they had to deliver you. Why they want you then? You special?'

Jenna thought about the way she had been trussed up and wrapped in blankets. 'I must be a hostage. Hostages only work when they're alive. What happens upriver? What's the dragon?'

'You don't know much, do you? Dragon, we calls him. Not *the* dragon. That's like . . . stupid. I better be going, girly.'

'No! I mean stay, please. Let me talk to you. People will be coming after me. To save me.'

Something flicked at the girl's face. Yearning? 'They better hurry. Got a boat for you.'

'I can help you if—'

'Ififififif.'

'—you promise not to feed my friends that beer if they turn up here.'

The girl snorted. 'Your mates can set me up, can they? With a brown cow?'

'Any colour you want,' Jenna said. 'They have lots of cows.'

'What about a hut and a man to work the land?'

'If you've got a cow and a hut, the men will come running,' Jenna said. 'Then you can choose.'

'What can you give me?'

'Me?' Jenna asked. 'I . . .' Then she saw she was about to lose whatever grip she had on the situation. 'What have I got? What have *I* got?' she said, to buy time.

'Yeah. What have *you* got?'

'Only the most precious thing in the world.'

'Which is?'

'Hope. I've got it. I can show you.'

'You can't show hope. Can you?'

'Oh yes, you can,' Jenna said. 'And I can do better than that. Come closer and look.'

11

Ram: determined, winning

It was a relief when the boatman woke Tog. Once again he had been dreaming about Jenna being next to him at the same as knowing she wasn't.

'This is the best place for you to disembark, my lord,' the boatman said. 'The river shoals here. We don't want that to happen.' He pointed to a big, upturned boat lying against a curling sandbar. The river plucked at a trailing rope. The boat was already filling with silt.

'Is that recent?' Tog asked.

'Yup.'

'Would the people have drowned?'

The boatman shrugged. 'Doubt it.'

'And you can't take us further?'

'This is just a punt, my lord. No good in open water.

You'll have to find another way from here.'

Tog's plan was simple enough. He freely admitted that Jenna was the key to his power with the British warlords and minor kings because his marriage had secured peace with the Picts. Now she was lost, that advantage had gone and all his support with it. He had to get her back. So while messengers went north from the Refuge to try and make contact with General Mailgwin's army, Tog would follow Jenna's trail and try and catch up with her.

Of course, the Roman map was a huge bonus for planning – better than magic really. It showed them that the Baridos, the river the fairies had escaped down, emptied out into the side of a huge estuary formed by a great river that snaked northwards into the mountains of Powys, while a tributary headed east into the heart of the country. But while the plan had felt good in the roundhouse, out here, under the huge sky, it felt puny. And when Tog looked north, all he could imagine was ancient forest, howling moors, empty mountains. How could he find Jenna in that lot?

The others were still asleep. Allanza was sprawled on his back, his huge frame crammed into the bows. Kai was leaning against him, looking sweet. Ordan, now asleep in the stern, produced a curious, strangled whistle from between pursed lips. He had insisted he come, pointing out that, as an adult, he could draw attention away from what he called the youthfulness of the king and his retinue. Tog still didn't trust him and Kai clearly could not stand him but there was something about him, some quality of knowing more than he let on, that made Tog want to keep him close – if only to find out what it was.

'Wake up everyone,' he said. 'This is it.'

They walked. Yellow sand, grey sea. Sun glinted on shallow pools. Birds' feet printed messages in the mud. Gulls cried. Waders waded. An island, flat and hard like a burned cake. Ribs of a wrecked ship. Across the estuary, rolling hills were dimmed by trees.

They passed a rocky headland and at last saw a boat coming in on the tide, bows smacking the choppy wavelets. There were two men on board, one at the tiller, the other managing the sails, and when they were no more than ten paces from the shore they turned so the boat was held still between the wind and the current, and something in the level blankness of their boatmen's stares made the travellers move their cloaks back to show their swords.

'Now I know what a cow at the market feels like,' Kai said as they watched the boat sail away.

They walked on.

They left a bloody sunset behind and walked though the

night into a clear bright dawn. Mist smoked from the dark coombs behind them; ahead the land was flat and the narrowing estuary pulled the forests of the northern shore closer. The next night Tog let them sleep for a while in a deserted hill fort and Ordan, who seemed to spend his resting moments sitting cross-legged and mumbling to himself, claimed the spirits had talked to him and blessed their journey. They endured a day of scrambling over slippery rocks while someone – or something – tracked them in the tangled thickets above the high water mark.

Then they rounded a headland and got stuck.

It was afternoon and they were exhausted, itching from the salt and damp. Allanza's fair skin was red from sunburn. They were too numb to think of a way of crossing a river that fed into the estuary in front of them. The brown water was eddying viciously and the mud looked like it could swallow a house.

Another thing was holding them up: the sight of a tall pole standing in the mud. It was three times the height of a man and a netful of geese dangled from it. The geese were still alive and taking it in turns to struggle. The scene – glistening mud, white feathers, orange beaks, the huge fresh sky – held the attention.

'We should wait here,' Ordan said. 'No man owning a fine net like that would leave it more than a day.'

'Why do we want to meet anyone?' Kai asked. The sun made his hair flare even redder.

'It is my belief,' Ordan said, staring out over the estuary. 'It is my belief that . . .' And he paused to stroke his chin. 'It is my belief . . .'

'For the third time,' Kai said.

'It is my belief in this matter that we should attempt to further our endeavours nautically.'

'What?' Allanza asked.

'Please don't encourage him to say it again,' Kai exploded. 'He's too fat and lazy to walk and so wants to go by boat. There's only one thing we need to do and that's to head inland. The river will narrow. There might even be a bridge.'

He glanced at Tog, stood up and started to move off. Allanza got to his feet, made as if to follow him, saw Tog hadn't moved and stopped. Tog felt torn between the need to move and a fear that they might be heading in the wrong direction. Also, he wanted to test Ordan's counsel. 'We're staying put,' he said.

'Is it because he's a gweat big man?' Kai put on a silly voice.

'No. I think there's a good chance someone will be along in a boat. We need to know where we are.'

Kai surprised him by sitting down on a tussock with a

triumphant smile stretching his face. 'Like the last two charmers? All right. Let's wait.'

'Tide's coming in,' Allanza said.

The mud ticked like a suckling puppy as the tide raced in. Kai looked increasingly smug until a coracle spun into sight, rowed by a man with one eye, no nose and not much hair.

He tethered the coracle to the pole and stood up. The tide had risen high enough for him to unhitch the net and drop it into the bottom of the craft. The geese lay in a hissing, undulating bundle.

Tog got to his feet.

'Good evening,' he said.

As the man turned, the evening sun flamed on the side of his head. As well as missing an eye and a nose, he was missing an ear as well. One sword cut, Tog thought. Left to right, probably from a horseman. Could have killed him.

'Evening.'

Very aware of Kai, Tog overcame his awkwardness enough to say, 'Any chance of a ride?'

'Where to?'

'Upriver.'

'To the place?'

'Is there a place?'

'Arr.'

'That's where we want to go. Can you take us?'

The man paddled the coracle to their tuft of a headland.

'There are four of us,' Tog said.

The boatman shrugged fatalistically.

Tog looked at Kai. 'Worth a try.'

'Arr,' Kai answered.

The coracle was a basket of willow covered with hide. What with the boatman and his bag of geese, there was not much room for anyone else. Ordan slipped in first and bagged the remaining space on the seat. Kai was next and the boat sank to a hand's breadth from the gunwales. Allanza was next and the water rose still further. By the time it was Tog's turn the only space was on top of the wretched geese, who made a soft but reluctant cushion. When he moved, he felt bones breaking and geese sighing. There was a finger's width between the water and the top of the gunwale.

Unworried, the boatman set off, propelling the craft with a swirling movement of his short oar.

'How do you catch the geese then?' Kai asked.

'Bend the ol' pole over and tether her, lay net on ground. Arr.'

'Arr?' said Kai.

'Tie her to pole, bait the net, wait for the birdies. Arr?'

'Arr,' said Kai.

'And when they come, as come they do come, pull the rope, pole jumps up, net jumps up, geese goes blimey, caught, damn and blast.'

'But why don't you pick them up right away?' Kai asked.

'I gets muddly, geese gets muddly, best to wait,' said the man.

'We're sinking,' Tog said.

Every now and again a wavelet splashed over the edge of the boat but, more serious that that, the little coracle was so strained that its sides were splitting and streaming with water. The only thing to do was heave the sack of geese of overboard.

'Sorry,' Tog said.

'Talking to me or the geese, lover?' the boatman asked.

'You could have let the geese go,' Kai said.

It was evening when the man spun the coracle into an inlet, held it against a rotting jetty, then set off without a word. At the end of a rough track was a big stone building, lights glimmering from high, slitted windows.

'This is a place,' Ordan said. 'There is no other.'

'Old Roman warehouse,' Kai said. 'Let's check it out but everyone keep their swords and packs close.'

An unpleasant wind followed them from the water and made the rough grass around them sigh. The warehouse doors were open to show a fire at the far end of the hall, two long tables and some benches. Bare stone walls were streaked with green. Birds twittered in the distant rafters. Broken tiles, feathers and old straw on the floor.

Four men were hunched over one of the tables, louse-grey sackcloth swelling their bodies.

'This sort of place is called an inn, or tavern,' Ordan said.

'No,' said Kai.

'Indeed, yes. In the lands of the Franks, such places are common. And you can pay for meat and a bed.'

He led them to a table, then rapped on the wood with his knuckles. One of the sack men stumbled to his feet, put his head through a doorway at the far end of the room and shouted something.

A girl came in: barefoot, thin, pale with rats' tails of hair falling over half her face. She pushed the hair back, blinked, then let it fall back like a curtain.

'We got sheep we got no pig we got nips we got b— And that's what we got,' she mumbled.

'Excellent,' Kai said. 'We all want sheep and nips. No

pig, I think. And a place to sleep, if you'd be so good. Anything to drink?'

Her visible eye swivelled, taking them all in. 'Nope. Nothing to drink. Nothing at all.'

'The men at that table are drinking,' Kai said.

'They are not,' the girl answered and slouched off.

'Well, this is splendid,' Kai said. 'Of course, we could have taken my advice, doubled back and followed the main road to Hot Baths, but then we wouldn't be enjoying such magnificent hospitality. What special thing do you like about it, Allanza? The warm and welcoming atmosphere, the promise of a really great meal, the company, the—'

'That's the gooseman, isn't it?' Ordan asked placidly.

The gooseman walked past them, went up to the table of seated men and started talking in a low voice. One by one the men looked across at them, then looked away. The gooseman approached.

'Found your way then?' he said.

'We're sorry about your geese,' Tog answered cautiously.

'No hard feelings,' the man said pleasantly enough. 'Either them or you. Wanna drink?'

'There's no drink,' Kai said. 'We were told.'

'Did you get your geese back?' Tog asked.

'Oh no. No hard feelings though. Wanna drink?'

Tog said, 'We'll pay if you can find any. And tell us how much we owe you for the geese.'

The man said they could settle up later and crossed the room to the doorway the girl had gone through. They heard a blow and a cry, then minutes later she came out with a vast tray: nips and sheep cooked into a fatty, grey sludge, and beer in rough earthenware beakers that put teeth on edge. Ordan ate heartily and pronounced it to be fine. The others picked at the food.

'If you take a mouthful of food, then a mouthful of beer, it sort of works,' Kai said. 'I mean, the fat kills the taste of the beer and the beer gets the muck down before you actually spit it out.'

Ordan banged the table and demanded more. His head seemed to be loose on his neck and when he reached for his beaker he knocked it over.

'Oh dear. The resident adult seems to be drunk,' Kai said. He blinked. 'And so do I.'

The room began to slide greasily past Tog's eyes although he was sure he wasn't moving his head.

He tried to stand but found he couldn't. His eyelids had a mind of their own and kept trying to close. Allanza was trying to push himself to his feet. He got further than Tog but fell over. Kai said, 'Sleep, sleep,' then had trouble closing his mouth. The girl from the kitchen was floating in front of him. The dirt lay in patterns on her skin that reminded him of the map. A dark bit here, a light bit there, a black mark . . .

Now she was really close and whispering, 'You got dreams, little king, but I got hope.'

She pulled the neck of her dress lower so Tog could see the skin between her breasts.

Like a dash of cold water, the shock revived him, but only for a split second.

He tried to say something but the harder he tried, the less he could. Then his head fell forward on to the table and his mind went dark.

12

The nightmare was small and awful.

He was tied by the wrists and ankles so he could not move and a little voice was calling him from a dark corner of the room. It made his neck hairs rise and his skin go clammy because there was nobody there – just a pile of sacks on the floor and a little pale head balanced on them.

'. . . she said it meant hope . . . she said it meant hope . . . she said it meant hope . . .'

Fear sat like a grey plug in Tog's throat and stopped him calling out. The sacks rustled. The head rose and floated towards him. Wake up, wake up, Tog said to himself, then realized that he was awake and the horror was real. He screwed his eyes shut.

'. . . the sign meant hope . . . the sign meant hope . . .'

The voice was small, flat and insistent, and was in his ear now. The head was whispering in his ear . . .

'. . . I want hope . . . I want hope . . . I . . .'

'Stop,' Tog managed to say, but his voice sounded weak.

'Stop? Stop? . . . I just want . . . she promised . . . she said . . .'

Close enough to touch now. His shoulders cracked as he tried to burst the ropes.

'I got light so you can see,' the voice said. 'So you can see the hope.'

Flint sparked, tinder flared and a taper caught. The head grew a body and developed features: hair, much dirty hair, an eye, a snub nose. The serving girl. She sawed through Tog's bonds, then began work on the others. Allanza rubbed his eyes. Kai sat up suddenly, said, 'Right!' and rubbed his hands. Ordan honked, rolled over and carried on sleeping.

'What happened? Where are we?' Allanza asked.

'Shh,' Tog said.

' 'S all right. Talk all you want. I gave you half sleep and the men double sleep, or you'd have been dead by now.' She throttled the air. 'Tried to keep you off it, like she said. She said I gotta help you, keep the secret, then the magic would work. Want to see it now?'

'She?'

'The queen, silly. Now I gotta show you the hope. That right?'

'If she said so.' Tog was slowly grasping that Jenna had been here and they were on the right trail. He took the taper while the girl knelt in front of them, pulled down the front of her dress to bare her bony ribcage and the hope, pricked into the ridged skin.

'It was three nights ago. She was all right. She gave me this.'

'What is it?' Allanza asked, crouching by Tog.

'One of Jenna's tattoos. It means she was here,' Tog said. 'They all mean something. A horse means strength. A heart means love. Bird's foot means speed. A bird in flight means hope.'

The tattoo rose over the girl's heart. A double curve cut by a single line, soot rubbed into pinpricks.

'How did you talk to Jenna?' Tog asked.

'She was with the Little Swords,' the girl said. 'That's what they call themselves. Everyone else calls them devils. Kids. They're kids been trained to kill. Dragon's big soldiers are called Swords. The kids are called Little Swords. The Little Swords are the worst, though. Everyone knows that.'

'So there's a connection between the Little Swords

and . . . the dragon,' Tog thought out loud.

'Dragon, like I said.'

'But who is he?'

'He's the big man around these parts.'

'Around these parts?' Kai asked sharply. 'What about the high king?'

The girl shrugged. 'Mebbe he's the big man 'round other parts. Here people don't pay him much mind.'

Just three days' march from my court, Tog thought. 'Tell me about the Little Swords.'

'The Swords, they're the army. Men. Grown-ups. Human, I reckon. But the Little Swords . . . Dragon's got this wizard called Merthen. People swear blind that Merthen makes 'em out of mud and blood and what have you but they love to get off their skulls on sleep and everything else they find and you wouldn't *make* something that did that, would you? No, you'd *make* it so it was perfect. Dragon and Merthen, they take kids and they *change* 'em but they remember what's happened and that's why they like the sleep so much. To forget. Lucky for you.'

'Lucky?' Kai said.

'Lucky for you they were so well out of it that me and queenie could talk. She said you'd help me if I helped you.'

'Sleep must be some sort of drug.' Allanza yawned. 'Certainly worked on me.'

'It's in a little box and it's grey and it came from a merchant and he came from far off. Anyone comes through here who's got stuff, we give 'em sleep then take their stuff for Dragon.'

'Let's go back to the beginning,' Kai said. 'Jenna was here . . .'

'If that's her name . . .'

'And she told you to help us?'

'If you helped me.'

'What do you want?'

'What I told her: a brown cow and a man and a home.'

'We can do that for you,' said Tog. 'Where are they taking her?'

'I'm not an idiot. I want my cow first,' the girl said. 'And mind it's brown.'

'We're in a hurry,' Kai said. 'Have you any idea who you're talking to?'

'The high king,' the girl said. 'Told you I'm not an idiot. Are you?'

'We haven't got a cow with us,' Tog said, 'but we have money that can buy you one. It's in my pack.'

The girl's expression said she had seen people like him before and knew their game. Then she lowered her head and muttered, 'You better come with me. Door's locked but I know about the tunnels.'

With some difficulty they woke Ordan, who said he was delighted to meet them three times before he opened his eyes and looked around. They dropped down into the hole by the pile of sacks into a tunnel, their knees scraping on fallen plaster, Roman bricks rough against their backs.

The tunnel opened out into the back of a furnace, its walls caked with greasy soot. Outside the furnace was a low, vaulted basement, thick with ash. Tog kicked something hard and light, and saw that it was the front of a skull: charred eye sockets, smoked teeth and all.

They followed the girl into another room lined with crammed shelves: sandals, shoes, cloaks, blankets, pots, pans, knives, spoons, boxes, bags. More things than Tog imagined existed in the world. A dark cloud spilled off one shelf and on to the floor. He touched it, then jerked his hand away.

Hair.

'All gets collected twice a year. Nothing goes to waste.'

Tog felt suffocated. Hair, he thought. Hair?

Kai got things straight. 'You kill people, steal their things and . . . Dragon's people come to collect it?'

'That's right.'

Then up a flight of worn steps into the kitchen. A black cauldron of sludge hung on a tripod by the fireplace, dirty meat skewers lay on the floor and wooden platters floated in a bucket of greasy water. Their packs were in a pile by the door, ready for sorting. Tog reached into his and found his purse. He hefted it in his hand.

'There's enough in there to buy a herd of cattle, a castle and crowd of husbands,' Kai said. 'Leave the money side up to me.'

'I'm no thief,' the girl said. 'Steal from you and the hope dies, she said.' She stood on tiptoes to get down a polished wooden box. Inside were the scrapings of a grey, sticky substance that smelled both rich and musty. 'This is the sleep. Almost out now. Mix it with beer. Can't make it taste any worse.'

'So, we leave now?' Kai asked.

Every bit of Tog wanted to get on Jenna's trail but something held him back. 'We should do something about this place,' he said. 'I mean, we can't just leave it so the next person to stay here gets murdered and robbed.'

'We're not in a position to stop anyone doing anything or help anyone right now,' Kai said. 'The girl's been paid. It's enough to follow Jenna into the unknown without stopping to save every Tom, Dick and Harry along the way.'

'If we leave the girl here, the men will kill her,' Allanza said.

'She'll slow us down. I don't understand you. This isn't about just saving Jenna. If we lose her, we lose everything. This is about saving the kingdom.'

'So is this,' Tog said.

'You pompous—'

'The king has spoken. We have a duty,' Ordan said surprisingly sharply.

Kai squared up to him. 'So what are we going to do? Hold a trial?'

'If the king wills it.'

'The king can will it until the cows come home. Who are you to come muscling in like this? Some big, ugly old—'

'Stop it now!' Tog said. He looked from one to the other. 'First thing: Kai, stop seeing problems as soon as someone makes a suggestion. Second thing: Ordan, people can disagree with me. Third thing: I know we've got to do something about this place and something to help the girl. Jenna promised. She saved our lives; we've got to do what we can.'

'She's gone,' Allanza said and nodded to the doorway.

In the hall, two of the men were lying in front of the dead

fire and two more were slumped over a table. The girl was checking the men by the fire, Tog thought. She left one, knelt by another, felt around his head with one hand and made a decisive movement. She moved to the next man and did the same, then she stood and walked to the table. As she lifted the head of the first man there, Tog saw the wet meat skewer in her right hand.

'NO!' he shouted.

The girl looked up. 'Just making things simple,' she said in a businesslike manner and pushed the skewer through the man's eye and into his head.

'You can't do that!' Tog dashed across the hall but his shouts woke the gooseman, the last man alive.

He opened his eyes, saw the skewer, and managed to grab the girl's wrist. The girl started to beat his head with her free hand but the gooseman ignored her. He had her wrist in both hands now and bent it back until the point was over the girl's heart. He twisted and pushed, the girl screamed and Tog threw himself across the table, scattering plates and pitchers, and slashed at the gooseman's neck with his sword.

The gooseman fell forwards on to the girl, taking her with him to the ground. Tog dragged him off. The girl lay on her back, staring at the high ceiling where the birds had woken and were chattering. Her fingers fiddled with the end of the skewer. The rest of it was buried inside her.

She said, 'Am I all right?'

Then, more faintly, 'I still got hope.'

Then, more faintly still, 'Brown cow.'

And smiled. And died.

At the back of the warehouse they found jar after jar of rancid oil. They poured it all over the things in the basement, and all over the tables and benches in the main hall. Then they put fire to it, waited outside until flames roared in the narrow windows, and walked off through a field. Kai managed not to talk until they could no longer hear the fire.

'I still don't think you can beat yourself up about it,' he said. 'You can hardly pretend she was innocent. She was part of the set-up. She knew what was going on all right. You can't run a tavern on the basis of killing your guests.'

No one answered.

'Well?' he insisted.

'I just think . . . we got off lightly,' Tog said.

'*We* got off lightly? We got off *lightly*? We were nearly drugged, throttled, robbed and burned. The bad men are dead and their home's been burned. How does that become *getting off lightly?*'

Tog walked on for a while. A heavy dew had soaked his

shins. His wet cloak slapped his legs. He breathed in the seaweedy air, and forced himself to notice the way the gulls tilted their wings as they floated past.

But Kai wasn't letting go. 'Well, how?'

'He means he didn't have to make a decision about the men and the girl,' Allanza said. 'That would have been the hard thing.'

'My lord takes his work too seriously.' Ordan sounded patronizing and put Tog's teeth on edge. 'My lord will tire himself if he does not give himself praise, the odd pat on the back. It is hard to be a king.'

'Especially if he doesn't have a country,' Kai muttered.

13

Boat: adventure, dying

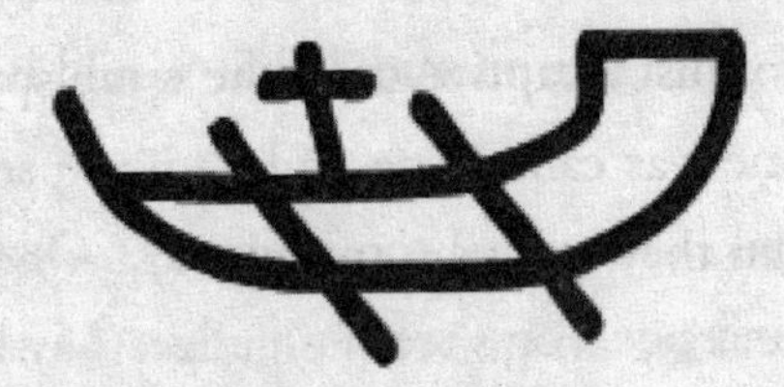

He's coming after me, isn't he? Jenna thought. Or did I just throw my hope away?

They had picked up the other boat now and were sailing up the estuary with the wind behind them, making horribly good time. A day and a night had passed since the warehouse, and the broad estuary was funnelling into a river. High rolling hills, blurred and bloated with forest, tumbled down to the river. By day the sun and by night the swelling moon swung across the sky as the boat followed the loops of the river.

The actual sailing was done by the tall boy and the red-haired one, and they were efficient and calm. When the wind dropped or blew in the wrong direction, the others rowed with surprising persistence, but for the most part they lay on the benches or the old fishing net piled in the bottom of the boat and talked. And talked. And talked. And Jenna, tied to the anchor stone by a rope around her waist, listened and listened and listened as the landscape unrolled around her.

She was not just a captive now, she was a spy.

The tall one was called Log and he was a sort of leader, deciding when they ate, who rowed and for how long. His voice was breaking and when he didn't think anyone else was looking, he stroked a mouse-fur moustache on his upper lip.

The only girl was called Pillows. A perpetual cold left red chap marks on her upper lip and she hawked and spat constantly.

The thin one who looked liked a ghost was called Nothing Happens In My Head. He was dark-skinned, dark-eyed, and lived in a world of his own, singing baby songs to himself in an endless cycle. If he was interrupted, he had to go back to the beginning and start again. Jenna couldn't see the point of him.

The big red-haired boy was called Fra Trouble Trouble. Most of the time he was practical and dependable but at any moment he could fly into a rage. He had nightmares in which he killed his best friend over and over again.

That left two more: the one with the shrivelled face and

filed teeth, who was called Toothache, and the youngest one, Face.

Face was beautiful, with skin and hair the colour of old honey, and huge green eyes. He spent a lot of the time looking at Jenna and even tried to smile at her once when the others weren't looking.

Toothache, to put it simply, was foul through and through. He could make his tongue bleed by flicking it against his teeth and did this to upset Face. He pulled the cat's tail whenever he could and talked about killing all the time – people he'd killed, people he'd like to kill, new ways of killing people he hadn't killed . . . Jenna got the message. The Little Swords knew how to kill so she had better be careful. But no one could stop her listening.

Toothache (sitting on Fra Trouble Trouble's chest, stripping a willow twig): 'Think he'll be pleased?'

Fra Trouble Trouble: 'He'll be pleased.'

Toothache: 'She don't look like much.'

Fra Trouble Trouble: 'You saying he's wrong?'

Toothache: 'No, mate.'

Fra Trouble Trouble: 'Better shut up now.'

Toothache: 'Because of . . . you know.'

Jenna was leaning over the side, her hands trailing in the water. Now she knew that they would be looking at her and her back started to prickle.

'Hey, you – freak face.'

She let them call her twice before she lifted her head, making her eyes sleepy.

'What you doing?'

She tried to read Toothache's face. 'Dreaming.'

Toothache got off Fra Trouble Trouble, rolled her on to her back and straddled her instead, knees hurting her ribs.

'Dreaming.' Toothache took her arm and pushed the sleeve up. 'You stop dreaming and tell me what all this is, girl,' he said.

'All what?'

'All these signs. Some of them are patterns.' He traced the swirls on her face that ran down her neck. 'But some of them are pictures. What's that?'

Jenna's wrist was circled by a zigzag pattern. 'That's an adder,' she said. 'It means my arm will be quick and strong and strike fast. 'Look.' She turned her arm over. On the underside, where the little pulse flickered under the skin, the snake's head was wrapped around its tail.

Pillows joined them. 'And what's that?'

That was Jenna's favourite. It didn't look like much – a fluffy bundle with a beak sticking out of it – but it meant a lot to her.

'That's a ptarmigan.'

'A whatigan?'

'In the winter in my country the cold is so hard that a man without shelter dies in an hour. But no matter how cold it is, the ptarmigan never freezes because its heart is like an ember.'

'So that keeps you warm?' Pillows asked.

'It used to keep my heart warm.'

With a filthy finger, Toothache pulled down the neck of her dress and traced the bird rising between her breasts.

'What's that one?' he asked. 'A seagull?'

'That one was hope,' Jenna said. 'But it doesn't work any more.'

'Doesn't work any more? You got any others? Special ones?'

'What do you mean?'

'You've got them on your legs and on your arms and on your feet and on your hands but now I can see you've got one between your tits but I'm wondering . . .'

Jenna went for his eyes with hooked fingers and tried to buck him into the water with her hips but he grabbed her hands and Pillows threw herself across her legs. She wrenched a hand free and went for Toothache's face again, registering how it lit up with shocked delight when she put a scratch down his right cheek and landed a good punch on his mouth. Then Fra Trouble Trouble threw himself across her, trapping her arms. Toothache giggled.

'STOP!' Log shouted.

Toothache looked down at her and winked. Blood dripped on to her from his split lip. 'Just having a bit of fun,' he said.

'You'll have the boat over.' Log's voice cracked.

'The plan said to bring her in. Didn't say anything about how.'

'In good nick.'

For a short while, it looked as if Toothache was not going to back down, then Jenna noticed that Nothing Happens In My Head's endless chant had changed. 'Three in one and one in three,' he said, then repeated it. Log looked at him, then all the others did too. Pillows and Face had joined in, then Fra Trouble Trouble, Log and finally Toothache.

'Three in one and one in three
Great is Dragon we can see
Warm is Dragon in our heart
Proper terror though is dark
Dark, dark;
Dark, dark
Dragon great and warm and dark.'

Jenna sat on the gunwales, goggle-eyed, ignoring the burn

on her wrists where Toothache had dug his nails into her skin, and the bruise on her ribs from Fra Trouble Trouble thumping her with his elbows. When they said Dragon the first time, they pressed their palms together in front of their chests; when they said it the second time, they pressed their hands over their hearts, and when they said Dark, they held their hands over their eyes.

The change in all of them was marked. They looked calm, at peace, carried away somehow, though she could not say how.

14

Coming across Nm was their first stroke of luck, Tog thought. Two days out from grain warehouse and about a day from the mouth of the estuary, their way was blocked by a wide river. The going had been hard: the foreshore was soft mud, the shore a maze of creeks. They had been bitten by too many insects and burned by too much sun. They sat down and watched the ebbing tide suck the water from the river's mouth.

'Too dangerous to swim at low tide and too wide at high tide,' Kai said.

'Lucky there's a boat, then.' Allanza nodded down the river where a long rowing boat, broad and deep enough to carry cargo, was coming into sight, steered uncertainly by a small, wiry man standing in the stern.

He waved, sat down suddenly, stood up again and drove the nose of the boat into the bank where it stuck in the mud. When the current started to push the stern around, the boat began to tip and the man scrambled to throw them a line.

'Going upstream?' he called. When they stared him down he added, 'If you are, I could do with a crew.' Another pause. 'All right, friends. I can't pay but when I pick up some cargo, I'll see you square.'

He was addressing Ordan, who nodded ponderously.

They settled down for the tide to turn so they could pull the boat to the bank. While Ordan chatted to the boatman, Kai and Allanza beckoned to Tog and walked him out of earshot of the bard.

'We're worried about Ordan,' Kai said. 'I know it just looks like I don't like him but there's more.'

'I woke up in the night and he was propped up on his elbow, staring at you,' Allanza said.

'He does seem to do a lot of that,' Tog said.

'And when I asked him what he does when he sits bolt upright with his legs crossed, you know what he said? Nothing. I am thinking of nothing.'

'Not really a crime.'

'And he seems so clumsy but I saw him catch a fly in mid-air without even looking. That's hard.'

'But you must admit he's not what he seems,' Allanza said. 'Suppose both he and Kradok were traitors?'

'He stopped Kradok escaping – remember?' Tog said.

'We thought of that. Maybe he wanted to stop Kradok getting the map for his own reasons.' Allanza's face, slightly blank at the best of times, ended up looking positively moony when he was trying to be persuasive.

'Then we need to find out what they are. I'm not scared of him.'

'It's just . . .'

'No!' Tog said, a little more forcefully than he meant. 'I don't want to change things now. He's our cover. See how the boatman talks to him and not us? That's the way I want it and he'll come in more useful when the river gets busier. I know our . . . bust-up happened because I forgot to listen but this is different. I *am* listening.'

'And then doing what you want,' Kai said.

'It's what I think is right.'

The boat was as long as three men lying end to end, and wide enough for two to sit side by side and row. It was built of overlapping planks knitted together with split hazel twigs, the gaps plugged with moss and mud. The boatman, skinny, balding, chatty, said his name was Nm and claimed to be a river trader whose crew had been poached by a rival. He was heading upriver – the town of Castlebright was just two days away and a man could pick up a cargo and a crew there.

Kai asked how he'd planned to stop himself getting swept out to sea when he hit the estuary. Nm told Ordan that he'd moored the boat and settled down to sleep but his knots must have slipped, because the next thing he knew the boat was drifting downstream. Allanza asked how big his crew normally was. Nm told Ordan it was four rowers and a helmsman. Kai asked Nm where he was from. Nm told Ordan that the river was his home. Allanza was about to ask another pointless question when Tog told them to shut up.

They let the current push them out into the estuary and were swirled around for some heart-stopping moments while the flow from the river met the incoming tide. Then the boat came round and the vast body of rising water started to carry them inland.

They took turns at the oars – two rowed, one rested, the other bailing. Within an hour their hands were sore, within two they were raw, but the dark hills were drawing in on either side as the estuary narrowed and they could see smaller craft plying their way up the banks.

Tog had busy thoughts but could get no purchase on them. They were in a boat. The boat was carrying them towards Jenna and they were making far better progress on the water than they were on land, but at the same time it was taking him closer to the dragon. It wasn't just the horror of the old warehouse, nor the army that had descended on the island like a storm, and like a storm had passed. It was a sense that the dragon had not just taken Tog's stronghold, but had stretched out his arm and ripped out his heart.

On they rowed. The hills on the left grew steeper and darker. A few settlements seemed to cling to the shore against the weight of the wild land behind. He'd seen forests before but here their endless depths and wildness were like a squeeze on his mind.

The boat slowed down as choppy water started slapping its bows.

'That's the Gwi coming in. The tide must be turning.' Nm pulled on the rudder to take them closer to the right-hand shore. Tog glanced over his shoulder and saw the wide river opening up on the northern bank. Something flashed past his eyes and hit the water with a splashy thwock.

'Arrows!' Nm shouted. 'Everyone row!'

He threw the rudder over, the boat heeling as the current caught it from the side. To avoid the arrows, they had to get right into the main current of the Gwi.

Thwock. Thwock-thwock.

'Pull! PULL. PULL!'

They rowed and the sweat fell into their eyes. They rowed until their hands were on fire. They rowed until it felt as if their backs had been beaten by chains. On their left the mouth of the river poured into the estuary with all the weight of the Powys hills behind it and on a patch of open land, half a dozen riders on small shaggy ponies waved spears at them. Past the river mouth the boat started to move more easily and after a while Nm pulled in under an overhanging willow tree.

Tog felt as if his lungs had been scorched by fire and when he dipped his hands in the river, he thought they would hiss. They collapsed over their oars, too tired to haul themselves onto the bank.

Tog couldn't sleep. His back felt as if it had been cudgelled and a row of blisters glowed white across his palms. And then there was the map, digging a hole in his ribs.

He sat up, and slid it from its leather tube. The parchment was pale like the moon and the black symbols on the back seemed to glow. He stroked them. They were the same as the ones on Jenna's back and he had to sit with the pain until it burned out.

He turned the map over and forced himself to think clearly.

If it were to be believed, the big river that fed into the estuary would take them a long way north, before it bent over sharply to the west. With his fingertip, he traced the one that headed north-east – the Big Straight Way, as it was known. That was the route the dragon's raiders had taken.

Next, he followed the line of the river but this time, instead of following the big one north, he followed a tributary that joined it from the east, not far from the estuary. The fact that it almost met the crossroads swelled in importance until suddenly the realization formed in his head like mist forming a raindrop: he was looking at the dragon's lair.

The power of the notion made his heart thump and forced him to stand. He tried to back up inspiration with reason.

One: the dead girl from the warehouse had said the dragon's base was somewhere in the middle of the country.

Two: Jenna's kidnappers and the army could both be heading towards it.

Three: You couldn't wish for a more brilliant location. Roads led from it to all point of the compass. Rivers too!

Another one headed to an estuary halfway up the country's eastern coast. If you had armies and they were mobile, you could control a country from that spot.

What did he feel? A measure of fear as these discoveries showed how formidable the dragon was. But there was elation too. Tog understood something about him now. He had conquered a little bit of him.

A sudden heavy rustling made him reach for his sword, but the big shape approaching had to be Ordan, accompanied by an extensive range of adult creaks and smells. The bard folded himself easily into his curious, cross-legged position and looked at Tog's feet. 'My lord cannot sleep?'

'No, he can't.'

'But he was using his time to unravel the mysteries of the map.'

'I was trying to work out where to go,' Tog said shortly.

'And has my lord?'

'He thinks so.'

'And would my lord be so gracious as to allow his humble servant to . . .'

To shut him up, Tog unrolled the map and held it out. Ordan's eyes brimmed with interest and something changed in the way he held himself. A tightening. A readying.

'You admitted you were interested in the map, back at the refuge,' Tog said.

'I said I was interested in such a wonderful thing, my lord. May I?'

Without waiting for an answer, he took the map at the top and bottom, ran a finger over the surface then held it up against the moon.

'Ah,' he said. 'My lord has read the words: "Behold the gift of Constantine"?'

'What of it?'

'It is not referring to the map itself but rather to a message hidden on the map. Would my lord hold it up to the light and tell me what he sees? I worry that my old eyes have tricked me.'

Tog held the parchment up against the moon. He could see nothing, just a tiny seed of moonlight showing through a hole in the parchment. And another. And another. Too many to be accident. The parchment had been pierced – a tattoo without ink.

'An X and an R on top of each other.'

'Or two Greek letters, Rho and Chi. That is the gift of Constantine – not the map.'

'I never quite got Greek,' Tog said. 'Some of the letters were different from Latin but sounded the same; some looked the same but sounded different. How do these two letters make a symbol?'

'Chi and Rho are the first two letters of Christos, Christ in Greek, and, when joined together, make a symbol of his name. Constantine had his soldiers paint the symbol on their shields before the victory that saw him become Emperor of Rome.'

'So the gift is the map, or the symbol?'

'That is the question. The symbol, I should add, perhaps predates the Christ and can simply mean "Good Fortune".'

'So it can work for anyone.'

'Indeed.'

'You know a lot,' Tog said simply.

'My lord himself knows full well that there is no better way to learn than wandering,' Ordan said. 'Across the sea, not three weeks' walk away from here, I can show you the cave where the Spring King sleeps, pale and sweet, as he is fattened on milk and pork for the sacrifice. I have studied in the libraries of Rome, been made welcome in the Courts of Clovis, and seen statues of giants rise from the deserts of Afreek. I have seen maps before, and tattoos, so for me, the mystery of your parchment is not the map itself nor the Pictish symbols on the back but the fact that they appear together.'

'So that would be why the dragon wanted it?'

'The fact that he has kidnapped the queen, a royal Pict, would seen to confirm it. It is this Pictish element that intrigues. Can my lord think of anything, anything at all, that would help? If he—'

'And tell you?' Kai's voice, sharp and sneering, interrupted. 'That would be convenient, wouldn't it?'

'Kai – what are you—'

'I'm watching out for you. More to the point, what are you doing? Can't you tell he's after something?'

'I know he's after something,' Tog said. 'And he's told me more than I told him.'

'My lord Kai is right. I was carried away. This conversation should have taken place as part of a council of war.' Ordan rose.

'So what do you know?' Kai asked. 'Is this map the reason you turned up?'

'I had no idea of its existence until that day at the Refuge,' the bard said. 'All I know, I put at my lord's disposal.'

'A likely story,' Kai said. 'From now on, you don't leave my sight.'

'I think I need to go back to sleep,' Tog said.

They set off again at midday. The tide pushed them around a vast U-bend in the river so smoothly it seemed as if the water was still and the wooded banks were moving. Night fell but the river was so placid they carried on as a huge full moon, as yellow as old teeth, laid a glittering path on the water. In the distance, the land opened up into a great flood plain.

Nm kept on screwing up his face, then shaking his head. Eventually Kai threw down the bailing scoop and said, 'All right. What is it?'

'Something in the back of my mind. Soon as I saw the moon, I thought, Nm: that old moon wants to tell you something. Question is, what is it?'

'Why is it that colour?' Allanza asked.

'Fires on the other side of the forest,' Nm said. 'Burn day and night, they do – something to do with the ghosts.'

'Ghosts?'

'That's what they say. You got to watch the woods there. Crammed full of ghosts, they are. They got flame coming from their heads and shine like the sun. They take kiddies to eat and sometimes grown men too. They're trouble. Between that and the town—'

'The place we're heading?'

'It's not Castlebright itself that's so bad, more the people, see. It's a greedy place. If you're a greedy person, that's all right. But if you're a needy person, watch out. They'll have you. They got people all up and down the river, watching out for . . . opportunities.'

'What do you mean?'

'They need workers, that's what I mean. Like I said, if you're a needy—'

Their boat lurched and their stomachs hollowed as a wave slipped beneath the boat. Its white, saw-toothed edge nibbled the bank as it disappeared into the darkness ahead of them.

'What was that?' Tog asked.

'More to the point, who are they?' Facing backwards as he rowed, Kai nodded at two craft, narrower and thinner than theirs, that were forging through the water so quickly that the bow wave glimmered white in the moonlight.

'Row, lads!' Nm shouted.

Tog and Kai took up their positions, measured the stroke set by Allanza and Ordan, then dug their oars into the water. Not too deep, not too shallow, watch the oar behind your shoulder, not too deep, not too shallow.

'Who are they?' Tog gasped.

'Slavers.'

'You're going on about ghosts when you're taking us into slave country?'

'Better chances for all us if we stick together. Now, row!'

It was a strange race, silent apart from the creak of wood, the splash of oars and the rush of water. At first they held their own, even drew away but as soon as the pursuers realized they had increased their speed, they did too and crept closer and closer.

Tog saw Nm's head turn from left to right as he looked for a place to put in, but there was a sheer mud wall on the right and forest on the left.

'How many are there?' Ordan gasped.

'Six in each boat. Too many to fight,' Tog answered.

'Ditch the boat and swim?' Kai said.

'Don't leave me, mates,' Nm said. 'I can't swim a stroke.'

'And while they're rescuing you, we'll be getting away,' Kai said. 'Whoa!'

Again the boat lurched but this time Kai and Allanza missed their strokes, tumbled backwards and Kai's oar slid from its rowlock into the river.

They rowed on hopelessly with two oars. The pursuing boats were long and low with sharp, raised bows. They surged closer, then separated and started edging up on either side.

Tog crawled to the bows where the packs were kept and unburied a bow. He fumbled the wrappings open, strung it, notched an arrow then very deliberately stood to show himself and his weapon. The boats steered away but kept up with them.

What now? He looked at the shore but there was nothing to see and anyway, they would be boarded long before they got there. He was struck at how quiet it had become . . .

. . . apart from a sort of gentle hissing sound.

'I'm just beginning to remember something, lads,' Nm said. 'I knew the moon meant something! The old god, he's down there in the water looking up and when he sees that moon, he wants a bit of it and goes chasing after it at the spring tides. Sometimes it's a little wave like the first one, sometimes it's a bigger wave like the second and sometimes it's a giant wave the height of man and it comes crashing down the river in a wall. And the reason you know it's coming is because it hisses. Row. Row. ROW!'

The panic in Nm's voice infected the rowers. They started to pull again. The hissing grew louder and now, when Tog looked back, he thought he could see a darker line above the river, fringed with white. A wave, racing down the river towards them.

The hissing grew to a roar. Low branches groaned and cracked as the wave tore at them. Their attackers began to draw closer.

'Stop rowing!' Tog ordered. 'NOW.'

The boat rocked. The shore line rose as the river shrank into itself, drawing breath. Behind them a wall of water was rushing down on them, a wave that towered over the boats. The attackers, surprised by the sudden slowing of Tog's boat, had to turn sharply towards it and were sideways on when the wave struck.

'ROW!' Tog yelled. Allanza and Ordan dug in and managed one stroke before the wave hit, knocking their attackers over. Tog felt the stern of their boat lift and the wind start to tear his hair.

'Row! Row!' Nm shouted again, then: 'Hold on!'

The wave picked them up and carried them forward on a rushing slope, so fast the trees on either side of them blurred. Tog heard someone shouting, then realized it was his own wordless yell of excitement.

'Bend coming!' he called.

Nm saw the danger. He pushed the rudder over but it made no difference. One minute they were in the middle of the river, the next they were rushing towards the left-hand bank. Nm cried out and ducked as the boat surged into the branches of an old willow tree.

Tog was too slow. One branch whacked his head, the other strong-armed him out of the boat and tossed him in the river. The water closed over him, eddies caught him, a small wave lifted him, threw him at the bank, before dragging him off. He felt a tree root under his hands and hung on as a series of diminishing waves lifted and pulled him, lifted and pulled him, lifted and pulled him . . . then stopped.

Suddenly everything was weirdly silent and he was totally alone in the river by a forest that was full of ghosts.

15

Another day, a different landscape, Jenna thought. Flatland and forest on either side of the river and, far in the distance, the grey lump of a huge hill. Could you have a desert of trees? If you could, this was it. The rickety settlements clung to the bank, as if the press of trees was pushing them into the water. The shadows were the days' sump of stale heat.

They stopped at one village to ask about the mysterious wave that has passed under them earlier in the morning and were told it was a river monster that travelled up the river a few times a year but no one could remember when. The villagers had no food to sell them and had only the sketchiest idea of what money was. Amongst themselves they spoke a different language. They kept their children out of sight.

They rowed on, Jenna tied in the bows of the boat and squinting against the dazzle of the river. She knew she should be planning her escape but all she could think about was Raindrops.

Raindrops was an idiot who lived in Jenna's family castle with the dogs. He was called Raindrops because that was all he ever said. Raindrops, raindrops, raindrops. It drove you mad. The only time he didn't say raindrops was when it was actually raining and he was standing out in it, face upturned, arms thrown wide, face stretched into a great big smile. People said that when he died, you would see his ghost as an empty shape in the rain.

Why was she thinking of Raindrops now?

Rain. It had to be because she missed the rain. She missed the way it stung her face. She missed the sweetness of it when she stuck out her tongue to catch it. She missed the way it brought out the brown, regretful scent of wet peat and heather. Her eyes drifted to a little settlement on the bank and a track that led northwards into the forest.

Toothache lay down beside her, and pinched her earlobe between two fingernails. 'I wouldn't,' he said. 'I know what you're thinking.'

'What have I got to lose?' she asked.

'What have you got to win?' he replied, and laughed

hissily through his sandy teeth. 'Very cut off these villages are. New girls are . . . popular. We carry on like this we'll make Castlebright tomorrow. It's a bit more civilized. More your kind of thing, queenie.'

'And after that?' She felt the fear dog wake up and stagger to his feet. 'Tell me.'

Toothache smiled and hissed. 'Wouldn't you like to find out why you're so . . . wanted?'

'Me? I thought you took me prisoner to get to the king.'

Toothache's burst of laughter was real and spontaneous. 'Him?'

'But what—'

'You're the one he wanted, little queenie.'

Jenna's mind flipped over and struggled like a beetle on its back. 'Why?' she asked, trying to hook on to anything that her mind could grip.

'Stand-by the sail,' Log called. 'Ready with the oars. Quick!'

Toothache winked before he slid back to his post and took up an oar.

Log had let the boat get close to the left-hand bank, so close Jenna could almost touch the leaves of the overhanging trees. Then she started.

A patch of sunlight on the leaves turned into a face: small, blank, framed by filthy hair. The shock made her shout out.

Another face appeared, and another.

'Get her down!' Log shouted. He swung the boat back into the stream. Pillows pulled her off the seat and pressed her head down until it was underneath it but in doing so, bumped her cheek against the boat's gunwale.

'Careful,' Log snapped.

'Yeah, careful. Idiot,' Fra Trouble Trouble echoed him. 'Anything happens to her—' He broke off. 'Anything happens to *her* and you're in trouble.'

From where she lay, Jenna caught an interchange of gestures and glances: a shaken head from Pillows, a finger drawn sharply across the throat from Toothache, red-faced guilt from Fra Trouble Trouble. Nothing Happens, who had stopped his muttering, breathed out and began again.

Jenna ran over the whole little incident. Fra Trouble Trouble had clearly been about to say: Anything happens to her *something*, and then tried to cover it up. If anything happens to her what?

Anything happens to her face? No. Anything happens to her . . . head, arms, legs, hair . . . Anything happens to her now, then . . .

'We're in the clear,' Log said, 'but keep her down anyway.'

'I'll watch her,' Face said. 'Please.'

Jenna didn't mind Face's sort of attention. He pressed his head into her side and looked up with his huge, clear, green eyes. He was holding the cat whose eyes were slitted with pleasure in a way Jenna felt was wanton.

'Hello,' he whispered in his small, husky voice.

'Hello,' Jenna whispered back. 'Can I ask you a question?'

'I think so.'

'Why am I being taken to Dragon?'

'Because you're special.'

Jenna felt the thought like a tongue feels a pebble. 'And is that why Toothache hates me?'

'Toothache hates everyone but especially you because if Dragon wants you, he must think you're special and, more than anything else, Toothache wants to be special.'

'Toothache's got nothing to worry about,' Jenna said. 'I'm just a hostage to gain power over the king.'

'Oh, I thought we were meant to get rid of him so we could get to you,' Face said simply.

That was it then. Confirmation.

'But why?'

Face glanced to the stern of the boat where the others were gathered, then shuffled closer to Jenna. 'Because you've been chosen,' he whispered.

'And that's why you have to keep me safe?'

Face nodded. 'We mustn't let anything happen to your beautiful secret!'

'Face! Leave your girlfriend alone,' Toothache snapped from the bows. 'Put a line out and catch a fish!'

'My what?' Jenna hissed.

Face smiled sweetly. 'Your beautiful secret!' he repeated and left her.

Ahead the forested hills were closing like a trap. I've got to escape, Jenna thought, or stop them. One way or the other.

At night the Little Swords tended to sleep on shore and she was left in the boat, arms tied behind her back and the short rope around her ankles tied to the wooden bow post. It meant, Toothache explained, that if she tried to jump overboard, her head would go down and her feet would stay up. Drown, in other words.

It was a good system – simple and efficient – and she could appreciate it. So, seeing as she couldn't unpick the knots they made, she decided she would have to unpick the boat instead.

The boat was built of overlapping planks of wood. Holes had been drilled through the overlap and a long lace of a fribrous plant was threaded through holes to press the planks together where they met. Gaps were plugged with moss and what smelled like fat. Left as usual to lie on the sail, she wriggled until her back was against the side and felt with her fingertips until she found the ties.

What's my beautiful secret? Jenna wondered. She managed to wriggle so she was close to the rope she had begun picking at the night before. Then she got her sore fingers on it and set to work. Was it her imagination or did it feel a bit looser? A bit looser and a bit wetter?

Strand by strand, fibre by fibre she tugged and nipped and when her finger nails softened in the wet, she rubbed the rough fibre between her bleeding fingertips and took a savage pleasure from the pain.

The next evening one of the rope rowlocks broke, causing a rare unscheduled stop. While Log and Pillows worked at it, Face tried his luck with the rod and line again. The low sun made everything golden. The cat looked at the ripples in the water as fish rose to flies.

There was a deep swirl in the water and the boat lurched downwards towards the water. The rod – a long piece of ash – was tugged violently from side to side. Jenna was tipped off the seat and even the cat was thrown off balance.

When Jenna struggled back up, she could see Face had managed to brace his feet against the side of the boat. He dipped the rod then worked it upwards, then from side to side. Under the water, something was stirring up the mud, tugging so hard the boat was tipping.

'It's an eel,' Fra Trouble Trouble said.

'It's a trout.' Pillows.

'Not in this river.'

A swirl. The river bulged.

'A pike!'

Jenna had eaten pike and found it tasteless and bony, so she wondered what the excitement was about. Now, as she peered over the edge of the boat, she could see how Face was letting it swim to and fro but all the time working it closer and closer to the surface. Fra Trouble Trouble and Nothing Happens were leaning closer to the edge now, looking down.

Face's arm was trembling. The thrumming line sliced the air.

'Make it soon,' Fra Touble Trouble said. 'He's almost at the surface.'

'Ready,' Face said through gritted teeth.

'He's turning. Rising. Now!'

Face dipped the rod then brought it up into an arc, using the pike's own speed to lift it clear of the water, an arc of tooth and sinew in a rainbow of thrown spray coming straight at Jenna who half rose, swivelled and clubbed it into the bottom of the boat.

'NO-OO!' someone roared, in fear, she thought.

Log had turned white. Pillows bustled into the boat and tried to grip the thrashing fish round the tail but it whipped round and sank its teeth, all million of them, into her arm. She screamed but still held on while Fra Trouble Trouble hacked at it with his sword. Back broken, the pike subsided, twitched and was still.

A moment's silence.

Pillows sobbed and held her forearm but Log ignored her. Stiffly he walked to the boat, ran his hands up and down Jenna's arms, checked her legs, then turned her round.

'It's all right,' said Jenna. 'I'm fine.' But was she? She breathed hard, as light burst through her head and the truth hit her like a big, swinging fist. She finally realized what was going on, what was so important about her, and it made her quite sick.

Fra Trouble Trouble and Nothing Happens had cut off the pike's head and were trying to make its jaws shut. Toothache was hawking a fishbone out of this throat. Face came and sat with her in the bow. 'Are you all right?' he asked.

Jenna turned so she was looking over the bows. 'Face, before the attack, were you on the island? You know, the place where the monks lived, and I lived?' Happily, she might have added, if only I'd known it.

'Yes,' Face said.

'You arrived before the attack?'

'Oh yes. We scouted. No one suspects kids – well, we kept Toothache out of sight, but the rest of us can pass for normal. He stayed on a little island with the cat.'

'And . . .' This was hard. Jenna thought of Vinny, chasing kids away. She wondered how often she'd not been alone when she thought she had. 'Did you look at me?'

Another smile, even more delighted. 'We were there a lot.'

'It's my skin, isn't it?'

'It makes you magic, doesn't it?' Like it was obvious, which it was.

Now Jenna knew why she had been thinking about Raindrops, and in particular why she had thought of him as an outline in the rain.

It was how the Little Swords looked at her. She was just an outline. A skin. What went on inside was of no interest to them.

Her skin, every pattern, every spiral, line and pinprick, crawled.

Her fate was written on her skin and there was nothing she could do about it, because once you had a tattoo that was it; it was part of your skin, part of your life, part of your fate. For ever. Which meant until you died.

Later that night, as the river gurgled round the bows of the boat, water rats bellyflopped into the stream and little creatures screamed as bigger creatures killed them, Jenna watched the slow spin of the stars above her as she picked away at the lashings. It had not struck her before that those pinpricks of light were tattoos on the blue skin of the sky. Half close your eyes, you could make them into any pattern you wanted: dots, swirls, jags, dogs, claws, birds . . .

Birds. BIRDS . . .

An idea, long buried, fluttered like a partridge in a sack. No, she thought. That wasn't possible. It was just a legend, just old fashioned, Pictish nonsense . . . The rope gave with a little sigh. She elbowed the plank as hard as she could and felt the seam gush.

'Help!' she called out. 'Boat sinking!'

16

Moon: possibility, change

Tog was up to his neck in water, hidden by a sprawling willow. The river fidgeted with its trailing leaves and swirled his warmth away; a small creature swam past him, a widening V following its nose.

When the reality of cold grew worse than the possibility of ghosts, he hauled himself on to the bank and curled up into a shivering ball. His friends were gone – his last sight of the boat had shown it riding the wave but disappearing fast. Would they come back and look for him in the forest? He hoped not. The sensible thing would be for them to push on to Castlebright and wait for him there. Just as long as he survived the ghosts.

Dawn couldn't be far off, he thought as he squeezed his knees into his chest and tried to stop his teeth from banging together.

He shouldn't be frightened of ghosts. Ghosts did not exist. He knew that. Everyone knew that. It was just . . . perhaps they did here, on the edge of the treacherous water and this immense, dense, green wasteland of forest.

Behind his neck, something rustled. He hugged himself even more tightly. Soft breathing.

Tog jerked his head round. Black leaves. Grey dawn.

A white face with round eyes.

Tog bellowed and convulsed. A tree shook as something huge rushed up it and he thought he could see a bulge where it hunched on a branch, leaning into the trunk. He didn't want to move in case it swooped, but he didn't want to go back into the river so he waited while all the birds of the forest yelled in the dawn.

The thing in the tree was a tall, thin man who wore a ragged cloak of black feathers and croaked like a raven. He had long toes with black nails and when he stood on the branch, they gripped like talons.

He plummeted down. The cloak, tied to his wrists and ankles, billowed. The creature was thin as a twig and stalked like a bird with careful feet and jerking head. Tog's skin prickled but fear lay lightly on him, like dew.

'Can you talk?' he asked.

A sad croak.

'I fell out of a boat,' Tog said. 'My friends are all in it and I need to catch up with them. Do you know how I can carry on upstream?'

The birdman put his head on one side as he approached Tog. He touched Tog's cloak and then his own.

Inspired, Tog flapped his a couple of times. The birdman chirruped, and climbed a tree, running along a high branch, before jumping across a narrow gap and disappearing into the foliage. Tog climbed more slowly, straddling the branches and shuffling along them. The birdman was waiting for him.

'Are you taking me out of the forest?'

He thought the caw sounded affirmative and followed the birdman along interlocking branches from tree to tree.

A slow way of getting around but probably better than getting scratched to pieces on the forest floor, Tog thought. Better still, the forest thinned suddenly and they dropped into a clearing.

A circle of huts was collapsing under two seasons' growth. Charred roof beams stuck out from the buildings like ribs. Perhaps it had been the birdman's home. Perhaps there had been a village of bird-people, all croaking and cawing together, thinking they were normal.

'Out of the forest and up the river, right?' he called out, just to make a noise, really. The birdman nodded with two sharp pecks and pushed through a veil of leaves and on to an old road.

Sunlight glinted through a vault of foliage. The air was thick and stifling. Black flies, fat as thumbs, pressed into Tog's face. When they kissed him, it stung. He grew hungry, then very hungry, then just achy.

At last the birdman stopped at a fast, narrow stream. Tog plunged his head into it, relished the splash of it on the back of his neck, rolled its freezing earthiness around his mouth. He could not believe he had been shivering just a few hours before.

A short distance downstream, the birdman was turning over rocks and plunging his hands into the water. He returned with four small, black crayfish, bit their heads off and offered two to Tog. Then he reached into his cloak and pulled out a small cloud of soot with an open, diamond-shaped throat. A fledgling. He chewed the crayfish, then fed the pulp to the fledging in a messy kiss. Relieved he didn't get the same treatment, Tog tried the crayfish for himself.

The meat was firm, slightly flavoured and good. He ate another, and while the birdman hopped off downstream to find some more, picked crushed shell out of his mouth.

The birdman returned with worms. Tog rubbed his

stomach and looked regretful while the birdman polished them off.

'I really do need to go,' Tog said. 'Shall I just carry on until I find a path that takes me in the right direction?'

The birdman tucked his hands into his armpits and flapped his elbows angrily. Then he hopped in front of Tog and, without looking back, strutted back to the path.

The heat grew as they climbed. The trees thinned and they came to a road of flattened stone and beaten earth. To the right it dropped between wooded ridges towards a distant glint

Tog pointed. 'There! The river. That way!'

When Tog set off down the road, the birdman attacked him, arms flapping, feet kicking. It was freakish, smelly and painful when he connected with a couple of good kicks on Tog's shin. When Tog backed away, the birdman attacked again, leaping up into the air, flapping his cloak, kicking with his feet. Tog dodged him, wondering what the trick was. The third time the birdman came at him, he realized that there was no trick; the birdman was trying to go for him like a fighting cock. On the next attack, he stepped to one side and clubbed his opponent on the back of his head with the hilt of his sword. The birdman went down and Tog set off again.

Away from the stifling mesh of branches, the air was

fresher. He glanced behind him, half expecting the birdman to be trailing behind him, but the road was empty.

He stopped, a prickle of unease, chilling his skin. Should he have just left him like that? Would it have been better to leave him tied up or even held him a prisoner? He looked at the woods on the left of the road and the scrub on the right. When he looked at the trees, he thought he glimpsed a flash of movement in the scrub. When he looked at the scrub, he thought he heard rustling in the trees.

Grow up, he said. He can't fight and, anyway, you're probably just imagining it all. Very faintly, he thought he heard singing. Now you're definitely imagining things, he thought, but, without prompting, the word ghost was in his mind.

What had Nm said: ghosts with flames coming out of their heads? It sounded unlikely but when he heard the faint singing over the sound of his footsteps, the sweat froze on his back.

It didn't sound like any singing he had heard before as it punched through the air in time with the steady crunch of marching feet. He peered down the road from behind a tree. He saw a cloud, and in the cloud silver and red things glinted. Armour. Closer still and he saw it was Roman armour – the sunlight glinting off the breastplates and the red plumes nodding.

Roman ghosts with flames coming out of their heads, shining like the sun, just as Nm had said.

Terrified, he backed further away, keeping an eye on the road but then felt a long bony hand wrap itself around his mouth. The birdman again! He panicked and lashed out but the birdman had wrapped his legs round his waist, and his arms round his neck and squeezed. He swung round, tripped, overbalanced, burst out of the trees and then there was bright sunlight all around him and he was lying on the road, surrounded by the ghosts of dead Roman soldiers. They had red eyes, hollow cheeks, grey skin. The armour was battered, tied together with plaited grasses. The plumes on the helmets were threadbare.

The birdman shrieked and buried his face into Tog's neck. Tog spat out dust.

'AVE,' he said weakly. Greetings.

There was a pause. 'VENITE,' a ghost said. Come.

Rough hands gripped his arm and yanked him to his feet. Ghosts didn't have rough hands, did they?

'UBI?' Where?

A sandalled foot prodded him. It was dirty and scabby and blood was oozing from a torn-off nail. Ghosts didn't bleed. One of the soldiers shouted at him so loud he spat. It was not Latin, Tog was sure of that, and not any language he had ever heard before – it was both harsher and more musical. When he didn't react, the soldier shouted, 'COME.'

Tog struggled to his feet, was tied by his wrists and pushed into the middle of the platoon. They relieved him of his sword – a quality blade – and commented on it, then the leather tube with the map in it, which excited no interest at all. The soldiers seemed to know the birdman; at any rate, he was greeted with a lot of merry hooting and then ignored.

Although he tried to push the thought away, Tog could not help thinking that the birdman had been trying to avoid this precise situation.

And he had ignored him.

Before he saw the town he smelled the smoke: a clinging stink that oiled its way into his head and stayed there. Straight lines of small wooden houses thatched with turf, straight streets, everything covered in a brown pall that erupted from two beehive furnaces in a field just beyond the walls. The air was bitter and leaves of the trees were spotted and covered with brown dust.

The soldiers hustled Tog through the wooden gatehouse, along a cobbled street, past open doorways where people sunned themselves. They were grey and their wrinkles were deep black, and when they called out to Tog's captors their language sounded harsh and musical. They stopped by a water trough in a large, stone flagged square. Tog drank and splashed his face. The birdman perched on the edge of the trough and tucked his head under his cloak. A soldier gave Tog's tether a couple of yanks.

'Stay!'

'I mean no harm,' Tog said. 'I am just trying to get upriver to—'

'Quiet!'

Voices came from the other side of the square where a door had opened. A group of men came out, some wearing ragged togas, but another who stood out in his bright-blue cloak.

Tog's mind sheered. He had seen the blue cloak before. He was back on the island, holding court, and an ambassador from the north was asking him about an attack, then saying something about Jenna. He had been wearing a blue cloak.

When he moved closer, Tog recognized the clipped white hair. That confirmed it. It had to be the same man!

He gathered as much of the leather tether as he could, yanked it out of the soldier's hand, then sprinted across the broken flagstones towards the group of men calling out and waving. 'You! Ambassador! The man in the cloak! It's me! The high king!'

Heads turned. The ambassador narrowed his eyes and Tog thought he saw a flash of recognition, quickly masked as if he could not believe his eyes. 'It's me! Artognu!'

A sudden yank on the lead jerked him sideways. He crashed down, thumping his head, saw stars and felt a sickening blackness yawn, and just managed to push himself on to all fours.

'Ambassador!' He stayed on all fours and watched the men approach. He heard their laughter, as if they thought he was good sport, but that didn't bother him now.

'Thank you. Thank you,' he gabbled. They were standing around him. One had barked out an order to the soldiers in the strange language.

'It's me,' he said, looking up at the ambassador. 'Artognu. Surely you recognize me?'

But the man looked at him blankly, pointed to himself questioningly, and shrugged with an embarrassed laugh. One of the men imitated him. 'Arth? Orth?' and pretended to cry. More laughter.

'And who is this?' another asked in a lispy, guttural accent.

'I don't *think* I've met him,' the ambassador said.

'Spoken like a true Gododdin! I suppose you wouldn't remember – you know so many little boys.'

The ambassador laughed again, coarsely.

Tog crawled up to him and held his knees. 'I'm sorry I didn't listen to you. I tried to talk to you. You said something about—'

His head, already aching from his fall, exploded as the ambassador reached down and cuffed him hard.

'Impudent little wretch!'

The soldiers were crowding round now, laughing. Tog couldn't stop the tears from coming. He managed to push himself to his feet. One of the men in a toga started to fire a series of questions at the soldiers. Tog tried to catch the ambassador's eyes but they looked anywhere except at him. He watched as his sword and the map tube were passed from hand to hand.

'That's precious!' Tog said. 'That's—' A soldier knocked him down. Tog tasted salty blood and understood something with utter finality. Whether the ambassador had recognized him or not, it didn't matter. Some mistakes were for ever and you couldn't regret yourself out of them.

He was led into a wasteland where a giant had chewed up earth and rock and fire, then spat it out again. Furnaces belched greasy black smoke and in the pall, runnels of molten metal glowed white, yellow and red. He was prodded on to a stone road that zigzagged up the hillside, keeping to the side to avoid the sledges that were being dragged along it. Full of ore on the way down, empty on the way up.

They stopped at a hole in the side of the hill framed by timber props, where a foreman was making marks on a tally stick. His gut was like a bulging grain sack and his legs were round as barrels. A skinny boy emerged from the tunnel, bent almost double by a rock-filled wicker basket on his back. The foreman hefted the sack without taking it off, dropped it back down on to the boy's back and carved a notch on to the tally stick. The boy staggered over to the sledge, emptied the sack of stones into it and shuffled back underground.

The foreman beckoned Tog over, pinched his biceps, pressed his cheeks to open his mouth and shoved him hard towards the mine entrance.

'Pick up,' he said, pointing to a stack of battered wicker sacks. When Tog didn't move he hit him. 'Pick up!'

'There's a mistake,' Tog said. 'You don't know who I am. I'm the high king. My friends have money. They can pay you. They could buy this mine. I could give it to you.'

The man looked at him and frowned. 'You are little king? Good. Here is your little kingdom. And here is your little crown and a little cloak.'

The man picked up a basket. A strap passed across Tog's forehead, his arms fitted through two more.

'Now go,' he said. 'Or I kill you.'

There was nothing Tog could say. He followed the crouching figure ahead of him.

Tiny lamps set in niches were too weak to light the way but gave Tog somewhere to aim for. Everywhere else the darkness pressed in like felt. Narrow tunnels wound downwards, opened up into bigger spaces and then narrowed down again. Pale faces loomed at him, then passed – children crushed under baskets of ore. The light became stronger and he found himself in a large underground cavern lit by torches. Naked men with whip-thin muscles stood on scaffolds and hacked the rock face with picks. Children dodged the falling ore and dropped it into the baskets. Basket-carriers waited in line.

'What happens if you don't work?' Tog asked the boy in front of him. 'There's a quota,' he answered. 'Don't meet the quota, overseer don't get paid. Overseer don't get paid, we don't get food. Every evening, the boy who's carried the least has to make it up in one go. That'll be you today.'

'Why me?' Tog asked.

'Because you're new. You're not hard. It's all right – everyone's slow at first. Then they get fast. Then they get slow again. Then they . . . We don't see them any more.'

'How long . . . have you been here?'

'Two months? I don't really know.'

'What happened?'

The boy shook his head. He was at the head of the line now. He closed his eyes as the first rock went in, and his thin frame shuddered. Again, again, again. Tog wondered how many journeys a day you had to make.

Now it was his turn. He hooked his thumb under the shoulder straps as he had seen the others do and braced himself.

The first lump of ore crashed against his spine and seemed to drive him down into the rock. He groaned and staggered. The next was even worse. And the next. Sweat bloomed on his forehead. How much more of this could he stand? Crash. Crash. Crash. The jarring pain went on. And on. And on. Then stopped.

'Move.' The child behind Tog kicked him. He set off.

The height of the basket meant you had to crouch so low you were practically on all fours, but if you didn't keep your back tilted up, the rocks slipped out and hit you in the back of the head. By the time he saw daylight ahead, two boys had overtaken Tog and shouted at him.

He made another journey. When he was standing in line on his third attempt, the boy behind him said, 'You've got to try harder. If the overseer thinks you've been slacking, he'll just load you up until you can't stand.'

'What happens then?'

The boy looked at him pityingly. 'He doesn't stop.'

Another journey and he noticed that it was getting dark outside. On the way back down, he passed the miners going up, made it back to the cavern and collapsed.

Supper was sloppy porridge and there was a barrel of water with a scoop that you helped yourself from. Tog was so tired and had so little force left in his hands that he dropped the ladle in the barrel and was cursed for it. The skin on his shoulders was raw; his knees and palms were on fire.

'Here.' The boy he had spoken to earlier unwrapped a length of fabric from around his shoulders. 'I want it back though.'

'What's it for?'

'For your back. You're going out again.'

'It'll kill me.'

'He'll kill you if you don't. They just don't care, see? You're just another body to sacrifice to Votan, their god.'

'I was told these people were ghosts.'

'We call them Romans. That's all I know.'

'Why don't you escape?'

'There's the overseer and then there's Votan. He's out there. He never sleeps. Even though he's got one eye, he sees everything. Where are you from?'

'Britain,' Tog said bitterly.

'What's your name?'

'Artognu the High King,' Tog said.

'Ridion,' the boy replied calmly, as if Tog's answer was as likely as any other. 'How come you ended up here?'

'I lost my kingdom and fell out of a boat,' Tog said. Self-pity was so thick in his throat that it choked the words.

'I was in the fields when they came,' Ridion said. 'They only took the children because grown-ups are too big to fit down the tunnels with baskets.'

'What happens to all the ore?'

'After they burn it and the metal comes out, the iron goes upriver. Some of the coal too – that's black stuff that stinks when it burns. They say a dragon eats it. Here's the overseer. Good luck.'

Tog lowered his voice. 'Listen,' he said. 'I'm going to escape and when I come back I'm going to stop this happening. It's not right.'

'How?' the boy asked.

'I'm going to lead an army here and we're going to free you.'

'Be quick. No one here lives very long.'

Then the overseer was standing over Tog. 'You bad boy,' he said. 'Bad boy, bad work. Come.'

Tog put his arms through the basket straps and braced

himself while the overseer picked through the lumps of ore.

Tog braced himself.

Crash.

He staggered backwards.

Crash.

The next rock knocked him to his knees. The overseer pulled him upright by the hair.

Crash.

Another rock smashed into his back. It was like a hammer blow, beating him down.

Crash.

He wasn't a king. He was a pile of rocks with a stone for a brain.

Crash.

A picture was jolted into his mind: that ambassador pointing and laughing at him.

Crash.

The next one jolted it out. He tried to find some anger to make him strong.

Crash.

He forced himself on to his haunches, felt for the wall, began to haul himself up.

Crash.

Muscles creaked. As he forced himself upright, he thought his head would explode.

'Good boy. Another?'

Tog braced himself.

'Very good boy. Perhaps Votan will not kill you.'

'Who's Votan?' Tog asked through gritted teeth, trying to get the basket balanced.

'Votan is our father. Votan lost his eye so he could read and write, then hanged himself by the foot from the Great Tree. If Votan sees you being bad, he tells us and we take you to the tree and hang you from it. Then his big black birds, Hunin and Munin, come and eat your eyes and then the rest. Now, go, go, go!'

Tog went.

The strap across his forehead took some of the strain off his back. If he stopped, he would never get going again. Now take a step, and another, and another. On he went, lit by the tiny guttering flames, step by step.

'Be good, little king. You see, I hear you. I hear all things in the darkness.'

Tog felt his anger, compressed it in his belly. Wait, he said to himself. Wait. The roof's higher in the next chamber. You can stand there.

It took an age to get through the low tunnel and by the time they reached the chamber, Tog's thighs burned like meat on a spit. Although he couldn't see the space around him, he could sense it ahead of him and it felt good. Now the low tunnel entrance was one step, two steps behind him. He slowed. Felt the overseer bump into him.

'Careful!'

Tog held his breath, let his anger power through his legs and, with a roar, pushed himself up and back, then let the weight of the basket drag him down on to the overseer. He heard him fall, heard him scream and the rocks crashed down on to his legs, and Tog, liberated from the weight, sprang forward.

As the overseer bellowed, Tog pushed on, felt the path rise – surely there was a left-hand bend, then a right, then it was straight to the top. He scraped his back, scraped his palms, pushed on, keeping low because if he hit his head at this speed, he'd be brained. But where was the daylight? How far did he have to go? Nothing ahead but darkness and more darkness. He was nothing. There was nothing. He fell forwards into nothing and it was a second before he realized that the lights above him were stars and the coldness was the clean night air.

He stood, stretched and then forced himself to jog down the stone track towards the town. He was like an arrow. Arrows didn't feel pain. Arrows didn't think. Arrows just went where you told them and did their job.

The smelting ovens were still roaring red as people fed

them coal, worked the bellows, paddled the molten metal with long poles. Tog found an empty barrow, dragged it through the middle of the works, trudged alongside a wagon that was creaking towards the town gates, walked up to the head of the oxen, held the halter behind the huge, solid jaw and slipped away before the driver shouted at him.

The town was laid out in a grid and so it was easy for Tog to move through the empty streets towards the central square. He heard drunken singing coming from the shuttered windows of a house on the edge of the square, and as he paused in the shadows a door opened and a man in a toga walked out, swaying drunkenly. Tog pressed himself against the wall, waited for him to go and then went to have a look.

The building had a balcony around the first floor and shuttered windows all the way round. Tog darted into the side alley and peered through a gap in the shutters. An inn of some sort. Bare rafters; a wooden staircase at the back. A long table, the ambassador at the head of it. Three men on either side. Jugs of wine. Piled plates. The ambassador was speaking, holding the rolled-up map.

'This will help me secure the concessions you ask for with my master,' he was saying, and he tapped the leather map tube in his hand. 'We have grain; you have coal. We can do business, if not today, then at some other time.'

'Another drink!' one of the other guests called out. 'For good sleep and happy dreams and a good thick head in the morning.'

'I must have my wits about me if I'm to set off for the north at first light.'

But he took the offered beaker, held it up to each of the men in turn, pretended to drink, then called out, 'Good night!'

He left, climbing wooden stairs at the back of the room. Halfway up he turned and put a hand to his head, as if he'd just remembered something. 'What did you say was going to happen to that boy?'

'Ah! The boy you are not interested in and don't know! Don't worry about him,' the men at the table called. 'His secrets and yours will stay in the mine.'

'Ah yes. Good night.'

'Ave!' The man threw his arm out in a Roman salute. The others stood, knocking benches over, and did the same. The ambassador raised his arm tentatively.

The men left after singing a mournful song. The innkeeper bustled in, finished off some of the wine left in the beakers and wandered off into the back. Tog forced the window and climbed into the room.

Bread, meat and cheese were strewn across the table. He

took a swig of sour wine and filled his mouth with food. Felt a rush of comfort. Picked up a knife and touched its point. Good.

At the top of the stairs was a corridor with lots of doors, all closed but for one. Tog peered in. The room was simple and empty but, more importantly, it had a slatted screen door, operated by a simple latch, that opened on to the balcony.

Tog crept around, peering through the slats. Most people were asleep. One traveller was paring his toenails by lamplight. The ambassador was in the last room he came to and was holding a smoking lantern above the map, peering at it closely.

Tog planned his moves. The latch was on the inside but he could flick it up by slipping his knife between the door and upright. The ambassador would hear. That meant he would have three beats, no more, to get into the room and get his knife in the man's throat. Latch, door, two steps, stab.

It all worked, or most of it did. The latch flicked up, the door flew open, and Tog was on to the ambassador before he could get a weapon or get away.

Instead he did something much more useful: he instinctively held up the thing in his hands to protect himself, and the thing in his hands was the map.

'Put that down,' Tog snarled.

'My lord?'

'You recognize me now?'

The ambassador breathed twice, then said, 'I recognized you in the square.' His voice, and eyes, were level. He settled himself on his feet but kept the map raised.

'I couldn't admit it. I mean, it would have done you no good and placed me in danger.'

'But I'm . . . I mean, I'm still . . . king.'

But the words felt hollow and tiny in his mouth. As soon he'd said them, he knew they had no currency.

The ambassador looked away. 'I'm sorry,' he said. 'Sometimes we . . . I have a duty. I have a responsibility to my people to make alliances where they will do most good. That is why I asked you about your defences. I hoped you would not fail.'

'But now I have failed, you must make alliances with someone else,' Tog said. 'So do it.'

'Do what?'

'Turn me in. It would make these people grateful.'

The ambassador opened his mouth, closed it, looked away.

'Come on,' said Tog. 'Who are they?'

'Teutons. Very few Roman legions were Romans. They took troops from all the empire as a way of bonding it together. When the legions were called back to help Rome ninety years ago, these people's fathers decided to stay. They've been hiding in the forest ever since. We wanted to trade – horses and grain for iron but they send it all upriver to the dragon where it's traded in his market. They gave me the map as compensation.'

'It's mine,' Tog said.

'I know. And I suspect it's important. The marks on it are Pictish but the map itself is Roman. My people . . . were poised between the two of them: the unstoppable Romans and the unbeatable Picts. This map is a mystery.'

'I may as well tell you it came as part of the queen's dowry.'

'Really?' The ambassador's face sharpened.

'You mentioned her at the end of the audience,' Tog said. 'I couldn't hear it. I tried to follow you but you'd gone and then I had . . . other matters to attend to. You said something like, "People are saying that the queen is the . . ."'

The ambassador shook his head. 'Oh that. The queen is the key. I wanted something from the meeting to take back with me. I'll explain more fully. Relations between my people, the Gododdin, and the Picts have not always been peaceful. Once we were united against the Romans, then, when they built the wall, we . . . saw which way the wind was blowing. The Romans needed grain and horses so we sold them grain and horses and grew rich. The Picture People, your wife's people, have only just forgiven us and with her marriage to you, it seemed that peace and stability might be established But it's all so fragile, my lord. Your father, the high king, just managed to persuade people that it was better to trade than fight and just managed to arrange the marriage with the Pictish princess. Now that she has gone . . . who knows what the Picture People will do?'

'But that phrase – the queen is the key. What does it mean? I heard the pigseys say it, or something like it, at my coronation, but forgot all about it.'

'Well, she's the key to peace.'

'Is that it?'

The ambassador looked uncomfortable. 'It's probably nonsense. It's an old saying, a prophecy almost. When things are bad, and people are just waiting for it to improve without actually doing anything, you say, "What are you doing? Waiting for the Queen of the Keys to ride over the wall?" Then recently this rumour started that your queen was the key to something else – that she had some greater importance. Of course, we want to find out what it means. There is one other thing, now we're talking of rumours and mysteries.' He made a *pah* sound as if to dismiss what he was going to say. 'In my country, there is a story . . . a story that three Roman emperors travelled to Pictland. Travelled there under treaty because they had heard of a great . . . marvel that the Picture People had somehow got their thieving hands on (no disrespect to the queen). In fact, that's why they came to Britain in the first place. It's nonsense. When could three Roman emperors come together like that?'

'The writing on the map mentions a Roman emperor.' Tog said. 'Constantine.'

'I saw. He was the last Roman emperor to visit the north and campaign against the Picts. I suppose the map could have been dropped by one of his generals, picked up by a Pictish raiding party who defaced it with their marks.'

Tog thought how Chi Ro, Constantine's symbol, had been pricked on to it like a tattoo without the ink. To him, that suggested a deeper connection between the Romans and the Picts, almost as if one was copying the other. Should he tell the ambassador? He decided against it. Instead he said, 'The attack . . . the one you tried to warn me against. It was for one reason only as far as I can see: to capture the queen. We know this warlord who calls himself the dragon was behind it but I don't know anything about him.'

'Depending on who you talk to, he's Old King Coel come back to life, the grandson of a Roman general, or just a mindless thug. We don't know. Somehow he's amassed a fortune, an army and has . . . a new way of doing things. He's set all his neighbouring kingdoms against one another and is making trouble in the east – after generations of living together, Saxons and English and Britons are at each other throats. Then he's got this religion – the Seekers they call them – and some people are saying he's a god, or even the Old King come back to life to save the country in its hour of need. The truth is, no one knows who he is but we're all aware of him – and his wizard, the one they call Merthen. Some say Merthen's the true power behind the throne and controls the dragon with witchcraft. People have seen Merthen – he goes out and about – but the dragon is always masked. No one's seen his face.'

The sound of shouting came in through the open balcony door. Torchlight flickered through the slats.

Tog looked out. 'It's a mob,' he said. 'Sounds like they know a prisoner has escaped,' he said. He looked at his knife, then at the ambassador. 'I really don't know what to do. My plan is to find my wife, kill the dragon and get my kingdom back.'

'And you're wondering whether to kill me so you can make your escape.'

'I don't want to,' Tog said. 'But you did let me go down the mines.'

'I could help you.'

'How?'

The ambassador shook out the biggest bag on his bed and held up a woman's hooded robe. 'It was for my wife but you need it more. Put it on and join the hue and cry. They're looking for a ragged slave, not a woman in a robe. Here, this is food, and here,' he reached into his purse, 'are some coins.'

'And the map?'

'It is yours. If you live and kill the dragon, will you remind your wife's people that the Gododdin still want peace?'

'You think I'm your best chance?'

'You're an opportunity.'

'Then we meet opportunities in the strangest places.' Tog peered out through the door. The square was filling up with people holding torches, shouting, banging on doors.

'I will repay you,' he said.

'We're giving each other life,' the ambassador said. 'It's enough. Now, the town of Castlebright is two days' walk up river. You'll be able to pick up news there, but be careful. They're not so kind to travellers with no money so make sure you hold some of it back.'

* * *

Tog slipped the robe's hood over his head and stepped out into the corridor. He followed a couple of guests down the stairs, then joined the happily bloodthirsty mob in the square. He was jostled and swayed out of it, down narrow streets, calling for himself to be strung up, and allowed himself to be carried all the way towards the southern gate. When the crowd shouted at the guards, he opened his mouth and roared with them. When the guard opened the gate and the crowd split up and started scouring the ditch below the ramparts, he skipped off into the woods.

It was the worst kind of wood to hide in: widely spaced oaks and chestnut trees, dried leaves that rustled, the ground cleared by pigs. Tog took off the dress and kept going steadily, lifting his feet up and putting them down carefully, making good ground.

Voices ahead made him drop to the ground and move forwards at a crawl. Guards were posted along a rutted forest track and the moon was only a few days off full and treacherously bright. He sank down between the roots and tried to think. As far as he could tell the town was behind him and the river in front, but he would have to work his way along the road until he found a place to cross.

Then he heard people in the forest behind him. Townspeople must be beating the ground. Tog headed left, skirting the road, but it was impossible to move silently and at speed. A voice called out from the road, and it seemed to be challenging him. He flattened himself up against a tree. It called out again and was answered from close behind. Panic hollowed out his head. He ran half a dozen steps, heard another voice and jinked away from that into thick undergrowth. Then the ground beneath his feet exploded with an ear-piercing scream and Tog was knocked sideways by what felt like a large, padded rock, and slammed face first into a tree.

He slid down, stunned. Screaming and crashing. Pigs! He'd stumbled on a family of sleeping pigs. He curled up as small as he could, listening to them crashing away. His pursuers ran past him, hooting and hallooing.

His chance. His right eye, which had taken most of the impact, was closing as he dashed across the road, forcing himself to ignore the jolting pain in his head.

The wood grew thicker. Rotten wood and brambles choked the ground. A shout to his left. A shout to his right. A shout from behind. Ahead, the undergrowth was impenetrable. Trapped. Blood roared in his head as he looked desperately around. Then close by, a little off to his right, a raven croaked.

Was the undergrowth a little less dense there? He found he could move relatively quickly. A nightjar whistled to his left. He went in that direction. The ground grew boggy and he came to a ribbon of water with a blackbird singing upstream.

He followed it. The ground rose. A skylark drew him away from the stream and he glimpsed moonlight through the leaves, pushed hard towards it and stopped dead on the edge of a great clearing.

It was blue and black in the moonlight, a solitary oak tree standing in the middle of it. Tog stared at it, exhaustion breaking over him in waves and he knew he had to rest. The wood behind him was suddenly terrifying.

He sprinted across the clearing, ignoring the unexplained crunch of things underfoot, the long fruit that hung twisting from the boughs and the terrible smell, sweet and bitter, that hung in the air. He swung himself up by a low branch and began to climb.

Then he saw where the birdman's whistles had brought him.

From a higher branch, hanging upside down by one leg was a dead boy, quite black with rot. Below him was another one, rather fresher. And right by Tog's face, where it was pressed against the branch, was a leg. And now, when he looked down, he saw the ground under the tree was covered with bones and from all the lower branches, bits of body hung like old fruit.

What had he been told? They hung bodies from the branches of a tree as a sacrifice to their god.

Tog climbed until he was above the hanging boys and found a broad branch. Roosting ravens, real ones this time, shuffled around him on the branches. One cawed. Another crashed through the branches, circled the tree and glided back. Tog straddled his branch, his back against the trunk, watched the birdman flap across the clearing towards him and felt the sweat dry on him. He shivered and worked the dress over his head, then put his head down on the branch and closed his eyes. Memories spun him back in time: the chase through the woods; the iron mine; the birdman; the boat sinking; the warehouse; the island . . . He was free. He had to remember that. Free.

His bruised eye beat time with his heart and throbbed him to sleep.

17

Flower: useful, pretty, breaking

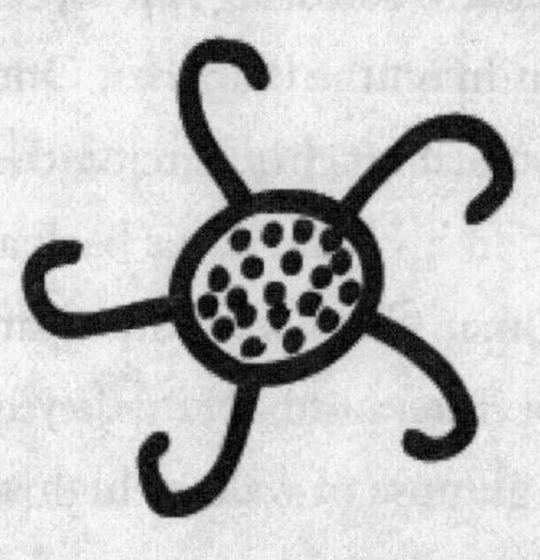

Now the boat was passing between fields that were worked by stout, sunburned people who stopped and stared as it passed.

Pillows had thought up a song about her and they sang it all day long.

Queen of nothing all covered in marks
Looks like a spider crawled out of your arse
Think you're so clever
But you're just thickture
Stupid crap queen with her stupid crap pictures

On and on it went while Jenna lay in the bows, trussed up like a chicken.

Repairing the boat had taken them half a day, much less time than Jenna had hoped, and then Pillows had noticed Jenna's torn nails and worn fingertips, and put two and two together. Being trussed up and left out for people to look at was punishment enough for her, along with the song and the wretched cat, which battered her eyelids when she blinked.

Jenna didn't see Castlebright properly because Log dropped a sack over her head before they reached the town, but she caught a glimpse of walls as high as cliffs and as the boat scraped into some hard mooring she began to hear a sort of simmering roar. It was, she realized with a shock, just the sound of people: hundreds, maybe even thousands of people.

The boat rocked as the Little Swords stepped off it and one of them dragged her up to her feet. Toothache. 'Think we'd leave you behind, did you? Face, you take your girlfriend. She gets away, we kill you.'

Face preferred not to use the rope they gave him but to wrap his hot little hand round hers as he told her what she was not seeing. 'There's a shop selling pots. There's a shop selling food. There's a guard. There's a shop and guard. Ooh! There's a great big black horse.'

Jenna had no idea what a shop was, nor how one could sell anything as basic as food and would have appreciated more simple advice like how to stop stubbing her toes. She noticed that people stopped talking when the Little Swords approached and she was certain she heard a woman cuff her child when they were past and tell it not to look at the devil children or he'd be cursed. And the Little Swords themselves were quiet, apart from Face.

A general change in the quality of the sounds and a lightening in the atmosphere made Jenna think something had changed.

'What's happening?' she asked.

'Nothing,' Face said. 'We're in the town square. It's really boring.'

Pride prevented Jenna from asking what a town square was but she sensed they were in the open after having been somewhere very closed. Why would a town want a square and how could people be in one?

'Where is everyone?'

'It's not market day so it's empty.'

'The square is where they have a market?'

'Of course. And all the buildings around it are important. Like there's a temple and there's a grain store and there's . . . I don't what they are. Big buildings with pillars.'

The heat bounced up from the flagstones. Big, smooth flagstones, her bare feet told her. No grass between them. She thought she had heard the liquid silver of falling water.

‘I’m thirsty,’ she said. ‘Really thirsty.’

‘Give her a drink,’ she heard Log say. ‘The rest of us go inside. We’ve got business with the council.’

Face tugged her towards the sound of the fountain and stopped when she could feel the wetness on the flagstones from its splashing. She could practically hear him thinking, so said, ‘It would help if you took the hood off my head.’

He lifted it above her mouth. It slid down again. To make matters more complicated, Jenna knelt, tipped her head under the stream of water and started to splutter.

‘No, no, no,’ Face said, and lifted the hood off her face. Jenna looked around, blinking in the harsh sunshine. She saw a field of stones bounded by rows of buildings at right angles making . . . a square. Obvious. The fountain was on the edge of the square, water falling from a metal pipe into a stone trough. People in the shadows stared at her.

‘I’d like to wash,’ she said.

Face didn’t answer.

‘But I can’t. My hands are tied behind my back. Do you know how to wash me?’

She glanced around. People were keeping their distance.

‘I can’t let you escape,’ Face said.

‘I know,’ Jenna tried to sound soothing. She didn’t like what she was planning but didn’t know what else to do.

Face loosened the rope around her wrists. She flexed her fingers, stretched, making her shoulders crack, then plunged her arms and hands into the water.

It was cold and the shock brought them back to life.

She stood, whipped a leg round, knocked Face off his feet, rolled behind him, and was about to apply neck-snapping pressure when suddenly she wasn't behind him; he was behind her. Worse still, he had grabbed her arm and was bending it backwards in a hold she didn't know. She could feel her elbow breaking and her shoulder twisting so far that the straining sinews squeaked like cat gut. She forced herself upright, tipped forward suddenly, felt Face somersault over her but instead of crashing into the water for drowning, he found the edge of the trough with his feet, sprang back, landed behind her, released and before she could turn, had kicked her in the side of the knee. Her foot, caught between two flagstones, did not move but the joint did.

Sideways.

Jenna went down. Pain took over that side of her body, shooting up and down her leg. She struggled to her feet but the joint ground loosely, as if the two surfaces had turned to granules, and she went down again with a scream, hands clamped round her knee, not really understanding what had happened.

Half blinded by tears, she looked up at Face, whose expression was concerned.

'You smashed my knee,' she managed to say.

'I'm sorry,' Face answered. 'I'm sorry. I had to keep you with me. I did say. You do understand, don't you?'

The odd thing was that Jenna, who had never been bettered in a fight before and had been about to kill pretty little Face without much compunction, did.

When the others joined them, they were bright-eyed, full of themselves, loud-voiced and it was clear they'd been drinking. They called for a stretcher and ordered four men to carry her to an inn. Every jolt made her gasp with pain and she was relieved when they left her in the corner and carried on with their drinking. She turned her face to the wall, eventually falling fitfully asleep against the background of their shouting. She did not know if she were dreaming or not when she felt boozy breath against her cheek and heard Fra Trouble Trouble slur, 'Yup, that's her.'

'The Crow Queen? Can I touch her?' A stranger's voice. An old man's voice.

'Get your hands off unless you want a slap.'

'Not even for another jug?'

'Now you're talking. Go on then. Touch her. But be careful. She belongs to Dragon and he don't like to share.'

Jenna screwed her eyes even more tightly shut and braced herself, but the touch on her shoulder was respectful, even as Fra Trouble Trouble called for another jug of wine and the party continued.

18

Barking dog: watchful, watched

Tog woke up stiff and sore with bark ridges stamped firmly into his cheek. A raven shuffled sideways down the branch. The birdman was crouched on the branch below, his head tucked under his arm, another raven asleep on his shoulder.

He peered through the leaves.

The clearing was on a cleared spur of land, and immediately below it the ground fell away in a series of wooded folds to the great horseshoe curve in the river. Tog thought about his friends. Had they escaped? Had the river taken them? Were their ghosts now dancing in the twists of mist above the flat, dark water?

And talking of ghosts . . .

Below him the flies were busy about the corpses. The

horror he felt the night before was replaced by a stifling rage. How could you end up here, hanging from a tree, after you'd been half killed in the mines? And why?

He heard voices.

A procession was crossing the field: two men wearing white robes and odd, pointed hoods, then three men carrying a ladder with a wriggling boy tied to it, then two more men holding a rope stretched between them.

With a shock, Tog recognized Ridion, the boy from the mine. Tog leaned over the branch to see what was happening, lost his balance and found himself slipping. Ravens exploded from the tree.

Tog, hanging upside down, his legs hooked around the branch, heard the chanting stop and silence, tense and thick, fill the clearing. Then a ladder pierced the veil of foliage below him. Before he had a chance to react, a man's head, still covered in the pointed hood, appeared. He looked to the left, then to the right, then down.

Then up.

His eyes widened, he gave a throaty cry, fell sideways off the ladder and crunched into the ground. Through the leaves Tog glimpsed him wheezing, limping and pointing backwards as he ran across the field shouting, 'Votan! Votan!'

An argument followed that the man won because first

one, then another, then all the voices started to call out, 'Votan. Votan! VOTAN!'

What had the foreman told him down in the mine? Votan was their god. He had given up his eye and hung himself from a tree to learn how to . . .

Tog hauled himself upright as another hooded head appeared below him. He roared angrily and bellowed, 'Votan' in a cracked voice. His throbbing eye made him realize how gruesome it probably looked – as if he had plucked it out. And he was hanging from the sacrificial tree . . .

He had to go for this while he still had the initiative.

The man ran away and Tog dropped to the ground, picked up a skull and leg bone for effect and walked across the grass to the men – correction, his priests – with what he hoped were god-like strides.

He felt a rush of wings as two ravens swooped down from the tree and circled over his head, calling.

'Votan . . .' one of the priests began.

Tog pointed furiously at the ground. Looking at each other, the priests lengthened themselves in the dewy grass. Ridion struggled into a sitting position to see what was happening, then quickly lay back down when he saw Tog, who poked him in the ribs with his toe.

'What makes you worthy of sacrifice, dog?' Tog shouted.

The boy whimpered.

'I know you as I know everything. I am Votan the all-knowing. Look at me, Ridion!'

Shocked eyes swivelled up. Tog widened his eyes and mouthed, 'It's me.' He saw the boy recoil, then gather himself. 'Speak, dog! Do you know who I am?' he shouted again.

'Yes, Lord. I think so.' Ridion's voice was shaking.

'Prove it. Who am I?'

'Votan.'

'And how do you know?'

'Because Votan hung himself in the world tree. He had only one eye.'

'Yes,' Tog said. 'I did.'

He heard a rustle behind him as if the priests were moving. He turned round suddenly.

'You so-called priests, crawl on your bellies and listen. Eat the earth. How many summers have passed since you were left in this land? Ninety? One hundred? How many winters have passed since you followed the Eagle? Ninety? A hundred? I have travelled far and I have travelled wide. I have given up my eye and I have learned the secrets of words and I have not forgiven you for following the Roman god.'

'Oh, Votan,' one of the priests said. 'We never forgot

you. We have filled the tree with sacrifices for you and you alone.'

'Dogs. Idiot dogs. Idiot lice that crawl on idiot dogs. I know who you have hung from this tree. Every last one of them has come to me and begged for vengeance. Why? Because, idiot dust on idiot fleas on idiot dogs, you have been hanging my chosen ones. Why did I pluck out my own eye? So I could keep one eye on the underworld while I wandered. And you: what do you do? You pollute its blessed darkness with the cries of children. I see into the darkness now, I see blood where some fat idiot overseer's legs were crushed. Am I right? Does the lost eye of Votan see the truth?'

'Yes, Votan.'

'Then free this boy. Free the others in the mine. This is my decree. If you disobey me, I will hang you all myself from the Tree of Knowledge so you can learn some sense.'

'And will you join us, Votan? Will you honour us by your presence?'

'I will not,' Tog said. 'Because you disgust me. But when you have worked in darkness for a hundred years, I will return. Now go, go before I vomit my guts on to you.'

Tog noticed that the man who had found him was looking at him and there was something intelligent in the way his eyes glittered through the slits in his hood.

'Perhaps Votan would show us a sign. He of all people would know how easy it is to trick us poor humans.'

Tog felt the attention of the others shift to him.

'A sign? Is it not enough that my servant, the raven man, is with me and my two ravens, Hunin and Munin, attend me? Is it not enough that I am here?'

The priests stood, and Tog felt a pressure coming from them he did not like.

'If you gave us a sign, Lord, we could return to our people and tell them.'

Tog picked up a rib bone and began to scratch in the bare earth beneath the tree.

VOTAN was quite easy to write. The priests looked at the ground, then at him.

'But that is the language of the Franks, Master,' one of the priests said. 'It would please us if you could write with our own, sacred letters.'

'Dog. Dog of dogs. Dogs of Rome. Dead dogs of a dead people, I write with these letters because you are not worthy of your own. Now go. Leave my holy place. You have made it filthy with your corruption. Go, cowards. GO!'

And that was the moment the birdman decided to make his appearance: leaping down from the tree, cloak flapping with a huge croaking cry. The tree exploded as the ravens launched themselves into the air, rose, fell, came together and finally circled the great oak in a ragged crown of black and the birdman, arms outstretched, cloak flapping, danced and hopped and croaked in triumph.

The priests ran. Tog's throat was sore, he was breathing hard but he felt as happy as the day he was crowned.

'Thank you,' Tog said to Ridion. 'That was brilliant.'

The boy dropped his eyes. 'Yes, Lord,' he said and took a step back.

'We really tricked them.'

'Yes, Lord.' Another step.

'You're not going, are you?'

'No, Lord.' Another step.

'Stay. Please.'

'I would rather go, Lord. I got into trouble for talking to you in the mine.'

'Yes. But now you're free. You don't think I'm Votan, do you?'

'The priests did.'

'No, they thought it was safer to think of me like that. As soon as they've calmed down, they'll be back.'

'Even so, you escaped from the mine. You hung in the tree. You can write.'

'There's no trick to that. I could teach you.'

'I'd rather keep my eye.'

'You don't have to—'

The boy turned and ran.

'Are you scared of me?' Tog asked the birdman.

The birdman cawed, lifted an arm and preened imaginary feathers.

'You were trying to help me from the beginning. You tried to keep me off the road, you guided me away from the town, you brought me here, you appeared just at the right moment to frighten the priests away.'

The birdman walked to the tree, and kicked around in mess of bones beneath it. He picked up a length of frayed rope and plucked at it hopelessly with filthy nails that curled like young ferns. Tog was very aware of time passing; he wondered how long it would take the priests to return.

'Perhaps you knew someone who died here,' Tog said. The birdman plucked at the rope and looked up.

'Perhaps you wanted to untie their bodies, but couldn't. Perhaps you brought me here to do it. All right.'

There were eight bodies and the sound they made as they fell was awful but as he climbed down, Tog felt he had done the right thing, even if he did not know why.

The birdman walked with him to the edge of the clearing. The fledgling, nestled in his hand, gasped for food. Ravens circled low above his head. The birdman cawed softly.

'Thank you,' Tog said. 'I don't know what else to say.'

The birdman pecked the air with his head, and stalked back across the clearing. Tog began to push his way downhill.

Tog found a narrow track along the riverbank and followed it – nothing else to do – and in the end it took him two days to reach Castlebright.

He saw dragonflies, butterflies and once a kingfisher flew past, a flash of blue and gold. His black eye opened and the bruises from the mine started to ache less. Fishermen exchanged meals for news of the world beyond the river and, because they knew he was passing, told Tog about their wives, their children and sometimes even where the best fishing spots were. No one tried to kill him, kidnap him, rob him, or demand anything of him and on the second night, he did not dream about Jenna or drowning or the battle on Fenny Castle.

But even better than that, priceless in fact, was the time he had to think.

If he was able to fool some priests that he was God, surely he would be able to play the king, for a while at least. It gave him a feeling of calm, as if everything in his head had settled into a new arrangement.

Encouraged, he studied the parchment until he had memorized every line and symbol on it. He closed his eyes

AMELIA HOWARD
2B3

HOMEWORK CLUB

OPEN TO ALL YEARS

and remembered the marks on Jenna's naked back. Now he thought about it, there were two very different kinds of tattoos on her skin: the ones that swirled like smoke up her legs and down her arms and the ones that looked as if they had been drawn by a child, mostly on her back: the ram, the moon, the barking dog, the wheat stem, the boat, the sun . . .

He sat bolt upright. How could he not have noticed this before? On the map the ram, the dog, the flower, the sun, the wheat stem, the boat and the moon described a rough circle.

Just as they did on Jenna's back.

On the map, a ridge of mountains ran up the centre of Britain, like the smooth bumps of Jenna's spine.

On the map, the land narrowed at two estuaries, one on the east and one on the west, before spreading out again, just as Jenna's body narrowed at the waist before flaring out at her hips.

It meant something; it had to, but what? The meaning was there but it was like a fish in a dark pool, tempting but elusive. When the walls of Castlebright came into sight around a bend, it was almost a relief.

19

Heart: vulnerable, understanding

Log was throwing a fit. Their drunken binge in Castlebright had cost them time. Instead of being bang on schedule they were almost a day behind. He started shouting when they woke up and carried on when they staggered into the boat, when Fra Trouble Trouble was sick over the side, even when they woke the next day, hungover and wretched.

'What's the panic?' Jenna asked Face, trying to care through a haze of pain that spread out from her knee and seemed to infect her entire body.

'We've got to get past the Wickwicks in time. When midsummer gets close, they go a bit mad. It's the drums. Once the drums start, there's no controlling them. Even Merthen's scared of them and if Merthen's worried, you know it's serious.'

When they talked about Merthen, they dropped their voices. If the dragon wanted them to go on their expedition, it was Merthen who gave the orders and set the schedule. He must be the dragon's enforcer and right-hand man, Jenna thought, and that was interesting. Some rulers wanted to be loved and they would use an enforcer to do their dirty work. Some rulers wanted to be feared, so didn't care what people thought of them. Dragon, from what she could tell, wanted to be loved.

But that was not the most important thing on her mind. Two little words, *Crow* and *Queen*, were.

Jenna could not believe that anyone outside Pictland had heard of that piece of superstitious nonsense, let alone an old man in Castlebright who wanted to touch her. None of the Picture People cared. It was just a bit of fun, wasn't it?

Jenna had first met the previous Crow Queen by accident. She was six and spent as much time as she could on her pony to get away from her sisters. She'd ridden up Big Hill but when she got to the top the mist came down, everything went grey and she got lost. As instructed, she gave the pony his head but instead of taking her home, he had carried her straight to the neep pits outside the Crow Queen's bothy and started nosing around in them.

It was a long, low building, with the hill as its back wall

and a single steep slope of dripping turf as its roof. Jenna was frightened – all the children knew how the old witch drizzled little babies in honey before roasting them – but Jenna was six and above all that, so she knocked on the door and when it opened said, 'I'm six years old and so tough you'd break your jaw if you tried to eat me but I want to come in because I'm cold.'

Wrinkles scored the Crow Queen's face like cracks in summer peat and her fingers were dark blue. She gave Jenna a cup of pine needle tea, asked her to tell her about her family, showed her the tattoo dye she was making, sucked her gums and then pointed out that the cloud had moved on and the sun was shining.

Jenna did not see her for another six years.

It was a warm, midgy, drizzly summer's day. Jenna was going spare because her pony was lame and needed resting and her sisters were talking about weaving and boys. When the old woman hobbled up, a wooden box strapped to her back, her mother screamed with delight, and her father, king or not, was ordered to take all the men off for a day and a night.

It happened in the big room, right there in front of Jenna's mother, aunts, three sisters, one niece, three servants, two slaves. Outside, Raindrops danced in the yard and the farmyard cock ranted at a circling buzzard.

The Crow Queen pointed to her, and Jenna of course burst into tears because she really did not aspire to the old woman's existence. The Crow Queen, slightly huffily, assured Jenna her lifestyle was a personal thing, and they got down to the matter in hand.

The world was changing, the old Crow Queen said, and the old certainties and traditions meant nothing any more. In the past, the Crow Queen had one simple duty: to choose a worthy successor. However, she had dreamed that Jenna was going to be the last Crow Queen and had been thinking long and hard about what that meant.

'What?' Jenna asked.

'When the time comes, the secret will no longer be a secret.'

'What's the secret?'

'It's a secret that the old Crow Queen passes on to the new Crow Queen.'

'So what's the secret?' Jenna repeated.

'You're not the Crow Queen yet, my girl. Now, let me get on with it.'

'Get on with what?'

'Putting the marks of the queen on your back. These are secret too so I have to do them myself. Everyone else clear off.'

And she opened up a long leather tube, unrolled a

parchment and kept on holding it up to the light while she copied the shape on Jenna's back, muttering to herself. *Now, I remember that you have to take that thingy and add that thingy and imagine a line . . . north. Why did I think of north? And what's the other thing? Oh yes, the crow marks the spot. Only Constantine found that out, the clever little weasel. The crow marks the spot.*'

It took the Crow Queen the rest of the morning and most of the afternoon to finish and when she was done, the pain was so bad that Jenna could hardly move.

'You lie still then, Crow Queen,' the old woman said. 'Lie still and think about what I've told you.'

'Am I the Crow Queen now?' Jenna asked.

'Yup. I passed it on.'

'So what's the secret?'

'What did I tell you?'

'That the old Crow Queen has to tell the new Crow Queen.'

'No such thing as an old Crow Queen,' the woman laughed. 'Either you are or you aren't. You are. I'm not. Hard luck. Ta ta for now.'

'But that's—'

'Cheating. I know. Oh, I almost forgot. There's a rhyme you have to know. Now repeat after me:

Promise to watch,
Death to use
Strong and warm
Moon at the top.'

Jenna repeated the nonsense to get rid of the old bat and wrote off the whole experience as yet another useless tradition that deserved to be lost. More irritating still, in spite of her mother praising the old Crow Queen's work as genuine folk art, the glimpses that Jenna got of the tattoos showed them to be ugly and amateur and certainly not worth the pain they had caused her. What was more, as far as she could see, there wasn't even a crow on it.

Back to reality, and back to the boat. Escape was impossible and yet had never seen so important. She groaned and tried to get comfortable. Her knee ached and throbbed and burned and hurt even more if she moved it. Face was curled up in the crook of her arm, and confusingly, she wanted him there even though he had probably crippled her for life.

'What are you doing?' Face breathed in her ear.

'Nothing.'

'Yes, you are. I heard your skin move.'

'Oh, that was just me trying not to laugh.'

Unexpectedly, Face began to cry. 'What is it?' Jenna asked.

'If you were one of us, I couldn't hurt you. I didn't want to hurt you but I . . . had to.'

'It's all right,' Jenna said. 'No, it's not all right, but think about it this way. It's my job to try and escape and it's your job to stop me.'

'Like a game?'

'Sort of. By the way, where did you learn that move?'

'Which one?'

'The hold that nearly broke my shoulder and elbow.'

'At training camp. Not everyone can do it. All of us on this mission were hand-picked.'

'And when you said that you couldn't hurt me if I was one of you . . . What did you mean?'

'It's one of our promises, when we become Little Swords. One of them is we love Dragon as much as he loves us and another is that we never hurt another Little Sword. Swords stick together.'

'And could I become one?' Jenna asked, without really thinking it through.

'That's the problem. You'd have to . . . You have to do something bad, so Dragon can forgive you. Then you get the training.'

'You're not bad,' Jenna said. 'If it's killing you're

worried about, I've killed men.'

Face sniffed. 'But this man was tied up. It was when they came to my village. It was dawn. They kicked down the barricades. Killed the guards. If you stayed in the house you were burned; if you ran, you were hacked down unless you were young. They just captured you if you were young. Made you lie on your face while they tied the old ones, the ones they hadn't killed, to trees. Then Merthen . . .' He hesitated. 'Merthen . . .'

'Merthen? Tell me about him.'

'He calls himself Dragon's teeth and Dragon's claws. He does what Dragon wants. Anyway, he gave me a knife and said Dragon wanted me to kill a man. "Kill him or we kill you," they said. So I killed him and now everyone hates me apart from Dragon. He's the only one that loves me.'

'It's a trick that wicked people know,' Jenna said, her voice trembling with fury. 'First they make you do a bad thing. Then, when you're feeling really awful about the thing you've done, they say they might forgive you but only if you do exactly what they say.'

'But it's true,' Face said. 'You saw the people in Castlebright and everywhere else. They all hate us because we deserve it, apart from Dragon.'

'If you hadn't killed this man, he would have killed you.'

She felt Face's head shake. 'He wouldn't.'

'You don't know that.'

'I do.'

Jenna sensed there was more, and waited. A thinning moon sailed across a gap in the clouds, an owl floated across the river, bats danced in the air.

'He was my daddy. He said it was all right but that didn't make it better.'

Jenna opened her mouth but the sense flew out of her mouth like a cloud of flies. To her relief, Face carried on talking. 'Then they took me to the Centre and Dragon told me that he could forgive me. He forgives everyone who gives themselves to him.'

'Does he indeed.' Jenna knew she sounded like her mother, but for the first time in her life didn't mind. Face snuggled further into her side, as if something in him had relaxed.

'And what did Dragon tell you about me?' she asked.

'Only that we couldn't fail. We have to get you back for the midsummer feast because that's when Dragon's going to eat the old world.'

'And what am I? The seasoning?' Jenna asked.

'I don't think so. I think you're going to make the new world. You and Dragon together. It's to do with your secret.'

A secret about which I understand nothing, Jenna thought. But I wonder if he knows that?

The river wound between low hills. Jenna dozed and woke and dozed and woke in a light mist of pain. A brown dog (a real one, she thought) followed them along the bank for a few hours, changing blue when it entered into her dreams and singing beautiful songs about bones and tails that wagged for ever. But when it started whispering about the smell of her skin, she realized it was the fear dog and forced herself to wake up.

The sound of whispering: the Little Swords were having a secret, night-time meeting.

'You shouldn't have told her,' Log hissed.

'But she didn't mind, honest,' Face said.

'She did,' Log said. 'She hates us. Dragon says we're different. Everyone hates us. Only he loves us. Only him.'

'But—' Face persisted.

'Dragon tells us it is so, so it is so.'

'It's just that—'

'I'd be quiet, sweetheart,' Toothache said, 'unless you want Log to slap a blasphemy charge on you.'

'But she listened—'

'We've all got a story. You just got to hold it in, Little Sword. Hold it in.'

'And seeing as we're up, we may as well row on,' Log said, then raising his voice above the protests, 'We're not past the Wickwicks yet. You wait till you hear their drums.'

Midday. Fra Trouble Trouble pushed his way to the bows and started to sniff the air, kicking Jenna out of the way.

'Meat,' he said. 'I smell meat. Smells like someone's roasting a pig on a spit.' He spat into the river.

'We should push on,' Log said. 'Come on. There'll be pig and beer for us back at the Centre. More than we can eat.'

'But I'm starving,' Fra Trouble Trouble said. 'I can feel it in my mouth. It's hot. It's fatty. It's—'

'Me too,' Toothache said. 'I'm starving. We'll just get a bite to eat and be on our way.'

'We'll row quicker with a good meal inside us,' Fra Trouble Trouble added. 'Help us get past the Wickwicks.'

'It's true,' Face said. 'And when did we ever get pigmeat at the Centre?'

Log opened his mouth, then closed it quickly. Jenna was sure he had been about to tell them to behave, but then had realized that he might have a mutiny on his hands.

'Well, we'll have to see,' he said.

The camp, the source of the enticing cooking smells, was pitched on a muddy bluff above the northern shore. Children with glistening brown bodies were jumping into the river from an overhanging tree, the clean spray making sudden rainbows. When Toothache steered the boat into the bank, they followed the party up the hill, chattering and making fun of the way Fra Trouble Trouble carried Jenna over his shoulder, like a sack.

The camp consisted of half a dozen leather tents. A few goats were tethered to stakes close to a hobbled ox and a pig on a spit was cooking over a fire, the fat hissing and flaring in the flames.

A child was turning it carefully.

A man stood. He was lean, bare-top and bearded, long hair tied up above his head. He kept his face impassive and asked them their business.

'Travelling up the river,' Logs said with an awkward grin.

'The girl is tied,' the man said, nodding to Jenna. They had gagged her and tied her to a tree on the edge of clearing before they went any further.

'Oh yes. She's simple, see? Talks all the time. We have to tie her, otherwise she'll roll herself down the hill and drown herself in the water. Can't swim. Heard about a healer upriver.'

A woman joined them. Like the man, she was lean, handsome and tanned. 'And who's in charge?' she asked. 'Are there no adults with you?'

'No one's in charge, really,' Pillows said. 'Well, Log's the oldest so if he says something we listen but—'

'Your parents. Where are your parents?' the woman insisted gently.

Pillows sniffed enormously, hung her head and dashed the back of her hand across her nose. 'Lost 'em. Pirates took 'em. All of 'em. Jus' tryin' to do our duty. Jus' tryin' to help.'

The woman's face softened. 'We have no problems sharing our good fortune with you. We caught a boar this morning – chased it right into our net – and we've been cooking him ever since.'

Her voice was low and concerned. Lovely, Jenna thought, and let her eyes drink her in, the woman and her man and all the children who were so happy in their care. But the way the heat blanketed the smell of wild flowers and cooking meat made her feel faint and goosebumps rose on her skin in spite of the heat.

Log said, 'Don't get me wrong: are there many of you?' He managed to look scared at the thought.

'Just what you see.'

Jenna watched him hide his fingers behind his back and count on them. Nine. He would be counting able-bodied adults. Too many for the scouts to take on, she most fervently hoped.

'The little one is hungry?' the woman said. Toothache had gone over to the pig and was trying to pull strips off it. The child in charge of the spit, not realizing what he was up against, was about to hit him with the basting ladle.

Jenna screamed through the gag and everyone turned. Toothache, whose hand had reached round to his concealed sword, checked himself, and flashed his sharpened teeth at her.

'I'll see what's up,' he said and swaggered over to her, knelt and put his face close to hers. Close up, the smell of his decomposing teeth was almost unbearable. 'Wasn't going to do anything. Just cut me a piece of meat. But now might be a good time to talk.'

He pulled the gag out of her mouth.

Jenna kept her expression blank. 'What about?'

'The little chats you're having with our Face.'

'I'm lonely.'

'He's your pet. Tell you about killing his dad, did he? The bad things that happened to him?'

'And your point is?' Jenna asked carefully.

'You feel sorry for him because he's so pretty but do you think I was always like this? Do you think I held myself down, forced my mouth open and took a file to my own teeth?'

For the first time Jenna looked into his grey, wizened

face, and tried to see the child in there. Really tried.

'I suppose not.'

'The worse we are, the worse was done to us. Face, he got off lightly.'

'I'm sorry,' Jenna said, abashed.

'I was happy once. You could . . . maybe with your charms . . . you could get that back for me.'

'I know you're clever,' Jenna said. 'You don't . . . follow Dragon the same way as the others, do you? You know he's not always right.'

'You think if you call me clever I'll turn into your little pet too?'

'It's true though. Dragon said that the bad things you did set you apart but when Face told me his story, I didn't think he was bad, did I? I understood. Same when you spoke just now.'

Toothache looked at her a long time.

'And I'll tell you another thing,' Jenna said. 'It made Face feel better to talk to me.'

'You think it'll make me happy too?'

'It's what you want. It's what you all want. To be happy.'

'Just give me charm like what Dragon wants!'

'Tell me what they made you do, Toothache. Tell me.'

'I . . . I . . .' Then he pushed her back roughly against

the tree. 'Get off me,' he blurted out. He leaned back, his eyes hurt and full of tears. 'You don't know nothing. You're as bad as he is. Just want to get inside my head and mash it up. Now you've made me hate you.'

He left. Jenna watched the sky load up with clouds as people stuffed themselves: the men carved the meat, the women broke the bread, the children made plates out of leaves. They ate, came back for more, and more, then lay back on the grass and chatted. Someone sang a sad song. Someone sang a happy song but Jenna thought the whole scene seemed to be *performed* in some way.

Was it just that the Little Swords were acting normal? Pillows had a baby on her lap. Face was laughing. Log was talking to the man and Fra Trouble Trouble was having a stick fight with a couple of younger boys, and playing nicely.

The heat pressed her eyelids down. Fra Trouble Trouble was doing handstands for the children now. It was a good act, she had to admit but still she felt this fear, even as he collapsed in a heap, then curled up, like all of the others. Curled up and slept in a pile, like puppies.

Jenna forced herself to stay awake by rubbing her face against the tree and biting her tongue. She forced her wrists apart again, trying to work the bonds down the back of her hand, then saw something in the clearing had changed.

Like ghosts, the adult travellers were rising. One fetched a long, dark roll from a tent. A net? The one they used for catching pigs?

They dropped it over the pile of Little Swords and when they leapt up – furious, shocked, struggling – tightened it around them until they were one big struggling mass.

And that was that. The adults conferred, then two stayed with the net, and the others walked off to the river.

Jenna redoubled her efforts – so far, no one had thought of her – and stretched and rubbed her bonds on a broken branch behind her. A last tug, the bonds fell away from her and she flattened herself in the long grass. Then a very strange thing happened. As she crawled deeper into the woods, the fear dog, who had been sleeping twitchily in the sunlight, staggered to his feet and started to follow her, grinning with his broken brown teeth and dribbling from his blotchy lips.

What was going on? The fear dog wagged his stumpy broken tail and hobbled closer. No! Jenna thought. This wasn't fair! He was forcing her back, telling her not to run. So she turned, just to see what would happen and the fear dog lowered his head. And as she began to crawl back towards the clearing, he gave a sigh and faded away.

20

Bird's foot: speed, stupidity

While he waited for a ferry with about a hundred other people, Tog looked across the river at Castlebright's harbour. Boats nuzzled the quayside like piglets on the feed. Porters carried towering bales into storehouses that lined the jetty. No sign of Nm's boat.

The town sat just above the river behind stone walls. There was a gate on the harbour and one on the other side, to judge from the steady stream of people and ox carts crossing the flood plain on a broad, dusty road.

Once Tog landed on the quayside, everyone started to move twice as fast as him. When a man trying to balance two huge oars on his shoulder walked past, it was almost a relief to take the back end and help him to the barge at the far end of the jetty. The mast was raised but its brown sail was furled and it was only half laden with bales of dyed wool.

The boatman had white hair, bandy legs and huge hands. He was the colour of old wood and looked as hard. 'If you're looking to work your passage upriver, we've got no places,' he said without looking at Tog. 'Why? The usual. Kings dying, armies on the move, drought, famine.'

'I need to find out if some friends docked,' Tog said.

'I've been here a couple of days. What boat were they on?'

'Rowing boat. It may have been sunk by a big wave – that's when we were separated. There were two boys my age, one my height and the other a giant, and an older man, sort of big and shambling.'

The man lowered his voice. 'Same every time, matey, same every time. The wave comes down the river once or twice a year on the spring tides. Next day the locals are out on the river picking up the wrecks and the poor so-and-sos who fell in. Any unmanned boat, or even a boat that needs their help, they just help themselves and call it salvage and the crews … well, put it this way, they don't take kindly to people with no possessions in Castlebright. It's a racket. If your friends were picked up, by now they'll have been charged and if you want them back, you'll have to pay. See what I mean, matey? This really isn't a place to hang around. Look, a steward's nosing about already. I'll tell him we've just taken you on.'

Tog saw a man in a reddish leather jerkin bearing down on them.

'Thanks, but I'll be all right. When are you leaving?'

'Meant to be taking on another load so on the afternoon tide, if we're lucky. Why?'

'If I can find my friends, can you take us upriver? We'll pay our way.'

'I doubt you'll get out of Castlebright,' the man said with a shake of his head. 'Still, I'll run it past the captain.' And he bent his head and began to coil rope.

The steward had a shaved head and small eyes that noted Tog's torn clothes, mad hair, bruised legs and skinned knuckles. 'By the powers invested in me by the municipal authority of Castlebright, I have the right to question you as to your means and motives for availing yourself of the facilities of this city,' he chanted. 'You may choose to accompany me on a voluntary basis or you may choose to be escorted. Either way, you agree to be held liable for any charges that will or may arise as a consequence of your decision. What do you choose?'

'I'll come,' Tog said.

A cobbled ramp led from the quayside to a fortified gate.

The street grew even more crowded and Tog gawped at everything he saw: there was a shop selling sides of meat, others selling earthenware flagons, vegetables in baskets, piles of salt. A man was beating out a copper bowl; another plaiting handles for buckets. It all made Tog feel bewildered and inadequate. Why ever did he think he could be king of all this, along with everything else?

They stopped in the town's main square. A temple took up one side; arcaded buildings the other three. A fountain played against the far wall. The steward led Tog to a door guarded by a single, hot-looking soldier, and ushered him in.

Behind the pillared façade was a large hall with small rooms leading off it. The steward knocked on the first door on the left and opened it on four men dressed in good-quality tunics who were sitting in a row behind a trestle table. There was money on the table, arranged in piles according to size, and from the expressions on the men's faces, it looked as if they had concluded some very satisfactory business.

'Chairman. I apprehended this person on the quayside with no apparent means of support and no stated business,' the steward said.

'Recommendation?' a clean-shaven man drawled. He was sweaty, jowly, his face darkened with stubble. His hair was curled into tight grey sausages, which he now touched, tenderly.

'To be referred to the—'

'I have got business,' Tog said. 'I'm looking for three people.'

'What three people?'

'Our boat capsized two nights ago.'

'Vagrants?'

'No – we were just passing through.'

'Vagrant?'

'I said, we were—'

'No, you.'

Tog reached into his bag and hefted his purse. 'I've got money.'

To a man, the committee members looked disappointed.

'If they are vagrants that are in our custody, you will be referred to the Sub Committee of the Council of Citizens.'

'But I just want to find out—'

'All matters pertaining to vagrants are dealt with by the Sub Committee of the Council of Citizens,' the man said. 'Sitting this afternoon. On payment of correct fee.'

Tog reached into his purse. 'How much?'

'Don't pay me – that would be most improper. A fee to cover administrative costs may be levied by the

Sub Committee and of course there is the question of your bond.'

'Bond?'

'In case you abscond. Returnable of course, as and when you present yourself, although we shall deduct supervision fees.'

'Supervision fees?'

'An escort shall be provided by the municipality. For your safety, of course.'

At an inn just off the square, the steward explained how the system worked.

'Listen – someone owes you money but can't pay, you deserve to get the money back from them. Right? So if they can't stump up with the cash, it's only right that they go to work for you until they pay it off. OK?'

'But a vagrant doesn't owe money,' Tog said. 'He just doesn't have any.'

The steward looked indignant. 'So tell me, who pays for the streets he begs in? Who keeps them safe? The city does, of course. And why is he begging in the first place? Because he wants money without working. Where's the fairness in that? None, so to even things out, we give them food and shelter and put them to work. That way everyone's a winner.'

'Free food, free lodging. Sounds good.'

'I never said it was free, did I?'

'So who pays?'

'They do, with their labour.'

'For how long?'

'That's where it gets complicated. Food and shelter doesn't come cheap.'

'So you put them to work, and then they have to keep working for the privilege of being put to work. For how long?'

'Depends on how hard you work. Believe me, it's better than the other way.'

'Which is?'

'If there's no work in Castlebright, we sell the debt on. People come from all over for the trade.'

'How does that work?'

'Well, they pay us what the beggar owes and the beggar has to pay them off instead of us.'

'So you sell them.'

'We sell their debt and give them the *opportunity* to pay it back. I know it sounds harsh but it's the Castlebright way. Look around you. This is a rich, successful, orderly town. In other words, our way works.'

He called the innkeeper over, who charged more for the meal than Tog thought was possible. The steward stood. 'The committee should be sitting now. Time to get on with it.'

The Sub Committee of the Council of Citizens consisted of the same people Tog had seen earlier, the only change being the mutton grease on their chins and wine on their breath.

'Well?' Tog asked.

'The Sub Committee of the Council of Citizens can confirm that three people were picked up by river stewards two days ago,' the chairman said. 'They were on the riverbank and placed themselves in the custody of the city by begging for transport.'

'I'll pay their debts,' Tog said.

'Debt payments are dealt with by the High Chamber of the Town Council,' the man said.

'I just want to free my friends,' Tog said.

'In exceptional circumstances, we can request that the High Chamber convenes.'

'I'll pay you double,' Tog said, and reached into his purse.

'You won't get anywhere with that attitude, young man,' the chairman said, but took the money. Tog left the room, walked round the square, and went back in.

In front of the High Chamber of the Town Council –

the same people as before, of course – Tog was asked to prove that he had sufficient funds to pay off the outstanding debts. He emptied the contents of his purse on to the table, which coincidentally was just the right amount.

The steward led him across the hall, unlocked a low door and threw it open.

Kai, Allanza and Ordan were sitting on the floor, tied by the wrists to hoops set in the wall at about waist height. If they stood, they would have to stoop; if they sat, their arms were pulled above their heads. Even so, Ordan seemed to be asleep. Allanza and Kai flinched.

'What do you want now?' Kai asked in a small voice. He was hunched and shrunken, his eyes scrunched shut.

'It's all right,' Tog said. 'It's me.' He tried to sound calm but a cold worm of anger twisted inside him.

'Tog?' Allanza asked. He blinked, turning his head this way and that.

'Free them,' Tog said. His anger grew as the steward started to fiddle with the knots. Allanza's and Kai's wrists were raw. 'Use a knife. That's going to take too long.'

'You'll have to pay for the rope,' the steward said.

'Do it.'

Freed, the captives fell to the ground, then struggled to their feet, eyes watering in the light. They stretched, rolled their shoulders. Kai took a step and Tog only just managed to catch him before he fell. Allanza and Ordan staggered into the hall and rubbed their raw wrists.

The steward unlocked another door and showed them their three swords, laid out on a table. Then he stood in the doorway, blocking their way, making himself big.

'Those are ours,' Kai said.

'Storage fees.'

'I gave all my money to you to free them,' Tog said. 'Look, I've got a good blade, worth money. I'll sell it.'

'No money, eh? That makes you all vagrants again and under our statutes, vagrants aren't allowed to be armed. In fact, vagrants are fined for carrying weapons, so under the powers invested in me—'

Tog's head caught him in the midriff hard, just below the solar plexus. He doubled up and fell. Ordan threw himself down, jamming his elbows into the man's gut.

'Kai, there's a guard by the main door. Check he hasn't heard. Allanza, can you tie this one up?'

'What are we going to do then?'

'Get some money, get new clothes and get out of here.'

With a sword in his back, the steward led them across the hall and called to the guard outside. When he stuck his head through the door, Allanza said, 'Hello,' and knocked him on the head with a cudgel he had found. They tied both men up, gagged them, then barred and bolted the door.

'Let's join a committee,' Tog said.

The committee, still seated behind a long trestle table, were dividing up Tog's money and didn't stand a chance. As the door slammed into the back wall, Kai and Tog lifted the table and sent it crashing down on to the four men, pinning them to the floor and sending coins flying through the air.

Tog jumped on to the unturned table and pointed his sword at the row of stunned faces lined up underneath it.

'Anyone moves and the chairman dies,' he shouted. 'You, take off your shirt!'

'No,' the man said. Flesh rippled as he jerked his chin. A red flush rose up his neck. 'I'm not taking orders from—'

Allanza smashed his cudgel into the ground. The man wriggled his arms free and began to strip.

'Take off your robes, rip them up, then tie up your friends,' Tog said. His head felt cool and spacey; his body balanced and fierce. He stuck his head out of the door. 'Steward. Come here and pick up all the money.'

The steward, who was in earshot said, 'I'd love to, master, but my hands and feet are tied.'

'Then crawl over and pick the money up with your mouth. Oh, and if we think you've swallowed any, we'll slit you open to get it back.'

* * *

The chairman had a keyring with five big keys on it. One fitted the front door, one the back, the third opened the prison cell and the fourth was for the store rooms. Worn clothing, old bowls, age-smoothed tinderboxes, and a few weapons were neatly stacked on shelves – all confiscated from travellers like themselves.

They took the best of the clothing, then Tog said, 'There's still one key.'

In a dark corner at the back of the hall, they found the door to a half-basement. A sweet, bitter stench lunged through the door as they opened it

A long room, empty, with a single barred window high up in the wall. Heavy chains hung from iron hoops that were riveted to the wall. The floor was covered with compacted filth.

When the committee members saw where they were being taken, they started to struggle and were pushed into the room at sword point

'You little brat,' the chairman gasped. 'You'll die for this.' His curled hair had come loose and flopped over his face. He tried to move it away by blowing, but failed.

Tog said, 'I'm going to ask you questions, and you will answer them. If you don't, my companion will kill you and I will ask the next man. If he doesn't answer he will die and so on until I think someone is telling me the truth. What's this room used for?'

'Gentlemen, gentlemen, gentlemen.' The chairman now adopted an oily tone. 'This is most unfortunate. Although we have been acting within our rights, we're men of the world and can see that we've upset you. Let's talk business. You have our money; what say we give you free passage out of here and say no more about it?'

'Wrong answer,' Tog said. 'Quite a lot of it's my money. Allanza, which is less effort? A blow to the head or a knife through the ribs?'

'I'll talk, I'll talk,' the chairman said. 'Not that there's much . . .' Tog turned on him. 'No, no. I'll tell you. It's slaves but—'

'Of course it is,' Tog snapped. 'But why are some chained up in here?'

'That's when we get a big consignment in. We store 'em then send them on. We just provide a service, that's all—'

'We were told to look out for you!' one of the men who had not spoken before interrupted. 'Orders.'

'From who?'

Colour drained from the chairman's face. 'Please, don't ask about them. We can't talk. Have you any idea what they'd do to me? To my family?'

'No one need know,' Tog said.

The man looked desperate and rolled his eyes.

'Oh I see, you're frightened your colleagues will tell on you if you talk. All right, we'll kill you all. Start at your end, Allanza.'

The general writhing was satisfactory, in a nauseating sort of way as all the men started to talk at once.

They were oppressed, it turned out; terrorized. No one could trust anyone else. When the Little Swords came, you did what they said or bad things – no, terrible things – happened. Innkeepers and shopkeepers who charged them disappeared. Farmers who crossed them would find all their stock dead within the week. He'd cornered the slave market, reduced Castlebright to a mere holding pen. He had spies everywhere.

'Who's he? Who are they?' Tog asked.

'*They*'re children who've been . . . changed in some way. They don't fear anyone. It's some kind of magic.'

'And were they here recently?' Tog asked.

'Three days ago. They rested at the inn out by the Eastgate.' A committee member, who had been silent up until then, spoke fussily. 'There were six of them and a special prisoner. A tattooed girl.'

'How was she?'

'We don't ask. The dragon wants money, gold, slaves . . . there's nothing he doesn't want. Nothing he doesn't have. He's got his own army. He's got his own wizard. He's got his own religion. If he wants a tattooed girl for whatever reason, he gets it.'

'All right,' Tog said. 'You've earned your lives. Gag them, chain them, leave them. We're off.'

In the town square, the stone walls glowed in the afternoon sun and cooked them like an oven. 'Is that it?' Kai asked.

'What do you mean?'

'This is where we find out about the dragon before we go charging off again. His troops. His headquarters. His resources. His track record.'

'And if we do, what then?'

'We can make a plan.'

They walked down a shaded alley and stopped by a little mossy fountain where clear water ran from a god's mossy mouth into a dark bowl. An empty house was full of pigs. Refuse lay around them in piles. Dogs watched them from the shadows. Tog's brain felt baked hard.

'We need to find out about Jenna. You heard the man in there. She was taken to an inn at the Eastgate.'

'But at least let me—'

'We stick together. It's just luck I found you, really, and we've lost days already.'

'Allanza, back me up here,' Kai protested. 'If we rush . . .'

But Tog was off, running after a bandy-legged, white-haired man who had just lurched out of a doorway at the far end of the alleyway. He caught up with the old boatman just as he was about to wander into a wine shop.

The man backed away, staggered, peered, then smiled. 'I know you. Kid from thish morning. No use robbing me 'cus I ain't got nothing left. Wasshappenin'?'

'We need to go upriver.'

'Upriver? Shame. We're not going anywhere and captain'sh furioush. He is. Furiosh. Mean' t'pick up more wool but the chief steward'sh dish'peared. Everyone lookin' for him. Hish wool, you see. No wool. No travel and we're a whole day late already.'

'We'll make up the money if we can get on the boat in secret. Lots of money,' Tog said. His mind was racing – if people were already looking for the chief steward, they had far less time than they thought.

'Shecret?' the sailor said loudly. 'I love a shecret. What's the shecret?'

Tog hustled him towards the dock. 'I'll tell you later but first I need some help. Sacks, I want sacks, and a cart.'

The sailor swayed and shook his head. 'Don't want much, d'you?'

'But first I've got to go check something else.'

'You wanna leave tonight, you better hurry,' the man said. 'Gates closh at shunset. Tide changes then as well. Gotta get off by then – if you wanna get anywhere.'

Tog looked at the sun, already low in the sky and reddening.

'We'll make it,' he said.

The Eastgate inn was easy to find but the innkeeper was surly, furtive and scared.

No, the Little Swords had not been in his inn. No, he had not served them. No, they had not had a prisoner with them.

Tog wondered whether to kill him, then decided to try one more time. 'All right. Let's do this the Castlebright way,' he said and placed a silver coin on the table. 'You know what I want to know, you just don't know how badly. If you tell me, you keep what's on the table but you've got to realize that I may get bored at any moment and take the money away.' He put another coin on the table. 'Of course, with every coin, I despise you a little bit more,' he added.

The man licked his lips and Tog put another coin down. Outside, he could see the low sun sinking. 'And the more I despise you, the more likely I am to walk away.'

'You don't understand,' the man said.

'I'm getting very tired of waiting.'

He reached into his purse for another coin, then hesitated. The man licked his lips. 'One more,' he said. 'One more. For my family. In case they find out I talked.'

The warmth on Tog's neck lessened as the sun slipped behind the rooftops.

'I'm not a bad person,' the innkeeper said. 'I've got a duty to my business. To my family. I'm taking a big risk here.'

Tog reached into his purse. 'Yours when you tell me,' he said.

'It was business as normal apart from … at first I didn't make anything of it. Then the rumours started.'

'What rumours?'

'You wouldn't have believed it. She just looked a mess with those marks on her. Blue. To me they were a mess and she was a mess, lying down and groaning. Face the colour of whey.'

'What?' Tog leapt to his feet.

'I'm just saying what I saw. She was hurt. Couldn't walk. Her knee was bound. Then they started boasting. Said she was the one and only, as in the One and Only. The Chosen One. She Who Will Remake the World. An old man paid to touch her.'

'Where was she lying?'

'In that corner. They kept on going on about how she had to be kept intact.'

Tog knelt where Jenna had lain and found what he wanted. Low down on the wall, three marks had been scratched into the rough plaster:

The bird's foot for speed, the crossed weapons for protection, but the third was a puzzle. It meant something so big it was invisible; something so important you might as well not think about it. He couldn't imagine what Jenna wanted him to think.

'Hey, we had a deal,' the innkeeper said as he walked out. Tog turned and threw the coin as hard as he could into the inn and he heard something break.

The cart that rumbled out of the dock gates was the last of the day. The guard was ready to close and bar the gates, and noted that the big man driving it looked incompetent and the man sitting by him was a very drunk sailor who was telling everyone they had a precious cargo and they'd better clear out of the way.

He squinted into the setting sun. The heat haze melted the horizon and as the sun hovered above it, it seemed to bulge upwards to meet it. Good. He could close the gates when they touched. Almost there. Almost there . . . He turned a professional deaf ear to shouts of *Stop thief!* coming from the main square and signalled to the trumpeter. The three hoarse notes drowned out the shouting and he put his shoulder to the one gate, then the other, catching a glimpse of the light westerly wind filling the sail of the last boat to leave.

They must be in a hurry, he thought. They'd left their cart on the quayside.

21

Tog slept through the night like a dead man and well into the next day, waking up with a head so full of heat that it felt as if it were bursting. The others were all up: Ordan was talking with the deckhand, Allanza was watching the sail, Kai was spreadeagled on the bales of wool in the hold, broiling. Tog felt them notice him wake up – and then ignore him. That suited him fine. All he could think of was the gap between him and Jenna widening. Eventually, he thought, the ties that bound would break. When you rolled dough too thin, its own weight would stretch it to breaking.

It was not until the second day from Castlebright, when the land had opened up into a huge flood plain, that the captain picked out Tog and spoke to him.

'We'll be at the fork soon – where you say you want to get off.'

'Where we do want to get off,' Tog said.

The captain shrugged. 'Suit yourself, but if you're seeking your fortune, there are better places. There are towns upriver where they don't try and enslave every traveller, and a man can make a crust by wheeling and dealing, as long as he keeps his wits about him.'

'Are you implying we didn't?'

'You're alive, aren't you? That means you came out ahead,' the captain said. He cast a shrewd look down at Tog. 'Of course, life shouldn't be that hard. It should be that a man can let his guard down sometimes. There were rumours that it was all going to change . . . that a new king was on the throne and a new age was dawning. The sailors said the wind was always going to be behind us. The farmers said it was going to be warm in summer, dry at harvest, wet in spring. Then we heard it was just a boy and we'd be better off hoping for something else.'

'Which was?'

'You hear a lot of stories on the river and the more you tell them, the bigger they get. Nothing to do with the truth, mind. They just get bigger.'

'Tell us. Please.'

'I'd rather keep quiet and just talk about what I see.'

'Which is?' Tog tried to keep his voice level.

'People looking for danger and I don't like it. It seems a waste.'

'Of what?'

'You name it: effort, hope, life . . . We haven't got long on this earth. I was learning my trade at your age, married a couple of years later. Now I've got two children, boys, one's six, the other's eight. I'm on this earth to pass on what I know and hope one day my boys have homes, a hearth and enough heart to look after their old man when he's too worn out to steer a boat. That's what it's all about. When you're young, you think you can conquer the world, seek your destiny and for a while you almost can. But destiny has a habit of biting back and if you haven't built something solid and strong, it'll kill you young. If you carry on like this, you lads'll be dead by the time you're twenty. I've seen it happen and I hate it.'

'Suppose we want to change things for the better?' Tog asked.

A bleakness settled on the man's face like thin snow on bare ground. 'Better for who? A man finds bread to stop his family starving and good for him, we say – the kiddies need to eat. But what about the family he steals from?'

And he stepped back and narrowed his eyes on the river

ahead. The deckhand beckoned Tog to the bows of the boat.

'Skipper's done a lot of thinking,' he whispered. 'He's a good man. I don't care how he got his boat. He's made up for it now and he could help you, you know, put the word about, maybe get you work.'

'We don't need work,' Tog said. 'We just need a boat to take us inland at the fork.'

'Everyone needs work,' Lol said. 'It keeps you busy. Stops you thinking.'

'About what?'

'About the way things are.'

'And if things could be made better?'

'Like the captain said, better for who?' Lol asked and spat wisely over the side. 'Better for who?'

Where the two rivers met was a half-abandoned settlement.

A couple of small boats were moored on the jetty, the muddy banks were lined with rotting sheds and two hulks lay in the water up to the gunwales. On their right, a wooden fort squatted on a low hill. Square fishponds lay below it but they were stagnant now and jellied with rot. The captain dropped the sails and Lol rowed the boat to the jetty.

The main river wound on ahead, broad, glittery and wide but the captain nodded to a narrow stream, overhung with willows, that fed in from the right.

The captain beckoned Tog to the stern where he stood, leaning against the big steering oar. 'Remember what I told you,' he said.

'We'll try. Thanks for keeping us safe.'

'For a while, at any rate. I don't know what you're chasing but I wish you luck. Perhaps I've chosen the easy way, although these days it doesn't feel easy. But perhaps it doesn't matter what you're doing, so long as you're doing it with all your heart and with all your soul.'

'And how do you manage that?' Tog asked.

'Everyone's got something they can do. The lucky ones have found it. Like you.'

'Like me?'

'You've got the mark. You're a leader. You're leading.'

Allanza pushed the boat back into the stream where it picked up enough wind to make headway against the current. The captain fixed his eyes upstream. Lol shipped his oars and raised a hand.

'If you need a boat, ask for Brin,' he called out. 'He's in the boatyard on the other side of town.'

Narrow streets of sagging wooden houses led back from the

waterside, empty windows opening into roofless rooms. No children playing with knucklebones in the street; no old people sitting on stools in the sunshine, just the sound of chanting from a ruinous warehouse and the boom-boom-boom of a man kicking his heels against a barrel. He was disinclined to talk and they pushed on through the settlement to the boatyard.

It was formed by two walls of stakes and a square building that opened lengthways on to the river. From it they heard the regular chk, chk, chk of axe on wood and found a man smoothing down a split-wood plank.

Utterly dumbfounded, they stared: at his skin, which was as glossy and dark as a plum; at his palms, which were pink; at his hair, which hung in great matted snakes down his back, and his beard, which was grey; at the chair he was strapped into, which was fitted with two large wheels.

Chk. Chk. Chk. Chk.

Bright shavings littered the dirt like blossom. He didn't look up until he had worked his way to the end of the plank and then felt along its length with a big rough hand.

'Brin?' Ordan said. To keep the focus away from Tog, they had decided that he would assume the role of leader when they were in public.

'That's me. You want food, I got none. You want money, I got none neither. You want a fight, I'll kill one of you before the rest gets me. You just decide who it's gonna be,' Brin said.

'We are in need of a rivercraft.'

'Takes a year to make a boat.' The man raised an eyebrow and ran a thumb along the edge of his axe.

'Then something smaller, maybe?'

'And where would you be going in such a hurry that you can throw good money into the river?'

'Er, round and about,' Ordan said hopelessly.

'Ain't no round and about round here. There's the big river and there's the small river and there's an upriver and there's a downriver and that's that. Maggot!' Brin called over his shoulder. 'Where's that straw-haired, straw-for-brains, sheep-faced fool? Maggot!'

Between piles of wood, stacked for seasoning, Tog caught a glimpse of movement on the slipway between the boatshed and the river. He thought he saw a flash of fair hair. His skin prickled. Thoughts roared.

'Maggot?' he said sharply. 'Is that his real name?'

'What d'you think? His parents named him that? Maggot's what I call him 'cos I can't remember his real name and he crawled in here like a maggot a week ago, begging for work. Said he'd fallen out of a boat and that should've told me what kind of an idiot he is. Now he lives off me, the maggot, but these days you can't be fussy about who you take on.'

Tog was running for the slipway as a boat splashed into the water.

'KRADOK!' he shouted.

The man in the boat turned and gave Tog a look of loathing and longing. There was no mistaking the strange, hot eyes, the shock of blond hair, but the man underneath had shrunk.

'Kradok. Stop!'

But he just bent his back and paddled. Tog threw himself into the dark water and swam after the boat, but it drew relentlessly away. Allanza and Ordan tried to track it on the bank, but the forest was impenetrable.

And Kradok was gone.

Tog splashed back to the shore and hauled himself on to the bank. Brin had taken up his axe and was back at work on his plank. 'Know him?' he asked.

'He was once a general in the high king's army.'

'He's a broken bastard now. I did wonder, though. Always watching the road and the river. Why's he frightened of you?'

'I don't think he is,' Tog said. 'Like you said, he was watching and waiting.'

'For you?' The black man spat. 'Then he's gone upriver

to snitch. That's the only way to make money here now. No trade, no jobs. No boats stop here now. No one dares and all because the town council – the council of elders – wouldn't take slaves. Christian, see? They abandoned the port and sit up in their stockade feeling good about themselves but there's no food, no work, no kiddies, no future . . .'

'No children? What happened to them?'

'Sent away to the old camp on Bredon Hill before the dragon took them. People think they'll be safe there but it's just a matter of time before he finds them and takes them same as he takes anything else he wants. I see the big boats heading his way carrying everything from slaves to that black stone that burns.'

'Have you seen him?'

'You don't see Dragon but you see his warlock all right. I've seen him close up. Very close up.' He put his hand in front of his nose. 'This close.'

'What happened?'

'He stopped by a year ago.' Brin's voice was flat.

'Did they want a boat?'

The man sucked his teeth. 'Not exactly. Most people run and hide when they go past. Not me. I'm clever, see? I was standing right there.' He pointed to the slipway and paused.

'Standing?' Kai asked sharply. 'But how . . .'

Brin talked over him. 'I'm standing there and the boat's charging through and Merthen's sitting in the stern and he sees me. Shouts something. Boat stops, then backs, stops in front of me, just holding itself against the current. Merthen, he calls out, "Who gave you your skin?" "My parents," I says. "Yes, but who gave your skin its colour?" he says. "Far as I know, I was born with it. Back in Afreek, we're all black, or so I've heard," I says. "Impossible," he says. "Undress." "Get lost," I says. He gives me a look like I'm going to regret that and the big boat rows off.

'Two nights later he comes back. With soldiers. They pin me down. Cut my hamstrings, hang me up by the wrists from the roof beams of my own shed, take my clothes off and he just walks round me with a torch, looking at my skin, while I hang there, twisting slowly. "Why are you doing this?" I asks. "For my master," he says. "We're searching." Then they cut my hair off, shave my scalp, look there as well. "How come the palms are pink but the rest of it's black? Maybe it rubs off." So they try to rub the colour off. "It's all black," he says. Not *you're* all black or *he's* all black but *it's* all black. Like there's me. And there's my skin.'

'He was interested in skin?'

'Nothing else, really.'

Whack whack whack, like three hammer blows, Tog's mind went Skin – Jenna – Map.

Jenna was marked all over her skin. Kradok wanted the map. The map was parchment. Parchment was skin. The map had the same marks on it as Jenna had on her skin. The dragon wanted Jenna. The dragon wanted to make her into a map.

Tog was almost sick.

22

There was a boat with three rotten boards that Brin was repairing. He replaced one board, and plugged the holes with his own mixture of wax and moss and shreds of old tunic. The boat leaked but he said it would hold for three days, as long as they needed.

He charged them. They left. A moon rose and they carried on through the night, rowing in shifts. A great hill rose from the plain and swung from side to side as the river followed its winding course. Old debris from winter floods clogged the lower branches of riverside trees. They passed under the old bones of a boat, bleached white, trailing weeds.

Now the river was squeezed between cliffs of red mud. A wind chopped the water and Tog was rowing badly, catching crabs and not keeping time with Allanza's steady stroke. It was a relief when Ordan called out, 'Boat ahead!'

They pulled into the side to watch it pass: a simple raft of logs with a rough shelter built on it, steered by a woman. As the raft spun in an eddy, they could see two women lying down in the shelter and four naked children with sunken eyes, still as dolls. When the helmswoman saw them, she screamed and veered away, jamming the raft into the bank so it began a slow spin.

'We can help,' Allanza shouted, but the woman screamed louder, panic stretching her face.

'What was that about?' Kai asked pointedly, when the boat had passed.

'Spooked by something,' Tog said.

'No, spooked by everything. And they were coming from where we're going.'

Tog acknowledged Kai with a bob of the head and a twisted smile. 'Better crack on.'

And on they cracked.

Tog's mind was stacked so high with thoughts he wondered if would overbalance the boat. Jenna was the One. They wanted her skin. Her skin had marks on it. Fear was a physical pain inside his chest, just below the ribs and just above his belly.

The harder we row, the less it will hurt, he thought, and shouted for a faster stroke, whacking hand into fist to beat time until both were sore. And although he stared at the surging V of white water pressed out by the bows, he seemed to be stuck in Votan's tree, except this time Kradok was hanging there, his face black, his hair a rime of blond icicles, and he told the priests that Tog was not a god, nor even a king, but a useless sack of wet bones.

He jerked himself awake, panic like a wind in his head.

'Why have we stopped?' he shouted.

'To rest,' Kai said.

'Do you want Jenna to die?'

'No, but we're no good to her dead either,' Kai said. 'You haven't bothered to notice what's going on around here. It's good land but it's empty. Correction: it's been emptied.'

'They were coming from where we're going. The land's not empty, it's been emptied.' Tog adopted Kai's hoarse, truculent voice. 'You think you're so clever. You think your words can make a point because you can't make it any other way. Listen to me. We are going to where we're going and if there's no one there, there's no one to harm us.'

'But who's doing the clearing?'

'We know that! It's the dragon or whatever he's called and we've known that from the start so nothing's changed and don't use it as an excuse to give up!'

But Kai wouldn't give up. His voice sawed on. 'But something has changed: Kradok. He's gone ahead to warn them.'

'And what do you suggest?'

'Take stock. Ask around.'

'We know Kradok came this way. We follow him to get to Jenna.'

'We—'

'We follow the king,' Ordan interrupted.

Kai snorted nastily. 'What's in it for you? What do you really want? He needs advice, not obedience. Look at him. He's a wreck. He's not thinking straight . . . he's learned nothing!'

'This is where we started,' Tog said. 'You don't think I'm up to the job.'

'And you never will be if you insist on doing everything on your own! If you'd ever listened, none of this would have happened!'

'So it's all my fault?'

'YES!'

Tog threw himself the length of the boat, knocked Kai off his seat, straddled him and started punching. Kai grabbed Tog's tunic, pulled him close and tried to wrestle him over. Tog broke his grip and had just got his hands round Kai's neck when he found himself being lifted up and away.

He was trying to shout but his mouth was a furnace and burned his words. He saw Kai scrabbling away from him, face twisted and tearful, and still he bellowed and roared. He felt arms around his shoulders and tried to fight them off but there were too many of them and then Kai and the boat split into myriad shards of light and however hard he shook his head, he could not shake the tears away. They just kept on coming and with them memories rose up, floated, flew apart, reformed: the fight on Fenny Castle; Jenna being carried away; rocks crashing on his back; dead boys in the tree ... His roar settled into a form of words he recognized as 'It's my fault and I can't bear it,' and they made sense, so he carried on shouting them and sobbing until he got too tired to say or do anything at all.

'I'm all right,' he said. 'I'm all right.'

He looked down the boat to see Kai sit up, flex his neck and look at him, resentfully.

'Good,' Ordan said. 'It's like sicking up a bad whelk. Painful at the time but good in the long run.'

'That is so disgusting,' Kai said. Tog inhaled snot and hawked. 'I suppose I have to say sorry,' he said. His voice was shaky and he felt lightheaded.

'Definitely,' Kai said. 'Starting with me.'

'Sorry I tried to throttle you,' Tog said. 'Sorry to everyone else as well. I . . . know it seems like we're just going forward blindly, but I think that's all we can do.'

He saw Kai flush, take a breath, then turn away.

'We have to keep going because sometimes that's all you can do. And you have to believe in me.'

Kai tilted his head this way and that, as if weighing the options. Then he shrugged.

'You have to say it,' Tog said, his voice coming under control.

'All right.'

'Say it.'

'I . . . believe . . . in you.'

There was a pause.

'That was a big thing to ask,' Allanza said.

'You're telling me.' Kai sounded indignant.

'No, mate, you don't understand. The asking was the big thing. Would you dare ask someone that? Would you take the risk?'

Kai said nothing, then shook his head.

'That's why we follow Tog. He's got the guts to ask.'

Ordan opened his mouth. Closed it, then smoothed his hair across his pate, his face quite changed, as if he had understood something.

The wind dropped and the heat built. The sky was a stretched grey skin, trembling with thunder, pulsing with light. They heard the wailing above the splash of the bailing and the creak of the oars. It rose and rose, then faded and faded, then rose and rose, then faded and faded. Then rose. Then faded. Crows circled a high bluff on the left-hand bank.

They moored the boat to a branch and walked carefully up the hill.

At the top they noted the trampled grass, the cold fire pit, the charred bones – pig, according to Kai – scattered far and wide by foxes, and, judging by the tracks, boars which had knocked down the shelters and chewed the cowhides. Dried blood on yellow grass. A goat and kid, both trailing tethers, looked at them from the edge of the clearing, close to a patch of recently dug earth that smelled of death.

Tog felt Jenna's presence like you sometimes felt a ghost. It was there and it was not there and he didn't know if he wanted to find a trace of her here. Standing with his companions on an open ridge, he felt shut in and alone.

He walked to the edge of the clearing and looked down the slope to the river. So suppose the Little Swords had smelled the feast, climbed the hill and then . . . something had happened. What did you do when you got to the top of the hill and were confronted with the camp? You wanted her out of the way but in sight. So you tied her to a tree!

The thought gave him a jolt of excitement. At last he had something to do. The tree needed to be a distance from the camp but visible.

He checked a silver birch sapling. Too flimsy.

Then a hazel. Too shrubby.

Then a young sycamore. The grass in front of it was flat.

He approached carefully from the back. There was a ring of smeared lichen round the trunk, where a rope might have rubbed against it. And there was the rope. He pressed it to his face and followed a trail of crushed grass into the woods.

Where it stopped.

Caught? No, there was no sign of a struggle. He cast around without success, then saw Allanza was pulling himself up into a tree on the other side of the clearing.

'Look at this!' he called out. Tog found Allanza standing on a branch, grappling with a young child. Holding it under the arm, he lowered it to Tog.

'No, no, please.'

The voice was cracked, faint and came from behind a clump of hazel. Tog crept around and found an old woman, barely alive, shrunk to a husk, lying on her side.

'Don't kill the child, kill me,' she cried hoarsely. 'Don't kill the child. Take it.' She was trying to wet her cracked lips with a tongue that looked white and dry.

'We're not killing anyone,' Tog said but the woman closed her eyes and whimpered: 'You're killers. You kill.'

Tog called Ordan. Allanza was holding the baby at arm's length. It had the loose skin of starvation, was listless, snotty and silent. When he tried to look into its eyes, they were blank.

Kai bustled over, red-faced. 'That's not what you do!' he said. 'You never hold a child like that!'

He took it, swung it round and held it close. After struggling for a while, the child went still and buried its face in his shoulder.

'It can't have eaten since all this happened.' He gestured to the clearing. 'Tog, go and get some bread from the boat and a bowl. Get hold of that goat and milk it. Water too. Allanza, check around – see if they left any food.'

By the time Tog had walked down to the boat and back up again, Allanza had caught the nanny goat and found a bag of chestnut flour hanging from a branch.

While Kai made a porridge he joined Ordan, who was kneeling by the old woman in the thicket. He had a wet cloth in his hand and was squeezing drops of water into her throat, then bending his head to listen, then letting her talk some more. The child sat cross-legged and fed itself solemnly with its fingers, looking from face to face.

'How old is it?' Tog asked.

'How old is *she*,' Kai correctly him fiercely. '*She's* about two, maybe a bit older.'

He wiped her face, trying to keep his own impassive but the mask was too soft and his feelings kept on breaking through: hope and worry, one after the other.

Blowing like a porpoise, Ordan sat down by Tog. 'I have important news to impart, my lord, from the old woman,' he said. 'She and the baby were part of a larger party of travellers. I imagine we met some of them on the raft. The old woman was considered too weak to travel, the baby's parents were killed and no one wanted it.'

He shot a look at Kai who said, 'Poor little scrap.'

'It will, however, delay us.'

Kai put the baby down. 'Here we go. Here we bloody go.' The muscles and tendons in his neck started to stand out – a sign he was ready to fight.

'Come with me, Ordan,' Tog said, and led him to the edge of the clearing, where they could see the river.

'When we met Kai,' he said, 'he had just buried his mother, father and his brothers and sisters. They were carried off by a fever and he was the only one that lived. I never realized it before but I think he misses them.'

Ordan looked calm and reasonable. 'I am thinking only of you,' he said. 'The food we have is suitable for us; it is not for a little thing like that. Do we take the goat with us? And if stops giving milk, go and find another? And if takes one full day to find the goat, or two? What then? And if the baby cries when we need to keep silent, what then? There is a story my people tell of a woman at home with her five sons and a baby on the breast when an enemy came. She lay low, and when the enemy came searching for her, she smothered the baby in case it cried so her five brave sons could grow up and take revenge. In times of peace, will people wonder if she were right? But in times of war, they ask, are you as strong as that woman? Now I ask you that question.'

Tog looked up as if the answer was hung in the tree tops. 'I don't know,' he said.

'Very well. Perhaps this will help. The old woman told me that when the Little Swords came up the hill, the travellers recognized them and attempted to restrain them by means of large net while they slept. They caught them all, except one. She was tethered to a tree.'

'I know. And?'

'She escaped.'

'Good.'

'But then she . . .'

'What?'

'Freed the Little Swords, armed them and, according to the old woman, supervised their massacre. She was then carried shoulder-high away from this place and into the boat.'

'Impossible,' Tog said. 'The old woman's lying. Let me talk to her.'

'The old woman is dead,' Ordan said. 'She stayed alive to tell me this thing.'

'It wasn't Jenna.'

'The girl she described was tattooed. Slim. And lame.'

Tog went back to the place where Jenna's trail had gone cold. This time, instead of looking beyond it, he followed it back, saw how it crossed the edge of the clearing to a wide area of flattened grass. Bundled up by it, a roughly woven net, cut open.

Ordan joined him. 'It doesn't mean a thing,' Tog said.

'It means we must make haste,' Ordan said. 'Surely you can understand that.' He lowered his eyes and backed away.

The sun banged on Tog's eyeballs but his mind was empty, like a box.

23

Sun: warmth, time passing

The first snap of the drum sent Jenna's heart blundering around in her lungs. So loud, so sudden, it was like the jaws of death closing. On the oars, Pillows and Fra Trouble Trouble both missed their stroke; Log jumped; Nothing Happens stopped muttering; Face went white; even Toothache flinched. Then another snap before a deeper drum started beating in a rhythm that shook her guts to jelly.

She saw Log shout, his face contorted but she could not hear him over the vicious thunder. She saw Pillows clamp her hands to her ears and Face struggle down the boat to huddle against her as if he were being beaten down by hailstones. Log was waving at her to get down and as she cowered in the bows, all she could think was that she could have avoided all this by letting the travellers take the Little Swords.

In another life she saw herself sitting on the bank of the river, and waiting for a boat to carry her back downstream. She rolled the days back. Saw herself bypassing the warehouse, taking a boat down the river, watching the island grow from a low, misty mound on the horizon to a strange mountain in the middle of the marsh. And there Tog would be, waiting for her, smiling a bit uncertainly . . .

The boat lurched; the daydream evaporated. The island was burned. The lake was red with blood and Tog, if he were still alive, would be following her into this.

The drums stopped together, as sudden as an ice sheer. Jenna pushed herself up but was immediately beaten down by the horror above the tree tops: the monstrous, shaggy, leaf-dripping green head of a giant.

On and on. The heat went out of the sun. The river sounded different, and grew choppier. Rapids? A ford. Jenna heard Pillows and Log discussing whether they were drawing too much water and would have to get out to lighten the boat. As it was, they scraped over, the rowers doubling up and complaining. Since the Wickwicks they all acted as if they had eaten bad meat.

Before her own imaginings went rancid in the heat, Jenna asked, 'What was that thing I saw? The giant, I mean.' She tried to keep her voice light.

'Don't ask,' Log said.

'But I want to know.'

'In case your little husband meets it? Like I said, don't ask.'

'But—'

'All right. She's the Greenmother, and at the midsummer festival she gets to eat a bellyful of humans. Now, let's just shut down, shut up and row on the Watergate.'

Which was a high wooden barrier that spanned the narrowing of the river, topped with heads on spikes. As the gate creaked open, maggots rained down and the water writhed with big fish.

'Almost home,' Log said.

'Yeah. Almost home,' Fra Trouble Trouble echoed. 'Time to get pissed. Time to have a paaarty. Woooh!'

'Wooh,' Pillows said.

They all looked nervous, and it wasn't because of the Greenmother, Jenna thought. It was the thought of coming home.

Before her hood went on, Jenna saw a wide road slicing through the woods, as straight as an arrow. The scars on the trees, where limbs had been sliced off, were still bright and white. The sun was on her left cheek. They were walking north.

She knew things were changing by the smell: first woodsmoke, then something else that uncoiled through the loose weave of the hood and probed her nostrils. It was sweet and stale, thick and sharp. Death.

Then sounds: a clink of a hammer on metal; the creak of a wagon; people shouting. A town or a settlement. The wagon jerked as people tried to climb on to it and the Little Swords yelled and beat them off. Jenna heard shouted congratulations, felt someone touch her then run away shrieking. The noises fell away and the wheels started make a hollow rumble as they passed over a long wooden bridge.

The wagon stopped. The rap of a fist on wood. The rumble and creak of a gate opening. A lurching roll across flagstones. Someone, she thought it might have been Toothache, whispered 'Relax' in her ear. She was carried up steps, more steps, then dropped on to a very soft floor. Before she could react, a door slammed and she was certain she had been left alone. She ripped the hood off her head, looked around and gasped.

What have I done? she thought. *What have I done by coming here?*

24

The room was dark – the only light came from an arrangement of candles hanging from the ceiling. In front of her a creature was staring at her from a forest. It was tall, with a human body and a dog's head. She turned. Another behind her, but he was squat and muscular, with the head of a bull, and thickly curled hair on his chest and legs that bent backwards at the knees. She turned again, this time coming face to face with a dog with three heads, huge red jaws and long white teeth.

Nothing moved. Torches hung, flared and smoked. The creatures were frozen as they emerged from a forest of grey tree trunks.

Pictures!

Jenna hissed, ashamed to have been taken in by such an

obvious trick and took stock of her surroundings properly.

She was floating on a field of twining roses and patterns of fabulous birds. The room was large and round with a low ceiling of beams and planks. The walls were covered with weavings, the floor with rugs. The table across the room was slender, three-footed, and on it was a jug, a real glass jug, wrapped in a green dragon to make a handle and a spout. She crawled to it and drank from the dragon's mouth. The wine was sweet and made her feel giddy and she looked for distractions when she realized what she had done.

Near the table stood a chest made of a dark wood, so smooth the torchlight flickered below its surface. She rapped it with her knuckles – the wood was as hard as iron! – and unfastened the hasp.

Wonder.

The chest was full of heavy, slippy, soft gold: coins, bracelets, chains, necklaces, chokers, rings, anklets, torcs . . . Jenna let bracelets drop over her hands until they covered her filthy, scratched arms. She wrapped a golden chain around her neck. There had never been gold like this back on the island. Tog had inherited a treasury from his father but had quickly spent it all – Kradok had told him that he had to pay the generals a loyalty fee, which took about half of it; the Abbot had claimed he had promised to build a new stone church in memory of his father, and that took the rest, more or less. She had offered him gold from her own dowry, hoping really that he would not take it, but he had.

But this chest of gold, more than she had ever seen before in her life, had been left in a prison cell . . .

Then she heard a knocking.

Was there a door? Of course there was. She had come in facing the Dog Man – so opposite him . . . yes. It had been painted over with more forest scenes but there it was. Seconds later it opened and four men in identical tunics carried in a gigantic copper cooking pot on poles threaded through strong hoops.

Water slopped out as they lowered it. Another man followed with a silver tray of small coloured bottles. The last person to come in was a woman, older than Jenna but not by much, with milky sunken eyes. Blind. She was carrying a robe. The men pushed past her and left. When Jenna moved a fraction, the woman's head tilted, then swung towards her. She felt her way to the edge of the cauldron and made a welcoming gesture with her hands.

Jenna said, 'What do I do?'

The blind woman worked her way to the little table. She picked up a bottle, took out a stopper, sniffed it, felt her way back to the cauldron and controlled the pouring of a thin stream of liquid with her finger. She stirred the water with her finger and the scent of flowers filled the room.

'It is the queen's bath,' the blind girl said. 'You get in.'

'What, all of me? In hot water? You want to cook me?'

The girl swallowed. 'Please.' She made her hands out, welcoming Jenna but also pleading with her.

Hot water for washing seemed like a strange idea but the oil made it soft as butter. Jenna lifted her skirts and stepped in. Her scratches stung, then the water carried the pain away. She allowed the bracelets to fall off her and on to the floor.

'When you are sitting, I can wash you.'

Jenna slid down so the water came up to her neck and it was wonderful. The blind girl came and out her hands on her shoulders.

'You are still dressed,' she said.

'Of course. You mean . . .'

'A queen should be washed.'

Jenna twisted in the water, made a V with her fingers and jabbed them towards the blind woman's eyes. She did not flinch. Still, Jenna hesitated. This dragon wanted her for her skin. Should she be exposing it, even to a blind girl, even under water? She lowered her head until the water covered her nose and blew bubbles. She moved her arms and legs. On the other hand, it would feel wonderful to be rid of the old rags that she had been wearing since she was kidnapped, she thought.

'What's the matter?'

'I'm thinking.'

'About what?'

'This is the strangest prison I've seen.'

'You are Dragon's honoured guest.'

'Don't creep me out. He kidnapped me. What does it involve, you washing me?'

The blind girl looked confused. 'Well, I take this thing called a sponge—'

'A what?'

'Sponge. And I rub it—'

'Give.'

The sponge looked like a sheep's brain. It was both soft and rough when Jenna smoothed it over her arms and legs, checking carefully to see that it left her tattoos. Good. No trickery there.

The blind girl poured oil into her hands and started to massage it into Jenna's scalp. She relaxed as the clever hands worked at her head, her neck, her shoulders. She bent her head forward and the fingers worked her neck, loosening the tight strands of muscle. She groaned at a particularly deep but necessary dig, then almost purred as stokes grew softer and wider, drifting out down her backbone then spreading out on either side. Lower. Wider. Lower. Wider until her whole back was covered. Until they were moving over the whole of her back . . .

Wrong. Very wrong.

She whipped round, grabbed one of the blind girl's wrists and a big hank of hair and dragged her head under the water. She ignored her struggles and waited until she blew bubbles, let her up, take a breath and then plunged her down again. She counted to five then let her up again.

'What are you doing?' she asked before the blind girl had even drawn breath.

The girl whooped and coughed and hawked and whooped again. Jenna waited until she stopped, then asked again, 'What are you doing?'

'Washing—'

She plunged her head under the water again, then brought it up again.

'Next time I will drown you. What were you doing?'

'It's my job.'

'Who?'

'Dragon. Merthen. Both of them.'

'How?'

'If I do what they say, they'll save . . .' Her voice tailed off. Jenna gave the now wet hair an encouraging tug. 'Someone, and if I don't, it will go badly.'

Her voice disappeared in a husky whisper.

'What do they want to know?'

'If you have marks on your back, I am to tell them.'

'And can you read them through your fingers?'

'I can tell from the feel of the skin where the marks are.'

Jenna slammed her palm down into the water. The blind girl flinched.

'What is it about the marks?' Jenna asked.

The blind girl looked panicked. 'You don't know?' she whispered.

'Why? Am I meant to?' She tightened her grip.

'I can't say. I've said too much. Please let me go. We're both prisoners. The best thing to do is go along with them. Just go along with them and try and survive for as long as possible.' A knock on the door. 'I have to go now. Please let me go and please . . .'

'What?'

The blind eyes filled with tears. 'Help me.' Then she raised her voice. 'Wait. The queen is not finished yet.'

And from behind the door a voice answered. 'She'd better hurry. Dragon wants her now.'

25

Jenna's robe was as subtle and as heavy as water, puddling in folds round her clean, bare toes. She had been carried on a chair into an impressive stone hall. At the other end of the hall, sitting on a pile of cushions, was a giant baby with a long green tail.

It's a dragon, Jenna thought, and a child with a shining face.

The dragon was man-sized. Its head, a full-face silver helmet, was smooth and fat-cheeked, with a horrid rude O of a mouth. Its eyes were green stones that caught the light and a green shimmering cloak fell over its shoulders and swept around like a tail.

On its right side was a line of people: soldiers, Little Swords, civilians. One by one they bent and whispered in its neat, shell-like silver ear, then lowered their heads still further to the round, immobile mouth, trying to keep their balance on a ring of gold coins that spread around the dragon's cloak. Jenna dimly remembered a travelling Dane whose boat had gone down in the outer isles. He had made himself charming with stories of giants and trolls and dragonish hoards and, from what she could remember, dragons were misers who knew and loved every single gold coin they had stolen. So the scattered gold was a test. Take me, it said, and see what happens. No one in the room so much as looked at it, even when their feet slipped over it. One of those coins, Jenna knew, could buy enough oats to keep a family alive for a winter.

She began to notice the cats. They were all built along the same lines as the one from the boat – some bigger, some smaller, some fatter, some thinner. In the boat, it had been the animal's take-it-or-leave-it self-sufficiency that irritated her. Here, the effect of seeing so many – sitting, lying, walking, watching, sleeping – was to feel belittled. So much mattered in this hall to so many people. The cats didn't care.

Sitting below the dragon on a stool so low that his knees were on a level with his ears was a man with thin lips and long, dark, straggly hair. Red-rimmed eyes stared at her from under the brim of a tall hat. He stared at Jenna and had not blinked since she was brought in.

When all the people had been dealt with, two shaven-headed soldiers lifted Jenna's chair and put it down in front of the dragon.

'Have you ever seen such glory?' the man with long hair asked her in a flat voice.

Jenna tilted her head and tried to look brave. 'Never seen quite so much *money*,' she said, to show she knew the difference. She was proud of the quite.

'My name is Merthen the warlock. Do you know me?'

'The Little Swords said you were an old faker. A perv. No one likes you. They laugh at you behind your back and say your breath smells like dead fish,' Jenna lied in a loud voice. She might as well have said nothing.

'Have you ever had a bath such as the bath you had and been dressed in silk like the silk you are wearing?' Merthen asked.

'Is that what the fabric's called? Interesting,' said Jenna.

'Did your bandit brat king have wealth like this?' He pointed to the scattered gold with a casual sweeping gesture. 'Behold the dragon. Behold his hoard. Behold his greatness.'

'To answer your question, not yet,' Jenna answered as loudly as she could, trying to ignore the implications of 'did'. 'And,' she added, 'I am beholding, but not because you tell me to. I suppose it's done to impress?'

'Remember this: Dragon knows you. Dragon knows your heart. Dragon saw you on the dungheap you called the island. He saw you pine. He knows your heart. You left your wretched husband before our people took you away from him. In taking you away, we were only obeying the call of your heart. Accept your destiny with the dragon. It is written. It is written on your skin. Resist and we crush you. We crush what is inside your skin.'

His words made Jenna tremble. The dragon leaned towards the tall man, then summoned the soldiers ranked behind. Its hands, Jenna noted, were fine and very clean and its wrists looked businesslike and strong. The glittering jewel eyes were pointed in her direction and she found it hard to keep her gaze fixed and level. The dragon tilted its head, first one way and then the other, a tiny gesture Jenna found very human. When the dragon rose and swept out of the room, she was not surprised when her guards lifted her chair and carried her after it into a small hall with large double doors at the far end. As Jenna entered, the doors were opened and the dragon stepped out on to a wooden balcony, where it was greeted with a huge roar. Merthen gestured to the guards to carry Jenna closer to see the crowd gathered below. When the dragon lifted its hand, people cheered. When the dragon lowered it, individual voices called out to save them. When the dragon turned to leave, they cheered again and when the wooden door slammed shut, they cheered even more loudly so it could hear them.

Jenna was carried down a corridor, and into a more comfortable room where a through-breeze from high windows billowed the rich drapes. Halfway down, Roman-style couches were arranged around a proper fireplace.

The dragon was sitting on one of the couches, and Merthen was lifting its silver head off. The dragon's shoulders were shaking.

With laughter.

'What did she call you? A perv? And a faker? That was priceless. Best thing I've heard all year. Oh, come on, Merthen, you've got to admit it was good. You do look a bit . . . fish breathy . . . Oh, never mind. Guards, bring her closer, so I can see her properly. That's it. Good room this. Warm in winter, less than stifling in summer. You all right then? Are all Picture People like you? If they are, we're for the north.'

The dragon's voice was light, confident, insufferable.

The dragon was tall with broad shoulders.

The dragon was clean-shaven with violet eyes and full, slightly upturned, well-defined lips. His nose had been broken at some time but that just made him more beautiful.

The dragon mussed up his hair, which was hat-flat, and gave Jenna a big smile. A cat leapt on to his lap and he began to knead its head. The cat stared at Jenna; she tried to not look at the cat.

'Sorry about the drama out there.' Dragon gestured to the doors. 'It all helps but I don't need to tell *you* that. Now, I'm starving – always am after brainwork. People ask you something and you just have to decide, there and then, what's best for them. It sort of becomes a habit and you don't realize until afterwards that, in fact, you've been concentrating hard for . . . ages.'

Two slaves carried a table to his side, and two more followed carrying an enormous metal tray.

'What have we got today? Chicken; partridge; sheep; fluffy bread, my favourite; pickles; mead – not sure about that, want to keep my wits about me with the queen in attendance – and some assorted veg. Some Greek guy, you probably know this, thought eating beans was a crime comparable to killing your own children, the theory being – Merthen, correct me if I'm wrong – that the bean looked like a curled-up baby and when it sent up a shoot in the dark, it was like a ladder that the soul climbed between life and death. Does that make sense to you, any sense whatsoever?'

Jenna continued to stare at him. She was not sure why,

but the fear dog had just wobbled into the room and was looking at her. It was a distance away still but she couldn't shift it.

'No? Well, maybe you like the Greeks. I've got nothing against them personally, I just think they're a bit overrated. Greeks say: eating beans is murder. British say: eat them if you can stand them. Greeks say: Know Thyself. British say . . . Actually, now I come to think of it, "know thyself" is good advice.'

He poured the cat on to the floor and it jumped straight back on to his lap.

'I know a Greek man,' Jenna said, and immediately regretted it because she did not know what else to say. Dragon's talk was like a glittering stream. You couldn't really stop it.

The stream ran on, not disturbed at all. 'I see – you want to find out what I know. Well, I do know about Melanius, though strictly speaking I would not put him down as Greek so much as Greek-ish. Bit of Jew in there, isn't there? A bit of Phoenician? A good Mediterranean mongrel, I would say. Now, I've got nothing against a mongrel but you and me, we're a bit different, aren't we? Pict and Briton. We know where we're from and we know what we're about. Now, eat. I want you to try that bread. Good, isn't it? White flour and yeast.'

'Of course,' Jenna said, not taking any but almost dribbling, it smelled so good. He knew about Melanius.

'Woman of few words. Hmmm.' His face changed and became serious, and Jenna had the overwhelming impression that he practised his expressions and could pick them like a craftsman picking a tool. Nonetheless, he surprised her with the next question: 'Just where do you stand on human sacrifice?'

'Where do I stand?'

'As in, what are your views?'

She straightened her back. 'Against.'

'Fair enough,' he said. 'But your father?'

Not to talk would be undignified, Jenna thought. To talk too much, obsequious. 'He knew it didn't achieve anything.'

'Now we're getting somewhere. And how did he know, or how do you know, that it didn't, or doesn't, achieve anything?' Dragon asked.

Jenna paused before answering. Was she allowing herself to be sucked in, or was this a chance to show what she was made of? She would talk, but keep it factual.

'Our people used to kill a man every spring and let the sacrifice bleed out into the first furrow,' she said. 'Then one year my father sacrificed a bull. Crop yield the same, give or take a pinch. Another year we couldn't do it. We'd been raided and lost too many cattle and anyway, the priest had been bribed to go over to another tribe . . . Then all the things the sacrifice was meant to give us – good weather, fertile ground – happened anyway. Best harvest for years.'

'And the people?'

'They were furious.'

'Thank you.' The dragon leaned across the gap between the couches and pressed his hand very gently on to her good knee, then withdrew. 'It's so good to talk to someone who thinks. We still do sacrifice humans and I'll tell you why. I don't think it's because we think it actually achieves anything in a cause and effect sort of way. I think we do it for a couple of other reasons. Firstly, there's tradition. I really believe in tradition. I think sometimes it is good to do things *just because* they've been done since time began. Secondly, I think it reminds people that life's a pretty serious business. Now, you and I know that. We were born to it. But I think it doesn't hurt to remind the others, the followers, if you will, that we're all on a knife-edge. We're walking along it. We fall, we cut ourselves or just disappear into the abyss and it's chaos down there. Believe me, I've seen it. When I took over this place, after my father died, there was enough gold in the treasury to support about a year's raiding. The tribes to the north were looking at my castle – it's one of the best in the midlands

– and I had to act pretty fast. I stopped the rot the first year, and three years later I'd turned it around and laid the foundations for what we've achieved. The secret was to give the people a sense of tradition, because if you don't have a castle and you don't have any gold, which is reality for most people, present company excepted, tradition is pretty much all you do have.'

'Yes,' said Jenna.

'Yes, what?' asked the dragon.

'Yes, life is a knife-edge and yes, I understand duty, and my duty is to my king.' She felt flustered, as if she had ambushed herself. Why was she thinking of Tog?

Dragon seemed embarrassed by her clumsiness. 'But of course. I know that? Did I question it?'

'No. I . . .'

'You wanted to straighten things between us. Fine. It's good to know what's what. We understand each other, don't we? We've both inherited a place in the world, a role. Me, I've got my little kingdom. You – you're who you are.' Then he enfolded her in his smile, and in spite of everything, she felt herself smiling back, as if they shared a secret. 'Honestly,' he chattered on, 'it's best to get these things out in the open, especially with someone you can share it with. Isn't that right?'

'I—'

'You can't do everything on your own.'

'No.'

'And this thing that makes you so special, you couldn't share it with him, could you?'

'What?' Properly surprised. Blindsided in fact.

'You couldn't share it because you didn't think it was worth anything. I do, though. I know what it makes you. You don't have to tell me anything. I understand – you've got to realize that – and I simply will not allow you, and all you have to offer the world, to go to waste.'

His eyes followed a soldier who walked across the room, bent and whispered something to Merthen, then Merthen rose and whispered something to Dragon and Jenna swore she heard the word Wickwick.

'Well,' Dragon said. 'I suppose you've had enough of me. I'll arrange for you to go back to your room. I've got some business to attend to.'

And Jenna was left feeling buffeted, confused and, shortly afterwards, furious, partly with the dragon but mostly with herself.

'Next time,' she said to herself. 'Next time I won't let him talk to me like that. I'll make him hate me.'

26

Wheat: life, bending not breaking

The child had stopped crying all the time and, under Kai's supervision, had grown plumper. He watched her jealously but they all wanted goes with her because she was a diversion.

'She needs to stretch her legs a bit,' Kai said. 'We all need a break anyway.'

Even though Tog knew he should be forcing the pace, he said, 'We're running low on supplies and that looks like an old settlement. Might be fields we could forage in, I suppose.'

'My lord, we should press on,' Ordan said, but faintly, as if he knew he would be ignored. Tog felt something about the bard had changed. Before, he had felt a stifled pressure, as if the bard had a plan and could barely hide his impatience at Tog's failure to carry it out. Now there was something else, but he had not quite worked out what yet.

He steered the boat to a collapsing jetty. The land around had been cleared once but now the wild oats and wild barley struggled with squitch grass in the field strips. Allanza took himself to see if there were any ripe seed heads amongst the weeds in the overgrown fields; the others lit a small fire. A patch of nettles showed where the village midden had been. Tog barked his shin on a plough that was hidden in the long grass. Ordan sat on a mound of stones that could have been a grave.

Suddenly an extraordinary scream, desperate and defiant, tore through the birdsong and the buzzing grasshoppers. Before they could react, a horse burst through the edge of the clearing and thundered straight for them. Its rider – slim, brown, crop-haired – was slashing down, left and right, at naked painted men clinging to its bridle. Half a dozen more figures burst into the clearing after it, covered in flaking red mud and armed with rough swords, rough spears and nets.

Allanza threw himself instinctively at one of the attackers who were trying to bring down the horse, got himself tangled up in the bridle and suddenly was being dragged out through the other side of the clearing.

But there was no time to think. In seconds, Tog was fighting with an armed man who seemed all arms and legs. He managed to land a punch but his opponent slammed a sword hilt into his temple, stunning him, and followed up with a series of kicks to his gut. From what he could see, the others weren't managing any better. Kai gathered up the child and was brought down; Ordan got hold of his sword but was surrounded and threw it away. They were tied at the wrists and ankles and left while the painted men cut down saplings. They threaded these through their ties, lifted them and ran off at a jog.

It was agony. Every jolt tore at the skin of Tog's wrists and ankles. If he tilted his head back, he could see a blur of grass and mud below his head. If he looked up, the leaves and sunlight flashed past his eyes.

'This is it,' he thought. 'I've failed.'

Suddenly, they were out of the trees and in a large clearing of beaten earth. There were huts all around, the river glinted a short distance away and towering above everything, very dark against the sky, a massive, swollen woman, made of leaves.

They were dropped on the floor of a hut and left. When the drums started, they shook all other thoughts out of their heads then turned the air to a jellied bog of noise that filled their ears and filled their mouths so they were deaf and dumb, clogged as earth, mashed to nothing. It went on and on. Tog forced his eyelids open and saw Kai's white face an arm's length from him, and beyond him the baby, lying like a broken doll.

The drums stopped. He closed his eyes and somehow slept.

27

He was woken by a voice that spoke as if it took it for granted that he would hear. It was soft, insistent and dreary. 'A good dog always warns you of trouble and never forgets a smell. Turn around. Turn around. Turn around.'

Tog wriggled until he was facing the speaker, saw a pair of fine leather boots, blue trousers encasing endless legs, the embroidered hem of a tunic.

'My name is Merthen. I am the dragon's warlock. You are Artognu and don't even think of denying it. The one with the child is Kai, son of Ecta, and the fat old man is Ordan, who claims to be a bard. Your court, high king, and army, rolled into one.'

The man himself was grotesque, with long limbs, tiny body, like a spider. His fingers, which he splayed for Tog's benefit, carried at least two rings each and his nails were pointed like claws.

'I do not like to waste time or words. You are captured. Your queen is captured. You will not escape. No one can escape the Wickwicks. It is your good fortune that we put them under strict orders not to eat you immediately. But you can thank Kradok for that.' Merthen's lips glistened like worms. Like worms they wriggled into a smile.

Kradok slunk in. He looked as if he had not slept or eaten since they had seen him at Brin's boatyard. He couldn't meet Tog's eyes.

'So there's the traitor,' Tog croaked. 'I suppose he warned you we were coming?'

'Warned me? Is the wolf warned of the lamb? The fox of the rabbit? Did you think you could take us? We own you, you and your wife.'

'No one owns the queen,' Tog said.

'Especially not you. The last I saw of her, she had just sat down to a meal with her new master. She was wearing silk and gold, and eating well.'

'What?'

'Yes. She arrived quite safely. I doubt we will need to use you to put pressure on her but you might come in useful.'

'Put pressure on her? I don't understand.'

'You wouldn't. Why would I lie? But no matter. We

have business.' He snapped his fingers and two painted men came in and pulled Tog to his feet. Merthen searched him, feeling in every corner of his clothes, then running his hands over every inch of Tog's body.

He stepped back. 'Where is it?'

'Where's what?'

'The roll of parchment.'

Tog's heart thumped. If he didn't have it on him, he must have left it in the boat. Yes, that was right. He'd left it in the bows on a pile of bags. He'd grown that careless . . .

'Why do you care?' he asked.

'That does not concern you.'

Tog looked at Kradok. It wasn't hard to sound contemptuous. 'I suppose the traitor told you we had it? If he betrayed me, he's certainly capable of lying to you.'

Merthen tilted his head. 'I doubt that. He is bound to us in ways you cannot understand.'

'Well, I'm sorry to disappoint you,' Tog said. 'I kept it as long as I could be bothered but then we used it the other night to light a fire. You should have chosen a better thief.'

'He's lying. He knows how valuable it is.' Kradok's voice was shrill.

'Too late now,' Tog said.

Merthen stared at him a good long while, then closed

his eyes. 'You were Kradok's last chance, of course. I suppose we will have to keep you alive a bit longer but don't think you have gained anything by buying time. Your life will be torture until I have what I want.' He paused. 'Of course, I could just give you to the Wickwicks now. Their most powerful goddess is the earth – they call her the Greenmother and like to keep her sweet. We, that is my master and I, applaud this ancient British custom and help them by providing sacrifices for them. Does that help you change your mind?'

'There's nothing to change,' Tog said. 'What's done is done.'

'A shame. With the parchment safely delivered to the dragon, the queen stands a far greater chance of living.'

Before Tog could answer, he left the hut. Then the drums started again and stunned them all into silence.

28

Crossed arms: protection,
fear, foresight

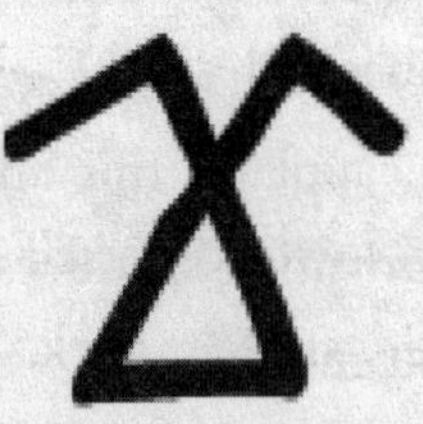

There were no windows in Jenna's room, so no day, no night and she had no way of knowing how long she had slept.

Someone had been in while she slept and lit lamps which choked the air with smoke. She had a headache and wondered if the wine she had drunk had been drugged, or whether she was just exhausted or whether she was just bad because surely only a bad person could sleep when they should have been planning to escape.

She unwound the bandages from around her knee and tested it. It was still puffy and tender but now, when it was strapped up, at least she could put some weight on it, and that was progress. She crawled around until she found the door and banged on it. The blind woman was there instantly with two guards behind her.

Jenna demanded partridge, white bread, honey, mutton, dried fruit, nuts, mead, wine, those agreeable green leaves and lamprey. Incredibly it was all delivered after a short wait, except the lamprey.

'Please stay,' Jenna said to the blind woman. 'I want to talk.'

The blind woman lowered herself carefully and sat with crossed legs and a very straight back. 'About what?'

'What's your name? How long have you been here?'

The blind woman said, 'You cannot ask me.'

'Why not?'

'It's too dangerous.'

'For who?'

The blind woman hesitated.

'Why talk to me at all?' Jenna asked.

'I was told to. I have to be kind to you.'

'You mean, if you talk to me, I might give something away? That won't happen.'

'Please. I'm not good at this. I have to find something about you. Something I can tell them. I'm begging you.'

'Will they hurt you? Oh, I remember. They'll save someone close to you,. whatever that means.'

The blind girl stood. 'This is a mistake. I must go.'

'Then I'll tell Dragon you displease me.' Jenna regretted it immediately because the woman's face distorted into an almost comical mask of fear. Jenna, whose entire upbringing had taught her how to mask her feelings and put up a front, felt tainted by it. 'No, I won't, but you must understand, if I'm going to help you, you've got to help me.'

'But if I tell you,' the blind girl said, 'you'll hate me.'

'I won't. I promise and if I do, what then?'

'I couldn't stand it. Not after what I've done to you.'

'You mean feeling for my tattoos? But I've forgiven you for that.'

'You don't understand. My name is Meryel. My husband's name is Kradok. He was your husband's man until I was taken and he was forced to work for the dragon. He betrayed your husband out of love for me, and now I am asked to spy on you out of love for him.'

It was dark the next time the dragon sent for her, but this time, Jenna felt prepared. She was woken by a knock on the door and Meryel brought her water and a towel. They didn't talk and Jenna felt light and alert as she was carried down the stairs. She closed her eyes and got her thoughts in order.

First, she would not be surprised by his openness, self-confidence or apparent respect for her.

Second, she would remember that he liked to be liked and would play on that.

Third, he exploited people's weaknesses to make them work for him. He was contemptible.

Fourth, she now knew that he had been planning her kidnap since before he had kidnapped Meryel. It meant she was valuable.

Fifth, Meryel told her that she thought something had gone wrong. There was something on the island called a mack or a mip that the army was meant to have found but didn't, and Kradok could have picked up, but didn't, and they needed it before Midsummer and that was barely a week away.

Knowing all this helped. It strengthened her hand and gave her something to do while the dragon tried to work on her.

Dragon was sitting in the long room on his own, staring at a small fire that hadn't quite caught and wouldn't quite go out. He had the silver mask on and the flames glittered in the green eyes. Cats were lying everywhere, except in one dark corner where one seemed to be killing something small and half a dozen others were sitting up to watch.

He took the mask off when Jenna had been put down

and smiled ruefully. He had forgotten to ruffle his hair and looked very young. Jenna convinced herself he looked stupid.

'How's the leg?' he asked. He was tired – his skin wasn't glowing and there were shadows under his eyes.

'You should know,' she said sharply.

He winced. 'Sorry. I forgot. Does it hurt?'

'Only when I run,' Jenna said.

He flashed her a smile, then said sorry again.

'I was trying to escape. I fought with one of your Little Swords. He beat me.'

'Of course. I could punish him. They were instructed to look after you, not tempt you into escaping.'

'No,' Jenna said. 'No. It taught me a lot. First time I was ever beaten in a fight. Shows I should pick my enemies better.'

She decided she'd leave that thought hanging between them to see if he plucked it out of the air. When he didn't, she asked, 'Out of interest, why didn't you instruct the army to kidnap me when they attacked?'

'Number of reasons. One, I don't quite trust soldiers, not the way I trust the Little Swords. Two, I expected more resistance. The whole idea of my raiding party melting away like that was to try and draw your army after it. We … didn't realize you didn't have an army.'

'Of course we have . . . It was elsewhere. We heard an attack was coming from the north.'

'If you say so.' He rubbed his face and went back to staring into the fire. 'Do you hate me?' he asked suddenly.

'What's not to hate?' Jenna asked.

He rubbed his face again. 'Of course. Of course you do. But in another life . . . I mean, there are things I have to do. You have been caught up in them but now I've met you . . . I would have done things differently. Look, life's a journey, right? You can't learn from your mistakes unless you make them and it's clear to me that I underestimated you, so I'm asking, please. Try and imagine a different life where we meet and talk and spend time together. What would you think then?'

Jenna was ambushed by a loathing so intense that it shook her like a fever. It was dark in the room but even so, she leaned away from the fire so the light would not fall on her face. 'Anyone in your situation who would ask that question to anyone in mine is . . .' She paused. 'Contemptible. Desperate. Pathetic.'

Dragon sighed. 'I was afraid you might say something like that.'

'So why ask?'

He looked her full in the face. 'I needed to know. I needed to know where we're going.'

'Wherever you say. I'm your prisoner.'

'I know,' he said. 'It's just I don't think of you that way.'

'How do you think of me?'

He held up a hand. 'I've just learned something about you – something I didn't know. It took a while but I finally had a debrief from the Little Swords. There were some initial inconsistencies but we finally worked out that, towards the end of the journey, they were captured and you rescued them. I'm not going to ask you if it's true – you don't owe me the truth but I really want to know why.'

Jenna swallowed. This was it then – the big thought she had been pushing to one side since she had arrived.

'Best way to find out about your enemy is to get up close. You'd know if you'd ever been in a real fight.'

'Is that it? Is that really it? You see, I thought that there might have been a deeper reason.'

'Not for me,' Jenna said. 'I'm as shallow as a puddle.' She wasn't going to tell him or anyone else about the fear dog.

But then he said, 'I don't accept that. I think . . . you know your destiny is here. With me. This is where you can test yourself. This is where you can explore everything you can be. I know you're honest with me. All I'm asking is that you're honest with yourself.'

Jenna felt a strand of resolution unravel, then Dragon did his cute head-tilting trick and she felt strong again. His attempt at a winning smile was replaced by a look of complete exhaustion. 'Sorry,' he said. 'Had to do an all-nighter and there's no rest tomorrow, or rather today. After you left yesterday Merthen was called downriver, leaving me alone. Sometimes it's nice to stay awake at night just because it's peaceful and it's good to sit and think. Do you ever do that?' he asked.

Jenna opened her mouth to say something sarcastic, then decided silence would be more contemptuous.

'Another apology due,' he said. 'You make me feel about nine years old.' Suddenly he gathered himself. 'Look, I know you can't walk yet and it's all my fault but do you think you could ride?'

'Ride?'

'It'll give you a better chance to spy.'

Clever, Jenna thought, and true. She bent her knee gingerly. 'I could sit on a horse while it walked but I wouldn't call it riding. And then I've got to mount it.'

'Don't worry. Stay there.'

'But . . .' She didn't protest too much. She really did want to get outside.

When the big door at the end of the room finally opened,

it let in a beautiful chestnut horse, led by a terrified groom with a just-woken-up face. It trod daintily over the rugs, nodding its head and blowing at the explosion of offended cats.

'What do you think?' Dragon said, rubbing his hands together. 'If the queen can't get to a mount, let the mount come to a queen. You'll need a hand, but if I lift you on to the table – my, you're light.'

Dragon's hands almost met around her waist and she had to lever herself up by putting her hands on his shoulders. They were wide. He felt as solid as a rock.

The sun was rising as they walked across the wooden causeway between the castle and the land. They skirted the town and climbed a low ridge. Below it, spread out for miles in the morning mist, was a massive army encampment. Row upon row of tents, roads between them at neat right angles, a good palisade around it and not a soldier in sight.

'They're away,' Dragon said. He was wearing yet another silver mask – a child, rather than a baby, with empty eye sockets. 'Always something to do. I mean, we keep the guard round the town and castle and we'll be increasing numbers for the Midsummer Gathering because you never know with crowds but I'm happiest when they're busy. You know that feeling when an army's just hanging around? It feels . . . it feels like a wasps' nest – all seething and buzzing.'

Jenna nodded sympathetically. She'd never had an army, but thought she knew what Dragon meant. These were matters that needed to be pondered. No wonder he was tired.

'And what's that?' she asked.

Between the camp and the town was a natural amphitheatre formed by a horseshoe-shaped ridge, cut into steps and facing the lake. In the middle of the bowl a wooden platform had been built; behind it was a high stack of timber.

'I think the Romans must have cut that amphitheatre. They built the tower – that's what you live in – and I've added to the rest of the castle. The platform is part of the general midsummer festivities. They've always been popular in this part of the world and I like to make a contribution. You see the way the sun's rising behind the seats? Of course, it sets right in front of them. Floods the place with light and looks like it's dropping into the lake. Very dramatic. It's a week away. You'll be here for it, won't you?'

She gave him a look. Caught his smile. 'Not funny,' she said.

'Got you,' he replied. 'I . . .'

'You can't tease me as well as everything else,' Jenna said. 'It's not fair.'

Dragon held his hands up. 'I know, I know.'

Jenna was about to say the same, when she wrinkled her nose – a dark, heavy, awful smell as if a breeze had just lifted the cover off something long dead.

'What's that?' Jenna wrinkled her nose.

'Just the camp. Slaves.'

'You keep slaves in a camp?'

'We hold them there.'

'How many?'

Dragon shrugged. 'People talk a lot of rubbish about slaves. Everyone has them; no one likes to think about the process. You know: capture, trading, distribution . . . We bring them here to a big centre for distribution. There are some problems – the smell is one of them – but we put the market upwind, make sure they're washed before they go up for auction. It's the little things that make a difference.' The mask turned towards her. 'I can tell you're shocked.'

'I'd never thought about it before,' Jenna said.

'How many slaves did your father have? Ten? Twenty? You never thought about them, I bet.'

More like five, Jenna thought.

'You see, my thinking is that if I give people choice,

they're more likely to get the right slave and everyone benefits: the client, me, and slave.'

'But the stink . . .' Jenna said.

'Slaves die like everyone else. Perhaps we haven't quite got that side of it sorted out. Merthen wants them to be burned but that means you have to organize timber duties . . . we'll get round to it. Still, that's for the future. Now I'm worried about that leg of yours. Let's get you back to rest.

On the causeway he said, 'I've been thinking. We can do this one of two ways. Either I keep you locked up in that room or . . . I give you a bit of freedom but you promise not to escape. What do you say? I'm going to be honest. I like seeing you but I can't have you with me every hour of the day. You'd get bored and it isn't practical. What say you can go up on the tower roof whenever you want and go into the rest of the castle so long as someone's with you?'

'What do you want me for?' Jenna blurted out. 'I don't understand anything.'

Dragon moved his horse so it butted up against hers and laid a finger across her lips.

'You know,' he said.

'But you haven't said.'

'But you know. In here.' He pressed his hand to his

heart. 'What you really want. How to be as great as you could be. Think about it, please.'

Jenna inclined her head.

'Good,' Dragon said. 'Good. That's made me happy.'

29

Bat: surprise, insight, speed

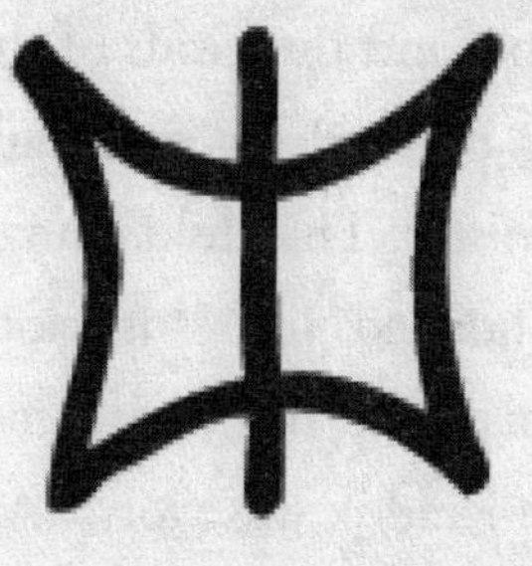

Merthen's boat had a bank of oars on either side, rowed by chained slaves, and a platform at the back where the wizard sat.

It was towing a raft made from dozens of tree trunks lashed together. Tied to the raft was the giant woman, and now Tog could see she was made from willow branches woven around a simple wooden frame. Her swollen belly pointed up at the sky. Her fat legs were the height of three tall men and her stumpy arms were slightly splayed on either side. Like flies round a cow, the Wickwicks whirred around their goddess in dug-out canoes and sang a high buzzing song. They were small, for the most part, and wore nothing but mud, which caked their bodies and hair.

Tog hardly had time to take it in before he was dumped in the bilges along with the others, between the two banks of chained rowers. They were stripped to the waist, thin, filthy and paid him no notice. Merthen was high enough to see over the prow and the heads of the sweating rowers. He was wearing a pointed hat and looked ridiculous but somehow more sinister. The child clung to Kai like a burr, with its fingers hooked into his clothing and its legs wrapped around his waist. But whatever happened to them, what happened to Kradok was worse. At first Tog thought that Merthen was resting his feet on a pile of old skins. Then the pile shifted and Tog saw it was Kradok. There was a lead round his neck and a horrid leather mask that drew his face out into a snouty muzzle. His hair bunched out between the straps and his hot, dark eyes peered out desperately over the top. Tog's mind went back to the night on the refuge when the witch had cursed him and said he would become a dog. Was this her curse coming true? He didn't want any part of it. But at least he now knew for certain how important the map was, even if he no longer had it.

At midday the lookout in the bows called out, 'Shallow water. We won't get over the ford.'

As the helmsman steered the boat to the shore, Tog levered himself up and looked over the side. The river was wide, shallow and fast here and bulged over the rocky bottom.

'Prepare to moor!' the helmsman shouted. 'Rowers, disembark. We're drawing too much water to clear the ford. You'll have to drag us over.'

The slaves wore big metal rings round their ankles. A long metal chain passed through this. The lookout knocked out big pins at either end of the chain, and the slaves, in a well-rehearsed routine, stood, lifted the chain and disembarked.

The helmsman jumped down into the hold and pulled the prisoners to their feet.

'Where are we going?' Tog asked.

'When the river's low, like now, the boat draws too much water to get over the ford with the rowers on board. But don't get your hopes up. You're staying put, though you might have to move to adjust the boat's weight.'

A small settlement lay on both sides of the river. Some coracles were moored to a jetty close to a single storehouse, its roof sagging like an old horse's back. A troupe of acrobats was rehearsing in an empty square: a giant with two slim boys standing on his shoulders. Another boy vaulted over a small, shaggy pony, landing with a thump, then sprung lightly backwards, his back an impossible arch, planted his hands on the pony's back, and held the pose for one breath, then another before twisting round, pushing up and landing on his feet with a small puff of dust on the spot where he had started the move.

The giant clapped. The boys on his shoulders whooped in high voices. From his wooden throne Merthen called out: 'I don't remember hearing of any tumblers in our land. I want the boat over the ford quick.'

The slaves dropped the last link of the chain over a hook in the bows of the boat and began to pull the boat forward, the helmsman leaning on the tiller to keep the bows clear of the bank.

Tog kept an eye on the tumblers, whose display had carried them closer to the boat. He felt its keel grind against stones.

'We've bottomed out,' the helmsman shouted back. 'We've got to shift the weight to the back, get the bows over the ford and then send them to the front. And the raft's trying to drag us backwards all the time. You three – move back quick!'

Tog made as if to move, tripped over the ribs of the boat and fell, catching Ordan and bringing him down. As they tried to stand, the keel ground again and the boat lurched.

'Can't move,' he called.

The boat listed as the current knocked the bows into the stream, then the drag of the raft pulled it back and it jerked over in the other direction.

'Get your dog to help!' the helmsman shouted at Merthen.

Again, the boat ground and lurched sideways. 'Do it, dog!' he snapped. 'But keep an eye on them.'

Kradok cut the ties round the prisoners' ankles. 'Help us,' Tog hissed. 'After this, there can't be anything left to threaten you with.'

Kradok growled. The slaves bent their backs and began to haul again. With a judder, the bows lifted and the boat moved again.

Then the stern caught.

'Stop pulling!' the helmsman ordered. 'Prisoners to the bows. Move!'

They stumbled across the hold, dipping the bows and freeing the stern as it rose over the ford. Tog kept his eye on the tumblers. The giant had walked closer and the vaulting boy was now sitting on the horse's back.

'Are we over it yet?' Merthen called.

'Just a few more paces.'

The giant looked at Tog, who nodded. Merthen shouted out a warning, but at that moment the giant took two swift steps that carried him up to the bows of the boat. The two boys on his shoulders stood up, balancing easily. One leapt on to the bows, while the other leapt on to the leading slave's back.

Caught by surprise he stumbled and fell backwards, taking the tension out of the chain. The boy on the bows unhooked it and dropped the end into the water. Immediately the bows of the boat began to swing out into the current. Kradok ran towards him but missed his footing and fell. Merthen rose to his feet, his face shocked and furious, and started to stagger towards them but as he was halfway down the boat, an arrow thudded into the helmsman's arm. He cried out, spun round, knocking the tiller and forcing the bows even further into the middle of the river. The keel caught and the boat heeled right over, throwing Merthen down.

Tog shouted, 'JUMP!'

One of the boys, beautifully balanced, ran to Kai, took the child off him, then leapt on to the bank with it. Ordan and Kai jumped the gap but as Tog prepared to make the leap, a hand clamped onto his leg.

Kradok was hanging on, his muzzle knocked sideways, teeth bared in desperation.

'Don't go. You don't understand! I—'

The boat tipped again, then began to grind against the bottom of the river as the weight of the raft dragged it backwards and into the middle of the channel.

Something in Tog responded to the desperation.

'Come with us,' he said.

'Can't.'

Tog kicked down again and again, feeling Kradok's head slam against the ribs of the boat. Still he hung on. Tog gripped the gunwales, dragged himself to the edge, twisted and let himself fall, relying on his weight to break Kradok's grip.

It did.

He splashed into the water, came up once but with his hands tied he could only take a quick breath before he went down again. The current caught him and turned him. He saw pebbles, weeds, a flash of sunlight through the water and suddenly he was yanked from the water and dumped on the bank. He coughed, felt a knife on his bonds, opened his eyes and saw Ordan sitting up and shaking his head while Kai lay a short distance off, spitting water, still holding the child.

In the river, the boat was beached sideways on the shallows, pushed on to its side. The Wickwicks were trying to hold the raft steady and there was no sign of the wizard, Kradok or the helmsman. The slaves were standing on the bank, looking confused. Then it seemed as if they understood the change in their situation because slowly they began to pass the chain through the shackles round their ankles.

A shadow passed between Tog and the sun. He looked up and smiled at the giant.

'Thanks.'

Allanza smiled easily. 'It was the women,' he said. 'The horsewomen. Don't call them girls. Can you stand?'

Tog pushed himself stiffly to his feet.

'Women?' But now he looked, the boys were very obviously women: skinny, burned dark brown and with hair cropped close to their skulls. All three were mounted now, sitting easily on their horses as if they were born on them.

'We've got to go,' Allanza said. 'They hate hanging around. They've got spare horses and they want us.'

'Who are they?'

'Friends, for now. Remember the attack when you were taken? I saved the horsewoman, we made contact with her patrol and now they're saving you.'

'But why?'

'I don't know. They wouldn't say. We've got to go though.'

'And the parchment?' Ordan asked.

'It was in the boat. I made them go back for it but of course that told them it was important and now they've got it.'

30

The horse-sister Allanza had saved was called Ran and the others were Argel, Mab and Olwyn. They lived on their horses, only stopped to sleep and played a cat and mouse game with the dragon's patrols. For example, if the enemy found a trail, they would lay traps or set ambushes for the horse-sisters. But the horse-sisters could often tell which trails had been discovered and would trap the trappers and ambush the ambushers. It was not a war they could win, but they couldn't lose it either and little by little they thought they were eroding the dragon's authority.

'Why don't you band together with the other kingdoms?' Tog asked Argel.

She was riding beside him and shot him a look of contempt. 'Do you think we would have dealings with men?'

Nettled, Tog said, 'They probably wouldn't have dealings with you.'

'And here's the difference between us. They ignore us simply because we are female. We have no dealings with them because men have ruined the world. Who burns villages, steals children, fights their neighbours? Men. Who rapes, tortures, enslaves? Men. But ask them what they're doing and why, you just get the same answer: keep out of it; this is man's business. And there's another difference. These men are only interested in power and the dragon knows this. He plays them. He makes an alliance here, a treaty there. If we made a treaty with any of the kingdoms, we would expect it to hold but they would only keep it until a better one came their way and then they would betray us.'

'You seem to have a low opinion of men,' Tog said.

'Could you do better than us?' Argel mocked. 'Even now, could you make your own way through the Great Wood? Go on. Climb a tree. Have a look.'

At her whistle the others stopped, held the bridle of Tog's horse so he could stand on its back and swing himself up into a tree. He climbed past the thick branches and higher and higher until he could feel the trunk sway with his weight. Up at the top, the sun was hotter but less stifling but all he could see were the tops of trees muffling the land in a thick blanket. That blue shape in the distance: could that be a mountain? No, it was just a cloud and in front of it, behind it and to either side were trees. Was that a hill? Yes, but it was covered in trees. There was no sign of the river, no sign of a road, no sign of a town, village or even a clearing. No smoke. No sound, just the dense dry rustling of leaves. He could have been anywhere, he thought.

'At least tell me why you were looking for us,' Tog said.

Argel put her fingers to her lips and looked superior.

They rode on until the sun was angling through the branches. Tog heard a fox bark, a kite shriek and then, at last, they reached somewhere: the trees thinned, the ground rose. At the foot of the rise, a stream fed a series of ponds.

As they stopped, lean, restless women slipped out of the thicker woods, arrows resting on taut bow strings.

'We found them,' Argel called out. 'One rescued Ran and we rescued the others at the ford. We sank the boat, and the wizard fell into the water.'

Bows were lowered, contemptuous faces looked away.

'Take them to Talar.'

Tog felt dispirited and bone-tired but the others, he noted irritably, were looking around and chatting. Allanza was carrying the child, Kai was distracting it by making faces, while Ordan was explaining to a non-existent audience that he heard legends of armies of women who cut off their breasts to make it easier to draw a bow, married each other and kept men for stud.

They stopped in a clearing. Huts made of uncut branches and dried leaves ringed it and in the centre was a huge old oak, dying apart from a thin crown of pale leaves from a few spindly branches. A woman, older than the members of the patrol, appeared from a small shelter. Her face was suntanned, bony and watchful, and her hair was scraped back from her face so tightly it seemed to stretch her eyes.

'These are the ones?'

'Confirmed.'

She raised an eyebrow. Tog could feel her take in his ragged clothes, leathered skin, crazy hair. 'They don't look like much but you never know. Is one of you called Artognu?'

Tog stepped forward.

'Stay there. Guards, be ready.'

Around the clearing, horsewomen put arrows to bows and held them ready.

'What's going on?' Tog asked.

'That is precisely what we are asking you. Sit there. I will listen to what my sisters have to say, then question you further.'

31

They were left by a pool of clear, dark water where golden beech leaves danced slowly in the current. Food was brought to them: flat bread made from chestnut flour, dried meat and an unpleasant form of cheese made from mare's milk. Each rider had their own store and they were all given a tiny bit by everyone, amounting to not very much at all.

The clearing filled up with women, all armed. Two archers approached and indicated they move to the centre of the clearing and sit on a log that was placed under an oak tree. Talar stood in front of them, legs planted solidly on the ground. She held the map tube in one hand and slapped it into the other palm.

'Is this a trial?' Kai squinting up.

Talar looked at him. 'It's whatever we want it to be. If you don't cooperate, we will kill you. If you do, you may be allowed to go free.'

'So that's the choice, is it?' Kai asked. 'Certain death or freedom maybe?'

'Or we might keep you for breeding – one or two of you, anyway. But that is to be decided later, along with the fate of the baby you brought with you.'

'Now hang on . . .' Kai began.

'Quiet. First, who are you?'

'What's that to you?'

'Cooperate or die,' Talar said, sounding as if she didn't care very much which they chose.

Tog looked at her, the impassive ranks of horsewomen arranged behind her, and came to a decision.

'My name is Artognu,' he said. 'Until three weeks ago I had the title of High King of Britain. I was attacked, my wife kidnapped and my army scattered. I am attempting to take her back with my friends Kai and Allanza, and Ordan the bard.'

'And who attacked you?'

'It was the army of the man who calls himself the dragon. We were following the river to his stronghold.'

'And do you have proof of this?'

'No.'

‘And you thought you could row up the river, through his screens of spies, past the Wickwicks, his . . .’

‘In all fairness, Kai didn’t,’ Tog said. ‘But it was all I could think of. Three weeks ago, I had not even heard of the dragon.’

‘And yet you call yourself High King? Why not travel with the high king’s army, surrounded by the high king’s generals?’

‘I thought . . . I thought my army had been scattered and we could make better time like this. Also, I didn’t want to advertize the fact that my wife had been stolen.’

‘She’s yours, is she?’

Tog swallowed. ‘I should have called her “the queen” not “my wife”. I am hers. I don’t know whose she is.’

Talar allowed herself a delicate snort. ‘Argel. Does this tally with what the tall one told you?’

‘He said they were on a mission to rescue a woman. He said that they had come from far away. He said they were travelling on their own and had had many adventures.’

Talar looked at Tog without expression, then spoke. ‘This is what we have heard and this is what we have learned. Our scouts have learned of an army, not a big army but an army, marching towards this part of the land on the West Road. This army is sending out its own messengers and they are offering a reward for information regarding a party of three . . . young men and one old man. This army is headed by a man called Mailgwin and he wants a message to be conveyed to the leader of these three young men: that the army is still loyal and he must meet them at High Cross in one week's time from today.'

'And when is midsummer?' Tog asked.

'In five days. And now I have a decision to make,' Talar said. 'Because it is clear from everything I have learned that the dragon wants you too and I owe it to my people to . . . do the right thing.'

'What do you mean?' Tog asked.

'She means, could she buy a bit of time off the dragon by handing us over?' Kai said.

'I could hand you over to him or any of the kingdoms that surround his land,' she said. 'Some of them might even be loyal to you, king.'

'But that will take days, weeks even!' Tog jumped to his feet. Instantly, the ground thumped and an arrow quivered in the ground between them. He swallowed, took one breath, then two. 'Something is going to happen on midsummer's eve – a ceremony involving the Wickwicks. Jenna, the queen, is going to be part of it. I'm afraid she might be sacrificed.'

'Argel?'

'The wizard was towing the Greenmother upriver.

Wickwicks were following.'

Talar shrugged. 'And then there is this parchment covered in strange marks you were carrying. Your tall friend thought it was important enough to go back and fetch but I have looked at it and I cannot see—'

A screech owl sounded on one side of the clearing, and another answered. Talar's eyes widened. 'That means danger,' she said. 'If this is your doing . . .'

'You brought us here!' Kai said.

'Quiet!' Tog ordered. The women dispersed to the edges of the clearing then melted away into the trees. Talar stayed with them and their guards, waiting, waiting. Nothing happened. The only sound was the gentle chuckle of the stream and the sighing of the forest. Then another bird call and a young girl, her hair shaved to stubble, was escorted over to Talar.

'Report, Mari,' Talar snapped.

The girl stood very straight. 'I gave the alarm. I saw movement. It was small. Not an animal.'

'If not an animal, was it human?'

'Yes. I mean . . .'

'Enemy?'

'I don't know. I . . . I don't know. Perhaps I was confused.'

'By what?'

'Something that happened earlier.'

'Report.'

'I smelled woodsmoke – no, an old fire. You know the way they smell after you put them out and they get wet?'

'There have been no fires here,' Talar said. 'You should have reported it.'

'It seemed so . . . small,' the girl said. 'Then I caught it again, but this time with the movement . . .'

Woodsmoke, Tog thought. Little people. Two more owl screeches.

'CONTACT!'

The cry came from the direction Mari had come from. They heard the hiss and thwock of arrows as the horsewomen shot into the woods, then: 'DOWN BOWS! Report any hits. Any incoming.'

No one called, but as they waited, Tog caught the movement out of the corner of his eye as something small and dark dropped through the air from a branch of the oak free. He marked where it landed, knelt and gently parted skeletons of leaves, until his fingers met something hard and sharp: a flint arrowhead.

Little people. The smell of woodsmoke. *Stone weapons.*

'No one shoot!' he called.

'What do you mean by ordering my people?' Talar snapped.

'I didn't mean to. I just know who's out there. Pigseys. Little People. They mean no harm.'

'Pigseys? Pigseys don't exist. They curdle milk. They tangle hair. Superstition.'

'They exist. We've met them – at least Allanza and I have. They like to keep themselves apart. If they're making contact, it's important.'

'For who? Why are they sneaking up on us?'

'They're not sneaking. They're secretive.' Tog hoped the pigsey in the tree would have the sense to keep still until he persuaded the horsewomen they were safe.

'If we don't know them, they're enemies. I can't risk it. I can't risk my girls.'

'Then let one of us go to them. They're all around us and could have killed every one of you by now if they'd wanted.'

Allanza glanced at him; he knew this last claim was an outright lie. With their stones axes and poorly strung bows, the pigseys fought as badly as they smelled. Their only weapon was stealth.

'You might turn on us too,' Talar said.

'All right,' Tog said. 'Put your best archer against a tree so no one can sneak up on her, and have her aim right at my heart. At the first sign of trouble, kill me.'

'And me,' Allanza said. 'I know them too.'

'If my king is putting himself in danger, I must as well,' Ordan said and stepped forward. Kai looked resigned and joined them.

'What's to report?' Talar called out.

'Nothing.' The calls came back from all around.

'Gron, Dera, Cyn: come here. Stand with your back against the oak tree there with notched arrows. Each of you take a prisoner. If there's any trouble, shoot them dead. Be ready for little people. Let them through. They are not Little Swords. Repeat, not Little Swords.'

'And don't be surprised where they come from,' Tog added. He looked up into the spreading tree above and said, 'You'll be safe now.'

Talar jumped back as the leaves above her rustled purposefully. A frayed rope dropped and a small figure wrapped in grey-brown sacking climbed painstakingly down from a broad, overhanging bough.

A surprised cry from the other side of the clearing caused a flurry of panic before Talar called out, 'Report!'

'It was just there, where I was looking,' a shocked voice called back. 'It came from nowhere.'

'Let it pass,' Talar called. 'Let the . . . little people pass.'

Half a dozen pigseys shuffled more across the clearing, all dressed the same, all with heavy matted hair swinging over their shoulders. They stood in rough order in front of

Tog and bowed quickly. He did the same.

The pigsey who had come from the tree asked in a blank, level voice, 'Are we ssafe?'

'Yes,' Tog said. 'The horse-sisters have promised.'

'It iss not important. It is important that we have found you. It iss important that we tell you thingss we know and you do not know. You have an enemy.'

'I know,' Tog said.

'He wantss the queen's sstory.'

'Her story?'

'She is the sstory and it iss not for him to have.'

Kai interrupted. 'How can Jenna be a story? Get him to talk sense.'

'A cup that holds water iss not water, it iss a cup of water. The queen holds the story like the cup holds the water. She is the vessel. She hass many names. She is the key. She iss the cure. She iss the crow. It iss all part of the ssame sstory that the dragon wantss to know.'

'What story?' Tog asked. 'Why didn't she tell me?'

'It is a sstory she hass to live, not tell. After she lives it then others can tell. But the dragon wants it. The dragon wantss to take her sstory. He wants to ssteal it. Eat it. Take it. The dragon iss greedy.'

'And if he does?'

'It will not be good for this world. Lissten. The pigseys

were here before the metal people came and before the Romanss came but we heard the Romans talking in their tent. All came to Britain to find the sstory. That is why it wass hidden where it wass hidden. Only the pigsey people could have hidden it better.'

'Hidden with the Picture People?' Tog said.

'The story wass as sstill as the mountains, ssolid like a rock. Now it is in the land of foressts and the rivers it will grow like a tree and sspread like water, thiss story. You musst stop it.'

'How?'

'With blood. There iss blood to make the change. Always there musst be blood. We go now.'

'But what is the story?' Tog asked.

The pigsey closed his eyes. 'Alwayss the ssame with the metal people. Alwayss the knowing and not the living.'

'I can't help it,' Tog said. 'Talar, will you let the pigseys see the parchment?'

Talar shrugged, then told one of the sisters to fetch the parchment and give it to Tog. He unrolled it. The pigsey looked at it with his weak eyes and sniffed it.

'Is this the key to the secret?' Tog asked. He was aware that Ordan had shuffled closer.

The pigsey looked at him. 'Sstory teller without a story,' he said. 'He knows that there are no ssecretss, only sstories not yet told.'

Ordan bowed.

'You want to tell this sstory? And you know why the Romans came to this island? The deep reason?'

As if hypnotized, Ordan said, 'To find a great treasure.'

'Yess. And this treasure is?'

'No one knows but some say it is the secret of life itself.'

'Ah. And is that the ssecret?'

'Some say that the treasure is not in the thing itself, but in the searching.'

'You ssay the ssame as the pigseys but in your own words.'

Kai could not contain himself any longer. 'I knew it.' he said. 'I knew he was after something!'

'Quiet!' Tog ordered. 'So that's it? The map is a clue?'

'And the queen,' the pigsey answered. 'And the queen. Now we musst go. we have sspoken.'

'You can't go now,' Tog said. 'You can't have looked for me all this time just to—' The pigsey held up a hand and amusement flickered across its smeared features.

'We do not *look for*; we ssee. We do not tell; we sspeak. Horsewomen. We thank you for not killing us and this is how we repay you: two dayss to the ssouth you will find a part of Dragon's army. They are looking for you and will be moving north tomorrow. King, the dragon has made a promise to his people that he will tell them the ssecret at midssummer. That iss before your army can reach him. And I can tell you this: she and Dragon musst tell the sstory together.'

'Jenna and the dragon?' Tog said.

The pigsey's face hardened. 'Ssecrets,' he said, and turned. This time they left, shuffling out of the clearing in their lopsided, halting way, disappearing almost before they reached the trees. They left behind a lingering smell of woodsmoke and putrid meat, and the rope that still hung from the tree branch. When Talar gave it the gentlest of tugs it fell apart and was absorbed by the forest floor as if it were made of nothing at all.

It was later, much later, and Tog could not sleep.

As soon as the pigseys had left, Kai had begged permission to put Ordan to death for hiding what he knew of the map. Allanza had pointed out that then they would never know what he knew, and he would hardly tell them now unless they gave him his life. Kai had suggested torture but Tog had vetoed that. For reasons he did not quite understand, he felt he was on the brink of leaving a deep, dark hole. He didn't want any more shadows on his soul.

Ordan had apologized but still refused to talk, outraging even Allanza.

'Why not?' Tog had pressed the bard, feeling self-conscious under the cool, mocking eyes of the horse-sisters.

'The danger is too great. I may have said too much already.'

'Danger to who?'

The bard had lowered his large square head. His back, round as a whale's, had heaved and huge cow tears had started to patter on the leaf mould. 'I cannot say,' he'd sobbed. 'The knowledge is too great.' And then, goaded by Kai dropping handfuls of earth on to his head, he had roared, 'Do you think I would do anything to harm the king? And do you think the pigseys would? And do you think I could say what they, in their wisdom would not? I CANNOT TALK ABOUT THIS MATTER!' Roosting birds had flown up from the trees with a creaking chatter. Horsewomen had drawn their weapons. Kai had jumped back, tripped on a log and fallen.

And Tog had found himself laughing.

'What?' Kai had said. 'What's funny about that?'

'Because it doesn't matter,' Tog managed to say. 'Nothing matters. I shall do what I shall do because I need to do it. Forget all the rest. Forget it. I don't know anything but everything's clear. Nothing makes sense and it all makes sense. Do I trust Ordan? I just don't care. Do I trust

Argel? I just don't care. It's a relief. That's all I can say.'

And he had gone to bed, filled with a wondrous, vacuous clarity. And now he couldn't sleep.

He sat up, his bed of dry of leaves rustling thunderously, but no one woke. Hugging his cloak around him, he walked to the pond and tried to touch the water without going through the surface, like one of those little insects – pondskaters, they were called. It took a finer touch than his.

Under the trees the horses stirred. Someone cried out in their sleep and someone else murmured to them in a low voice.

The country was sick and Jenna, not *he*, was the cure. She was also the key and the crow and the cup. He unrolled the map and tried to stroke the lines to life. Nothing. The map of Britain was like Jenna's back. Jenna held a story like a cup held water. A cup ... Something shifted in his head but he could not catch it. Jenna was going to live out the story with the dragon. His heart hurt so he punched it. Talar sat down beside him.

'Leaders sleep less than their people,' she said. 'Even young ones.'

'I felt young, for just a minute, when Kai fell over. Everything was clear. Now it's all muddy again. Can I ask you a question: are you a tribe?' It was a relief to think about something different.

'No. We are companions, brought together by shared stories, as the little man might say. And the stories the sisters tell could make a stone weep.'

'You don't seem to like men very much.'

'It was men that wronged us.'

'And they made you so fierce?'

'No, they made us angry. Then we made ourselves fierce. Now answer my question: that parchment the little man knew about. What do you see in it?'

'It's called a map,' Tog said. 'It's Roman – a picture of the country drawn in ink on parchment – and it must have been important enough for a Roman emperor to put his seal on it. I thought the pigseys might tell me straight out what it really means but that's not the way they do things. They make you work things out for yourself.'

Talar said, 'You are thinking about this in the wrong way. My sisters and I have found that we have to think of everything as if the world is new and we are creating it – otherwise we fall into the old ways. Let me tell you about this mystery. If it is prized by men, it is about one thing only. Power. That is why the dragon wants it.'

'And if he wants it, I should try and stop him, whatever

it is. And then I should find this thing and use its power myself.'

'Are you sure?'

'If you let me go, that is.'

'I meant: are you sure you should use its power?'

'It's all I can think of.'

'Perhaps you are right, and perhaps you are wrong. The question I have to ask myself is this: if you beat Dragon and take on his power, will you be better than him or worse? Do you have an answer?'

'A month ago, I would have said better,' Tog said. 'Now . . . I just don't know. I don't want to be like him but the truth is, I've never had that much power so I don't know what it will do to me. I might turn into a monster. I might even turn into the dragon.' And he laughed.

Talar looked at him long and hard before she answered. 'If nothing else, you're trying to be honest. What do any of us know? I am going to release you and just ask three things. Firstly, please keep this power away from us. Second, give us the woods. Third, leave the child you brought with us.'

'That won't be easy for Kai.'

'Nothing is easy for that one.'

'He's not a bad person,' Tog said, feeling queasy, checking the feeling and realizing that it was because he was judging his friend and passing that judgement on to . . . another leader. So that was what he did now. Talking, leader to leader, at night, while the others slept.

The horsewoman looked at him levelly. 'Yes or no?'

'If you can persuade him, then yes. And yes, the woods are yours, for what my word is worth. Now I've got to ask you a favour. Can you give me a guide to take me to the dragon's lair and can you . . . can you keep my leaving a secret from my friends as long as possible? I think it's best if I do this on my own.'

'Are you sure?'

'Yes.'

'And what do you want them to do?'

'Make contact with General Mailgwin, then join me as quickly as they can.'

'And the map? Did I gather that the dragon wants it too? Shouldn't you leave it here?'

'No,' Tog said. 'I want it with me.'

'You think you can bargain with it?'

'I don't know.'

'By finding out the truth, you risk losing everything.'

'I've got nothing left to lose,' Tog said.

'I have rather a lot, so be careful.'

32

Dawn. In front of Tog a dead swan lay on the brown margins of the lake, an arrow through its side. From the reeds, he looked across a stagnant lake to an island reached by a wooden causeway. It rose to a small hill in the centre. On top of the hill stood a castle, surrounded by patched stone walls, with wooden watchtowers on each corner. Inside the walls were barracks and storehouses and in the centre, at the highest point, stood a hall and a square tower built of blocks of blood-red stone.

Tog's guide was a horsewoman his age. Like Talar she kept her hair pulled back. It showed a scar that ran from the corner of her eye, down her face and on to her long, thin neck.

To the east of the castle lay the marketplace, warehouses,

slave-hall, and a shanty town, she explained. It would be a good place to hide so long as Tog kept his head down – every other person there was a spy for the castle. They traded information like apples or oats.

She left Tog with a green hooded cloak. 'Talar took it,' she said. 'The Little Sword killed her friend. Jumped down from a tree and slit her throat. Talar chased it for a week before she caught it.'

The cloak was stiff with blood. 'Don't worry about that. The more blood on their clothes, the better.'

'Thank you,' Tog said. He almost meant it.

'Good luck,' his guide said. 'It is true you've given us the woods?'

'Yes.'

She gave a small smile. 'Then I should give you something. People are saying they've seen the queen.'

Tog's heart leapt. 'Here?'

The woman nodded.

'How is she? What was she doing?'

'People are saying she goes riding with the dragon. If you wait by the causeway, you will see her. She often goes out at sunset.'

Hope to misery in two dozen words.

Tog skirted the castle, avoided the patrols and joined the

stream of wagons, merchants, farmers, buyers, sellers, hawkers, trampers, beggars, thieves and outright nuts heading to the town from the north.

The road was hard and narrow, its ruts hard as brick. Walkers stuck to the wide grass verge where Tog got talking to a rangy man with a nose like a rudder and a loud, rich voice.

'Here for the Midsummer Gathering, little brother?' the man said.

'Hoping to find some work,' Tog replied non-committally.

'Good luck but, as Dragon says, "put not your trust in the hearts of men for it is a false trust. Search for the truth and all will be well." '

'I'm not from round here,' Tog said. 'People I've met on the road have been vague about the Gathering.'

The man punched him on the shoulder. 'And that's because of the mystery,' he said. 'Surely even you would know that?'

'No, I missed out. No one spoke of such matters in my home.'

'This is not the religion you pick up in the home,' the man said. 'This is the religion of the road. It is Dragon's vision of unity and oneness. We're all brothers, all seeking the same thing. At the Gathering the dragon will set the

Seekers on a new path and turn us into a holy army with one aim, one lord, one goal.'

'But what is this thing that we're meant to be seeking?'

The man expelled air in a noise that sounded like 'Hoosh'. 'You think I'd give you my hard-won wisdom just because you happen to be sharing the same patch of road with me?'

Tog tried to sound contrite. 'Sorry, brother. I didn't mean to pry.'

'I mean nothing by it. Try to make it to the Gathering, friend. On the other side of the town there's a godless place – an old amphitheatre where they say the Romans played their filthy games. We're taking it over, brother, making it ours! What's happening? What's going on?'

Ahead, a clot of people had formed on the verge, slowing the crowd. Tog followed the man as he pushed his way forward, straining on the tips of his toes to get a look and thought he caught a glimpse of a small building about as tall and not much wider than a man, with a pitched, tiled roof.

'A shrine! A new shrine, brothers!' Someone called out ahead. Tog pushed his way towards it until he reached a solid mass of people that would not budge. He tried to move back but too many people were pressing in from behind. The crowd started to sway forwards, then back and

Tog could only stay upright by hanging on to the shoulders of the man in front. Someone grabbed him. He staggered, was kicked, hit, and felt the crowd close round him. Panic gave him strength. He pushed upwards, found a gap, pushed harder and this time, instead of trying to stay upright, climbed. He got his shoulders out of the press, wriggled up, used the crush to support him and suddenly was surfing on top of the crowd. He caught a glimpse of the shrine, a baby's head, silver, expressionless and shining, set on a background of green, then slid down a surprised, plump traveller and looked around.

He was on the edge of town. Houses were built of any material that came to hand: split logs, wattle and daub, turf or a mixture of everything. If there was a street vendor, you guessed you were in a street but travellers built shelters or put up tents more or less wherever they wanted. On three sides the forest shrank back from the shanty town, trees showing white scars where people had torn off their limbs for firewood. On the fourth, a high wooden palisade surrounded the grain stores and slave market. Tog wandered past market stalls, trying to get a feel of the place, but plagued by a growing sense that he was being followed. He had noticed there were three types of people in the crowd: those that kept their heads down, those that met his eyes and looked blank or curious, and those that met his eyes and looked away. Spies. He had to do something before he was picked up, so he hid behind a building and dropped the Little Sword's green tunic over his head.

It was stiff, smelled musty and was slightly too big for him, which was fine. He pulled the hood over his head and down his forehead as far as it would go, found a barrel near the causeway, and settled down to watch and wait.

After an hour, he watched a man in a green cloak and a silver mask ride out, followed by a slim woman, a girl really, in a dress of blue silk and a golden mask that looked like a bird. They were riding side by side and from the way their heads nodded, talking like friends. It was only when the girl lifted her hand to push her hair back that Tog saw the tattoos on her arm and recognized his wife.

33

The world: everything or nothing

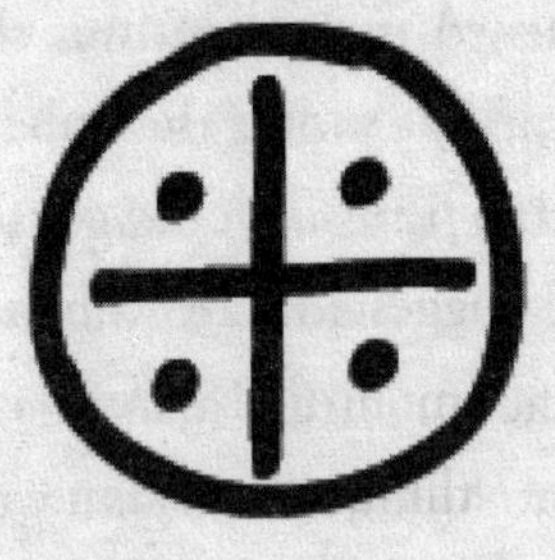

Jenna leaned against the parapet and looked out across the muddled rooftops of the town to the dark and endless waves of forest. She rubbed her hand against the rough stone and tried to get her thoughts in order. The cat from the boat had found her and rubbed itself around her ankles.

That morning she had seen two very different sides to Dragon and it was . . . intriguing. The first side was competence in action, and she rather liked it. Attending the dragon's public court, her seat had been put close to his so she could observe. She watched as people whispered in the dragon's ear. She watched as he tilted his head on one side to signify thought, then dispensed advice.

Local issues. A farmer claimed a neighbour had stolen

half his cattle. Bring the neighbour here next week, Dragon said, unless you want the Little Swords to investigate? Another wanted his son to join the army. Imagine him dead, Dragon said. Still interested?

Affairs of state. A neighbouring warlord wanted to ask, without actually saying so much, how much it would cost to keep the Little Swords from raiding his lands. Another suggested an alliance to invade a neighbouring kingdom. From his clever line of questioning, Dragon found everything there was to find out about the warlord's own army.

Dragon's soldiers, shaven headed, insect-like in moulded leather breastplates, were a constant reminder of his power; the gold on the floor a constant reminder of his wealth. In a room off the main chamber you could hear a constant hubbub as people did business. Money was levied and spent; ideas were tested; people thought along the same lines. Most impressive, Jenna thought, as she pretended to pick up tips.

She saw the second, unexpected side to him on the ride.

She was getting rather used to the whole process. As they walked their horses down the causeway and into the town, people moved away but then lingered and stared. The guard rode a respectful distance behind. Jenna felt her gestures become stiffer and more formal. Because the mask narrowed her field of vision, she had to move her head in order to see anything at all. She no longer just looked; she showed people she was looking. Then she found that when he talked, she was exaggerating her gestures. She was no longer talking, she was acting the talk as well. It all rather went to her head and it didn't exactly help that Dragon, for once, was quiet and hesitant and that made Jenna gabble.

Where does the mask come from?

Might be Roman.

Roman? Really? That's so interesting. Have you ever met a Roman? I have, once, can you believe it, holed up in a falling down villa, quite senile as a matter of fact, well, the man was. His wife was quite normal. They had a son, I think. I wonder what it was like growing up in Britain if you knew you were Roman.

And then, because some instinct started warning her not to talk too much about Romans, she rambled on about her own childhood and this, at last, got a response. Dragon laughed bitterly and said that he always wondered what it was like to have two parents and brothers and sisters and to be allowed to do things like ride out on a pony and be gone for day or two and live off trout and bilberries and oatcakes.

'So what was your childhood like?' she asked.

'I didn't have one,' Dragon said simply and bitterly. 'My father didn't believe in children. Just small soldiers. I—'

They were riding on the ridge above the castle, alongside a small stand of silver birches. A dog, which had been sleeping in a patch of shadow by the track, woke up, saw the horses, leapt to its feet and crashed into the wood.

Dragon started as violently as the dog and yanked on his reins. His horse reared, turned and was suddenly galloping down the track, scattering the respectful guards. Jenna turned, noted the guards' enquiring faces and said, 'Something spooked the horse.'

She urged her horse into a jolting trot, ignoring the jarring pain in her knee, and caught up with Dragon as he slowed down to cross the causeway into the castle.

'Did you see that?' he said rather too loudly. 'That bloody dog frightened my horse.'

Hooves clattered over the wooden planks.

'Are you all right?' Jenna asked.

' 'Course I am. Point is, are you? I mean, suppose your horse had taken off like that? Would you have been able to control it?'

'No,' Jenna said, thinking she was sure that he had made the horse rear, turn and flee. 'No.'

'I'm sending my men out. I'm having that dog killed.'

'It'll be far away by now.'

'It's a menace. A bloody menace!'

'I see a dog when I'm scared!' she blurted out.

He narrowed his eyes. 'What?'

'I see . . . an old dog whenever something frightens me so I know . . . sort of . . .'

A soldier ran up and spoke urgently to the dragon, who dismounted without a word and strode off. Seconds later he was back, standing by Jenna's mount, looking up at her. She was sure his eyes were swimming with tears.

'I forgot,' he said. 'I've been so long on my own . . .' He held up his arms and Jenna swung herself down lightly, but on landing found that her hands lingered on his shoulders and her mind had framed two unasked questions: what's wrong? Can I help?

She could tell him more about the fear dog and how she had discovered that the only way to beat him was to advance. Then he would say, 'I didn't think you were scared of anything.' And she would say, 'Oh, I'm scared all right. A lot of the time.' And he would say, 'You really are the most extraordinary—'

A crash of thunder jerked her out of her daydream and she shook her head angrily. The late sun was dragging down a heavy lid of clouds behind it. Darkness built like pressure. Jenna clenched her fist and whacked her ribs above her heart – traitor! – and tried to make herself think of Tog. Please rain, she thought. Flatten me, then wash me away before I find out what I really want.

34

Walking down the street wearing the Little Sword's hooded tunic, Tog felt as if there was a repellent, invisible barrier around him. If he stood still, people swirled past him like water round a rock. If he moved, he slid through the crowd like a blade through fat.

Little Swords, he realized, had a reputation. Good. He would take advantage of it.

He saw the bridge ahead. A cart was stuck half on, half off, its wheel lodged in a pothole. The guards were cursing the driver and as Tog walked past, he gave the flat-eared mule's rump a thwack with his hand. It whinnied, backed, struggled. Tog walked on, waiting for someone to curse him, but nothing happened. His feet thudded on the wooden planks. He watched the water glint between them as he passed. He looked up to see the gatehouse loom in front of him; the shouting mouths of the spiked heads, the ragged eyes. Two guards here, standing roughly to attention. He put his head down, hawked and spat as he passed. Then he was in the thickness of the wall; then he was out and inside the castle of his enemy.

He let out a breath and looked around. A street with low buildings on either side led straight to the stone tower. He passed a few closed doors, looked into the first open one. A barracks. Rough beds arranged in rows. Ten in all. Eight buildings. Eighty men.

Close by, he heard the definite chink, chink, chink of a hammer on metal.

He turned down a gap between the buildings and stepped over a rough fence into a chicken run. An old women sat in the front the henhouse, shelling peas. He smelled cooking and thought it came from a big building the other side of the tower. Of course – feeding all those men two or three times a day meant dining rooms and kitchens. And then they had to be armoured, armed, clothed and shod . . .

He felt himself shrink, then caught himself. He couldn't compare himself to this. For now, he had to see his insignificance as an advantage and he would fight the way he had been taught when he was a woodcutter's boy – by turning the enemy's strength to his advantage.

He continued on his circuit of the tower. A bell rang and he shrank back into a doorway that creaked open behind him. Warm rotten air billowed like a cloak. Something shifted. The hair on the back of his neck rose in cold hackles as he turned to confront it. In the darkness he saw two rows of beds, each with a shape on it.

'Will he come?' a voice asked from the darkness, weak and eager at the same time. 'But will he come?' Tog smelled pus and rot.

The voices outside were louder now, and backed up by crunchy, confident footsteps.

Tog backed into the room, holding the door open a crack as soldiers walked past, easy and relaxed on their way to a meal, Tog thought, or coming off duty.

'Will he come? When will he come? We are ready. Blessed be Dragon.'

Tog imagined the sick and wounded sitting up, falling out of bed like soft logs, crawling across the floor to him. He did not turn round, just slipped out and started moving quickly so the air could rinse him clean. He wasn't looking where he was going and found himself on the edge of a dusty square with the tower looming high on one side. A huge bank of earth had been piled up against the wall to support it and an oatmeal line of mortar zigged and zagged up the scab-coloured blocks.

He paused. To cross the square would make him feel too exposed. To walk around the edge would put him too close to the buildings that surrounded it.

He turned to retrace his steps but as he did so thought he caught a whisk of movement, as something flicked into a gap between two buildings.

Thunder sounded and a sudden, shocking gust of wind raised dust devils in the square. Tog blinked, ducked behind the corner of a shed and peered out. There!

A small figure, dressed in green, running across the square. Now he heard voices off to the right. Better hide in one of these sheds. The first one stored freshly cut timber: too risky. The next was empty, with cobwebs across the entrance. Tog crawled in under the cobwebs, sank back against the wall and tried to slow his breathing down.

He had made it. He was inside the castle, had found a safe haven and, what was better, could look down a narrow gap between buildings at the cracked side of the tower.

And what he saw made him very interested indeed.

The sun had found a gap in bulging, copper clouds. Shadows now picked the crack out and showed that it was deep and wide. Better still, the mortar used to fill it was lumpy and rotten. The usual story: a botched repair on a

Roman building, and he tried to memorize every zig and zag in the stonework.

When Jenna appeared, he thought he was imagining it. Her hair was held up in a band that glinted, the way she wore it for formal occasions. She looked clean; when she lifted a hand to wave a fly away, the sleeve of her dress moved expensively.

He watched her hit the parapet, her frown, then her face sharpened with longing before softening into something else. His own heart knotted. He knew that expression. He had seen it in the glow of firelight, in the white blaze of moonlight, in the golden glare of summer. It had always been for him; he thought it was only for him. Now he was not sure.

35

Jenna looked around her room with disgust. The hangings stank in the warm, damp air. They were threadbare. Rotten. Oppressive. The gold in the chest was someone else's, as was the silk robe she was wearing; she had just noticed old sweat stains on it. Angrily and spiteful, she ripped a seam apart, then tore a strip from around the hem which she wrapped tightly around her bad knee. She could hardly stand now without the feeling that something was scraping inside her bones. It was the trotting that did it, trotting after Dragon, who hadn't climbed the steps to see her and hadn't checked that she was all right.

She lay down on the carpets and banged her head a few times, then stopped. A sound, the tiniest vibration, seemed to be coming up through the floor. She found the edge of a rug and pulled it back. There was another one underneath, and another under that, and then a layer of smelly rushes and under that a floorboard. She pressed her ear to it.

Voices, and one of them was Dragon's! He was in the room underneath hers. She was gripped by a furious curiosity but as she flattened her head against the wood, the voices grew fainter.

That did it. She hobbled to the door, opened it, and checked the landing. All clear. Stairs weren't too bad; she could bump down them on her behind. On the landing below, there were three doorways. One led to the stairs, the other to a room with a wooden cage in the middle of it, gnawed bones on its floor. There was a third and this was open a crack.

Jenna pushed it open.

A long passage. Using the wall to steady herself, Jenna hopped and stumbled along it. She passed an empty room; a room stuffed with broken furniture; a room with dancing ladies painted on the walls. Right at the end of the corridor was a narrow, curtained arch. She inched the curtain to one side and found she was looking down into the great audience hall behind Dragon's throne, just as Dragon himself swept into it, followed by Merthen with a terrible creature following on a leash – a man on all fours with a leather muzzle over his mouth.

'I told you, Merthen, it's not something I can help.' Dragon's voice was strained.

'Not on your own, but with my help, all manner of change is possible.'

'Ever since my father told me about the hell hounds, I've just never been able to stomach dogs. They look at you all happy and trusting but I know they're just waiting for to me fall and then it's jaws and red teeth and tongues as they tear me to pieces. That's what going to happen at the end of the world, you know. The hell hounds—'

'So some say, but they're just stories. Scary stories for little people.'

'The Pict sees a dog when she's scared.'

'As I said: scary stories for little people.'

Jenna blinked, waited for him to contradict the wizard but he didn't. Instead he said, 'She just . . . blurted it out in that mad accent of hers. All right. All right. What am I meant to do with this creature?'

'Let him approach,' the wizard said. 'Let him see your greatness. Let him quiver. Let him tremble. Dog!'

The dogman approached, fawning. Dragon leaned back but Jenna could see it was all he could do to stop himself running away. Her face was burning with shame. Was she a blurter? Was her accent mad?

'And this is meant to achieve what?' Dragon asked.

'You get used to him, then we introduce you to real dogs. May I suggest you kick him?'

Dragon extended a toe and prodded the dogman in the ribs. The dogman fell and showed his belly.

'Has the blind woman anything to report?' Dragon asked absent-mindedly.

'There is only so much she can do. I almost feel for her. I've let her stroke him. It was almost pitiful when she realized what her husband had become. And you, my lord. Has your way worked?'

'It takes time,' the dragon said. 'She does not know her own mind and it would help if she did but I am . . . weakening her.'

The blind woman? Jenna thought.

'Weakening?'

'She looks forward to seeing me. She wants to touch me. When I helped her down off her horse this afternoon, her hands lingered . . . if only there was more time to find out what she knows.'

'My way is quick,' Merthen said. 'I'd rather her back was off her bones and in my hand.'

'But she counts for much more alive. A marriage. An alliance . . . A new start and . . . the secret. The way to remake the world.'

'We could just threaten to strip her, in public, at the

gathering. She might talk then. She's proud. She couldn't take the humiliation.'

'I need one more chance,' Dragon said. 'In fact, it may have done no harm to at all for her to see me frightened. Girls like to see a bit of vulnerability, or so I've been told.'

'And don't forget she felt rejected by her own husband. Perhaps now is the time to pretend to take her into your confidence?'

Dragon tipped his head from side to side. Then he bent down and touched the dogman like a child daring to touch a snake.

'I did it, Merthen! I did it. I actually touched it!'

Jenna pulled back. She crawled back to her room, back to the solid, indifferent weight of the cat, so shocked and depressed she felt almost ill.

At first she could only drift in a mist of self-hatred. She had been duped, seduced, made to look an idiot. It followed she was an idiot tart, addle-brained, weak-hearted and a traitor. How many dozens of slaves does your father have? You and I, we understand this and that and everything like why slaves must die and we are the way we are. By pretending she was as rich as he, by flattering her, he had been slowly slicing away at her past with a knife so sharp she had not felt the cuts. Well, she had recovered in time and seen sense before those cuts had bled her dry. Now she had to do something about it. Revenge and self-recrimination could come later.

First things first. Dragon didn't know what the secret was. Now she knew that, he couldn't bluff her into saying anything. She would be dumb. She would be silent. She would never let him find out. But, but, she thought . . . it would be good if I knew the secret so I could have the pleasure of not telling him.

In the treasure chest she found a large silver plate, which she rubbed into a shine with a handful of silk. Her image leapt at her, more clearly than she had ever seen it before. She lay on her tummy, hands cupping her chin and gazed at her face: the swirls of blue that rose up her neck and curled so delicately around the jut of her cheekbones; the delicate fronds of the world tree on the ridge of her thin, straight nose; the crescent moon, lying like a cup in the middle of her forehead; the two hawks that stood like guards on either temple. When she closed one eye, she could see the eye drawn on its lid, so even when she was asleep she was watchful and alert. Back home, she could make children laugh when she blinked.

But this was no laughing matter.

She blew on the silver and gave it another polish, then shrugged her robe off her shoulders and tried to use the mirror to look at her back. That didn't work. Suppose she propped the mirror against a wall, lit another lamp, and put them either side. Dim images swam in the depths of the silver but they were so vague . . .

A tiny flicker of the flame warned her that the door was opening. She whipped the robe back on and turned in one movement. The blind woman stood there, shoulders hunched.

'I came . . . I came because I wondered if you wanted something.' Her voice was roughened by crying.

'You and I have got a lot to talk about,' Jenna said. 'Come.'

The blind woman approached.

'Sit,' Jenna said.

She knelt and put her hands in her lap.

'I'm going to come straight to the point. I, umm, I heard Dragon and Merthen talking. I know what he thinks of me now – not much, and I saw your husband. I'm sorry. I had no idea.'

The woman nodded.

'I realize now you must have thought I was pretty stupid. I never realized how bad Dragon was.'

The woman sniffed.

'We can help each other, you know.'

A tilt of the head.

'I need you to . . . tell me what's on my back.'

'I don't understand.'

'I think you do. I want you to do it now, like you did on the first day. Read the marks with one hand and trace what you're feeling on this silver tray.'

'I'll try. But suppose I tell Dragon what I've found out?'

'Then I wouldn't blame you.'

The blind woman turned her head away from Jenna, then said, 'There is one thing I heard: the Wickwicks caught your husband. No! Don't cry! He escaped. He was rescued or taken by women.'

'Women?' Jenna blurted out. 'What do you mean?'

'Some people say they're half human, half horse. Others that they're the most terrifying fighters. Others that they keep men like men keep women, inside their homes and doing chores. All I know for certain is that Dragon hates them and they hate Dragon.'

'Well,' Jenna said. 'Let's hope they don't make Tog cook. He'll poison the lot of them.'

'Will he come and rescue you?'

'Yes,' Jenna said and found she was very close to tears. 'Yes, he will. And you. Right. Let's do this thing.' Jenna shucked the dress from her shoulders, straightened her back, reached behind her and put the blind woman's left hand on her back and her right hand on the silver tray.

Her skin crawled as fingers touched her, first moving in quick, horizontal lines, marking each symbol with a quick press, and then, at last, returning to the first, just under her left shoulder blade.

Jenna switched her attention to the finger on the silver tray and followed its movements.

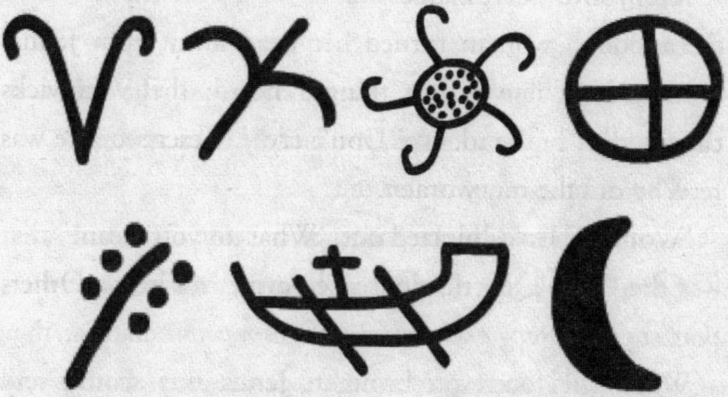

'Ram,' Jenna said to herself when she had made out the first shape.

'Ram, bird,' at the second.

'Ram, bird, flower.'

'Ram, bird, flower, sun.'

'Ram, bird, flower, sun, wheat.'

'Ram, bird, flower, sun, wheat, boat.'

'Ram, bird, flower, sun, wheat, boat with the moon in the middle.' Because the crescent moon, while it was not in the middle, was under the ram.

'May I go?' The blind woman sounded exhausted.

There were memories in Jenna's head that weren't so much stirring as bouncing.

'What? Yes. Of course. Oh – can you get someone to bring me food? Lots of food.'

Ram, bird, flower, sun, wheat, boat with the moon in the middle.

Ram, bird, flower, sun, wheat, boat with the moon in the middle . . . the moon in the middle. The moon.

Why did the moon stand out?

Surely it should be the moon at the top. Of course, that was the Crow Queen's nonsense rhyme: *promise to watch, death to use, strong and warm with the moon at the top*.

When the food was brought, Jenna was sitting very upright and very still as if the slightest disturbance would shake her into bits. She ate mechanically, her mind repeating the rhyme, then the signs, then the rhyme. Then she screwed up her face and tried to remember the one thing that she hadn't really bothered to think about at the time: the position of the signs of her back. It was very important. Very, very important.

When she thought she had it, for the first time since she had been taken captive, she started thinking of escape and when the blind woman returned to ask her if she wanted anything else, Jenna said, 'Yes.' She spoke very intensely and quietly for a minute or two, and then, when left alone, lay down to rest.

36

Tog was huddled behind a broken wagon and trying to rest before storming the tower. But the argument that suddenly broke out close to him was too interesting to ignore.

A man snapped, 'I don't care about your special orders or commendations for delivering some princess to the dragon. I heard you were in disgrace for getting captured and letting yourself be rescued by your own prisoner. No more special missions. Just kitchen duties from now on. Get lost.'

'So your orders are to round up any scouts you see and escort them to the main hall? And that's all right with you?' A boy. Sneering. Surly.

'Orders are orders. I'd have the lot of you drowned in the lake like sick puppies.'

'And you believe that one of us is really a terrorist infiltrator?'

'I believe you're all rotten to the core but word is, it's an infiltrator in disguise.'

A distant rumble so deep it seemed to shake Tog's bowels. Then another. Then a sharp crack.

'That's a storm,' the younger voice said. 'Tell you what, I'd rather be in held in the guardhouse than searching the castle right now.'

Rain whacked the ground so hard that dust jumped. Tog sneaked a look and saw one of the Little Swords walking away, his lips pulled back over pointed stubs of teeth. His mind went all the way back to the Refuge and the man saying that one of the fairies had hissed at him through fangs. His heart quickened.

Lightning flashed through the bare thatch. More thunder. More drops, each one bigger than the last until they were the size of blackberries. They balled on the earth, then turned it to mud, started to fall in a solid sheet, then boiled up the mud into a brown flood. The blackest clouds Tog had ever seen billowed up from the west. More lightning, followed by a crack of thunder even louder than the one before. The rain increased to a steady driving roar. The thatch started to drip and Tog risked a quick glance out of the hut door. To the right, a soldier was walking along the wall, keeping close to it for the meagre shelter it offered, staring at the ground. It was what you did in the rain, Tog thought. How can I turn that to my advantage?

Water was running off the ground outside now, gurgling into the hut. I could run, Tog thought, but where to?

He pulled a loose piece of stud timber from the wall. It was as long as his arm, dusty and not quite heavy enough, but would do. He pressed himself against the shed wall to the left of the door, and waited.

A slight lull in the downpour. Tog heard splashing footsteps.

He'll come in here to shelter, he thought, and the guard did, stooping under the flat curtain of water that now fell in front of the door. Tog brought the length of wood down on the back of the man's head with as much force as he could. It snapped, but the man went down on his hands and knees. Tog knocked his helmet off and whacked him again with the stub.

The guard collapsed. Tog flapped his stinging hands then dragged him to the back of the hut, took his helmet, tore off his cloak, and rolled him over so he didn't drown in the rising water. He put on the helmet, threw the cloak over his shoulder and trudged out, stooping. Down the alley another guard raised his hand and trudged on. Tog did the same, waited, then ran down the alley, across the yard and started to climb the earth slope that was piled up against the tower.

The water was sheeting down the tower wall. The earth slope was slick and steep. Tog dug with his fingers and dug with his toes. Halfway up, he began to slide down and could only stop himself by flattening his body against the slope and grabbing handfuls of earth until he found a rock, which he hung on to. It held. Slowly, filthily, he began to inch his way up again.

The slope was concave and steepened as it got closer to the wall but the earth was looser and easier to dig into with his hands and feet. Nonetheless, when he finally reached the great rough stones of the wall, his arms and legs were trembling from cold and effort. The storm was overhead now and the rain was getting stronger, cascading down the tower walls. Could he make it? He felt for the gap. The mortar had crumbled to sand. He had a chance. He made a handhold, kicked a hole with his toes and began to climb.

37

The first clap of thunder shocked Jenna; the second got her moving as the cat leapt off her and up the wall. She looked around. No way out down the stairs. No windows . . . hold on! Just because she could see no windows, it didn't mean there were no windows. What did the hangings conceal?

Lifting the first revealed nothing but rough stone. And the second, and the third. But under the fourth she found something interesting: a significant crack that zigzagged across the wall from bottom left to top right. Crumbly mortar – barely more than sand and pebbles. She picked again and a big chunk fell out. She reached in and dug with her fingers, scratching and scooping until she cleared away the mortar on two sides of a block, then pushed and pulled. At first nothing seemed to happen. Then she felt it grate a hair's breadth, first one way, then the other, as it moved on its bed of grit. She worked it harder, a little flame of delight rising inside her. Now it was grinding, rocking to and fro, and she was able to get her fingers behind it and pull.

The block slid towards her so suddenly she had to move backwards to get a better grip and try again, but with a huge heave she pulled it half out of the wall. She crawled over to the table and fetched a lamp. It was hard to see but she thought that behind a layer of rubble, she could see the back of the next block. She closed her eyes. Please let it be the outside, please let it be the outside, please . . .

Ignoring the scratches on her arm and roughened ends of her bleeding fingertips, she began to pick away at the next layer of mortar.

38

Tog found a sort of system. Right hand into the mortar. Make a hole. Take some weight. Scrape a hole with left foot. Take some more weight. Raise right leg and make hole higher. Push up and make hole with left hand. Stretch up right hand. And so on. Sometimes the blocks were jutting out and he could grip them or step on to them without having to kick out the mortar. Sometimes a stone in the mortar mix was wedged in the crack and would not budge. Once he slipped and was left hanging by his right hand and only just managed to get a foothold before he fell. Rain rained; Tog climbed and climbed . . .

Jenna realized that the rubble and mortar she was pulling out was wet. Rain must be getting through, she thought, which meant that the mortar on the outside was rotten too. She scrabbled and dug and at last felt cold air blow on to her face. She was through! One last effort now.

Water was sheeting down the side of the tower, freezing Tog's hands. He turned his face up into the waterfall. Lightning showed the top of tower against the sky.

Almost there.

That was when a lump of mortar fell from the wall about him and landed in his eye.

Jenna was certain the last block had moved. It was big. There was no way she could drag it in through the thickness of the wall. She would just have to push it out and hope no one noticed. She braced herself and shoved. Good. A tiny movement. She pushed again. A bigger movement. Excellent.

Tog blinked the stinging mortar out of his eye then looked upwards so the rain rinsed it out. It was painful, a shock, but he had hung on and could still move. He climbed two more steps before he next looked up and this time saw the wall begin to move.

With the block teetering, Jenna gathered herself and gave

it an enormous shove. It rocked, tipped, rocked, and fell.

Tog shouted as a block of stone, as big as his head, seemed to float out of the wall and tumble towards him. He let go with his left hand, swung round on his right as the block shot past him, felt his grip begin to go on the slick stone, swung back, reached up with his free hand . . .

. . . which appeared like a ghost in front of Jenna's face as she wriggled through the hole. Her scream was like an echo of Tog's as he blindly gripped her wrist. Jenna screamed again, struggled, strained her neck, teeth bared, rain pounding the back of her head as she stuck it outside and saw Tog . . .

. . . who saw Jenna.

He stared up, rain falling into his open eyes and open mouth. He couldn't even say her name. Jenna grabbed the neck of his tunic with her free hand and he found a toehold. She pulled, he pushed and slowly the soaking, freezing, mud-spattered high king of Britain wormed his way though the hole in the wall and the queen held him, feeling the cold and wet press upwards through her clothes until it lay on her skin. She straddled him, knees pressing into his chest, and cupped his face in her hands, bent down and pressed her lips to his cold lips and found the warmth behind them, then kissed his cheeks, his eyes, his lips again.

'Hello,' he said.

'And you're alive,' she said. She pushed mud off his face with the heel of her palm, sucked the cuff of her dress to try and get the rest off. She failed and held his freezing face again. 'I didn't know . . . I didn't know if you would be coming. I only just heard that you were close.'

'And I thought you might be . . .' An expression so quick it could hardly be called one warned Tog that some things should wait until later. 'I didn't know how you would be,' he concluded.

'Well looked after, as you can see.' Jenna gestured to the room. 'My knee's hurt but it's getting better.'

'What happened?'

'I got hurt trying to escape.' She could be proud of that, at least.

'And you were kept in here all the time?'

'Not all the time. He takes me out to try and win me over but now . . . I don't know what they're going to do. They want me because of my tattoos.'

'I know,' Tog said, relieved that she met his eyes as she talked. 'We worked that out. You're famous. The queen is the cure; does that mean anything to you?'

Jenna shook his head.

'And did you know that the tattoos on your back are the same as the ones on the map?'

When he showed the parchment to Jenna she frowned. 'I've seen that before,' she said. 'The old Crow Queen used it as a pattern when she was tattooing my back.' She recited, "*Promise to watch, death to use, strong and warm with the moon at the top.*" It sounds nonsense until you think about the tattoos but even then it doesn't make much sense. Wheat means promise and the barking dog means watch. The boat means death and the flower means usefulness. Strong and warm – that's the sun and the ram, and the moon's just the moon. So the rhyme is about the tattoos on my back.'

They lay on the carpeted floor, the map unrolled between them. Tog tracked each symbol with his finger as Jenna said the rhyme.

'Do it again,' he said. 'Just the symbols.'

'Wheat to dog,' Jenna said. 'Boat to flower. Sun to ram.'

She watched his finger cross the map diagonally one way, then another, then from top to bottom.

'If you put the moon at the top, it makes the Chi Ro,' he said. His voice sounded strangled and airless.

'Crow?'

A little sun burst in Tog's chest. 'Chi Ro! Crow! Cure! Key! They're all the same. You're the Chi Ro Queen, not the Crow Queen. It's the symbol of the Emperor Constantine. It's on you and it's on the map!' He held it up so the light shone through the pinpricks in the parchment and showed the symbol. 'The pigseys said you were a vessel; you were carrying a story. This is it, or part of it. And suppose . . . suppose the map is meant to show us something more, like the key to the secret.'

'So anyone who wants to find out about the secret needs me and the map.'

'Yes,' Tog said. 'Your rhyme spells out the clue. The clue leads you to the Chi Ro. Does the Chi Ro lead you to the—'

He broke off as heavy footsteps banged on the stairs, coming towards them.

'Get the map out of here!' Jenna said. 'Run!'

'No! I can't leave you.'

'I can't run! I'm injured. My knee!'

'Not after all this!' Tog looked around the room. Hangings flapped as the wind gusted in through the hole in the wall. He noticed the table, delicate as a skeleton.

'Which way does the door open?' he asked.

'Inwards.'

'Pull as many hangings down as possible! Rip them in half!'

While Jenna tugged and tore, Tog smashed up the table and wedged the door with two of the broken legs. He quickly tied two torn halves of hanging together to make a decent length of silk, then tied one end to the remaining table leg. Next he tore a couple of hangings off the wall and draped them over his shoulder like a cloak. The door creaked as someone tried to push it open. A pause, then it thudded as a shoulder hit it.

'That will never hold us,' Jenna said, as Tog pushed the length of silk through the hole in the wall, anchoring it with the table leg laid across the opening.

'Follow me out.'

'We can't go down there!'

'You won't have to.'

She watched him wriggle through the hole, gave him time to get clear, then followed, wincing as her bad knee scraped against the rough stone. As she reached down with her good leg, she hoped Tog had the sense to get out of the way, hoped the wedges would hold the door. The gust of wind and rain caught her and she was soaked as suddenly as if someone had thrown a bucket of cold water over her. She looked down, a cold pit opening in her stomach as she scanned the wall and the muddy ground far below for Tog.

He wasn't there.

When the wet hanging, securely knotted into a loop, hit her on the back of the head, she was so shocked she nearly fell. She looked up and saw Tog looking down over the battlements almost within reach above her. He'd climbed; the knotted hangings dangling down were just a decoy! She slipped the loop under her armpits and allowed herself to be hauled up.

'We've got to time it perfectly,' Tog said. 'They'll find the hole in the wall, look out, see the hangings and run after us. That's when we try and get down.' He was peering over the parapet, trying not to show too much of his head.

The roof of the tower was wet stone; the stairs descended from a rough wooden shelter.

'Now,' Tog said. 'Get on my back.'

Jenna was shocked at how skinny he felt when she wrapped her arms around him. She tried to make herself light as he ventured down a couple of steps. They heard shouts and echoing footsteps, growing fainter, and set off. The door to her room was open but there was no sign of guards. Still, Tog paused and they took the flight slowly, stopping again to listen.

Jenna nearly cried out when the door on the landing opened a crack and Meryel said in a quiet voice said, 'Who is that?'

'It's me,' Jenna said.

'Are you escaping?'

'Trying to.'

'How?'

Jenna felt Tog's back stiffen. 'Do I know you?' he said.

'I . . . I don't know what you mean.'

'Help us,' Jenna said.

'I don't know,' the blind woman said. 'I think—'

'You're Kradok's wife,' Tog said. 'He's a traitor!'

'Whatever he did, he did it to save me. You don't know how he suffered.'

'Jenna. You'll have to get down. I'll have to kill her.'

'NO! She's helped me.'

'But she must help her husband. Don't you see? Look at her. You can read her face. I didn't come through hell to rescue you just for—'

'We can't,' Jenna said.

'We must!' Tog loosened his sword. The blind woman backed away from him.

'No!' Jenna said, and this time she sounded definite, not desperate. 'Leave her. Please.'

'But . . .' Tog said.

So it came to this again. Suddenly he was full of doubt, out of his depth and not knowing what to do.

'It's all right,' Jenna said. 'Meryel, do what you have to

do. Do what you must but remember, we all have friends in unlikely places. Tog, you can't run with me on your back any longer. Let me rest on you and I can make my own way.'

'But she'll betray us!'

'It want make any difference. Trust me! Please.'

They moved down the corridor and into the hall. Tog's feet slid on coins. Outside, torchlight seeped under the big double doors. They heard a guard stamp his feet. Of course it was guarded! Tog turned, suddenly feeling all the tiredness of the climb and his long, long journey. Upstairs he heard shouting and thought it was the blind woman, sounding the alarm. He took a step forwards, then back, then realized that he didn't have the faintest idea where to go or what to do. Jenna held him.

'Why did you do it?' he panted. 'Why didn't you let me kill her?'

'You must trust me,' Jenna said. She turned his face towards hers and kissed him on the lips.

'It's him, isn't? It's Dragon. You gave me a chance and I blew it. Now you know the secret and you're going to give me up.'

'I am not giving you up. And don't give up. Just trust me,' Jenna repeated.

Behind them he heard the big double doors to the hall

crash open. In front, a line of guards poured into the room, silent on their feet but rattling slightly as shield clicked on breastplate. There was an airless hiss as all swords were unsheathed and then the wizard appeared, looking tired and irritable, Kradok scuttling behind him on all fours.

'Let her go or I'll cut your hamstrings,' Merthen said briskly, taking control. 'Guards – put him a deep cell. My lady, Dragon wants you. He is worried that you might have hurt yourself.'

'I'm fine,' Jenna said.

'In spite of the brat's best efforts, I see. Ah, there's your servant. Help her. Come on,' he said to the blind woman who appeared at the top of the stairs. He covered the ground to Tog in two strides, reached into his pocket and extracted the map.

'And this time, we really have exactly what we want,' he said.

Tog was led down steps, a long damp corridor, more steps, then thrown into a long damp room. White mould bloomed between the bricks. Light came from a small barred window high in the end wall.

He hauled himself up by the bars and looked through the window. The grey surface of the lake lapped its sill.

Drained by the rain, the dawn sky was weak blue. On its far side he could see the huge figure of the Greenmother, standing now against a backdrop of a grassy amphitheatre. What did Jenna mean: it's all going to be fine. Fine for her? Had she betrayed him? Should he have trusted her? Could he trust her? It was this again: trust. He was back on the island, trying to do things his own way and failing. He had promised himself that he would listen to her but now she had asked him to do the impossible . . .

Bolts rattled, the door crashed open and a young man swept in.

Tog's hatred of him was instant, instinctive and gut wrenching. He hated his blue eyes, black hair, broad shoulders and the calm decisive way he scanned the room and clearly found it all right. When they rested on Tog, they weren't curious – quite the opposite in fact. They didn't look at his ragged clothes or even search his face. They just latched on to his eyes and stayed there out of a sense of efficiency.

'Right, questions and answers,' he said. 'Who am I? What am I doing? What's going to happen to you? There are a couple of things I want to get straight. I'm not in this for kicks. I'm not random. This is part of a plan and you're caught up in it, all right? I don't expect you to understand but at least listen. I know who you are. I know your story. I know you have a claim – a pretty weak one but a claim – to be high king. The problem is, I don't think you're right for it and I think I am. When I was your age, I was planning this. When my father died, he left me a broken-down old castle, a wizard and a few old soldiers. I've built all this up myself and now I want to move. The country is ready for me. The small kings are ready for leadership but I offer something new. I'm not just one of them with a bigger army. I've got the ideas. I want a united country. I want people to be excited by being British. I want them to feel we have our own traditions and our own religion. But it needs a change. That's what Merthen does. He's a specialist in changing people. He can change men into dogs, children into soldiers, peasants into Seekers and a mob into a state. But if you promise change, you have to deliver and then you've got to keep it coming. I'm not interested in getting old. I'm not interested in losing my fire. I'm interested in keeping going. And that's where the Crow Queen comes in.'

'Jenna doesn't know anything of this,' Tog said. He felt like a twig trying to stand in a flood.

'That's the beauty of it.' The dragon looked out of the little high window and inhaled. 'Do you know what the biggest change any of us will experience is? The first is the change from nothing into life. The second is from life back into nothing. But the big one, the big change is from man into god. And that's what I intend to do.'

'Become a god?'

'Be reborn, again and again and again.' He glanced at Tog and snorted with delight. 'I can read you like a book. He's mad, you're thinking. Off his tree. Doollally. Maybe he's so mad that I can escape while he's talking. Maybe he's so mad that his people will rise up, desert him and follow me. Wrong. Wrong. Wrong. This secret is the big one. Three Roman emperors were after it, a truth that was tortured out of prisoners in the dungeons of the imperial palace hundreds of years ago. Christian prisoners – ah, now I've got your attention – Christian prisoners who knew a secret. Christian prisoners who knew that their Christman left a treasure behind and it was smuggled out of the Holy Land, carried across the sea and the land, carried across the Channel, carried into Britain and carried into the most godforsaken spot of this entire country, where it rains half the time and snows the rest and the people draw pictures and kill anyone who comes close. Pictland. Oh, don't look all grim. I know you've worked this out. You should be laughing. Crying. Grinding your teeth in frustration because you know.'

'And . . . you don't?' Tog said.

'It's a cup. It's filled to brimming with his blood and it

never cools and it runs for ever. I know this and everything but for one little thing. A point on a map – and don't pretend you don't know what a map is. Now, here's the deal. I go to your wife and tell her that if she doesn't tell me, I burn you alive in the Greenmother. And then I come to you and tell you that if you don't tell me, I strip your wife naked in front of the biggest crowd ever assembled in one place, and cut the skin from her body. And when she sees you begin to burn and when you see the knife go into her flesh, I promise, one of you will talk and tell me what you know. So,' and he turned on his elegant heel and strode to the door, 'which one of you is going to talk first? You have a short while to decide, while you try and imagine what being skinned alive will feel like. To the woman you love. Goodbye.'

39

So, knowing you are going to die feels like this, Tog thought. Funny, when I may be the only person in the world who knows how to find the secret of eternal life.

He was standing on tiptoes, watching the sunlight on the lake, thinking he had never seen anything more lovely. Bitterness, blankness, anger and sadness washed over him. He felt weightless.

He remembered his first night with Jenna, the wonder of being with someone who only wanted what you wanted, and you wanted only what they wanted and all the things you wanted were bigger than the world, bigger than the sky, bigger than heaven and earth. He remembered things that counted for nothing at the time but now seemed so precious because they had not mattered: looking at clouds, climbing a tree, stealing cider, sending a skylark up into the sky . . . Everything mattered now. He cried, he scraped his knuckles, he rattled the window bars. Nothing made any difference because nothing would affect the outcome. The door would open, the guards would take him to a boat, they would row him across the lake, they would stuff him into the Greenmother and they would set it alight.

What he didn't guess was how much last things mattered: how the oarsman's knuckles whitened as he pulled the boat through the water, how the sun felt on the back of his head, how a fish sounded as it jumped for an evening fly and how green the grass looked, how blue the sky and how high the little, grey-lined clouds were. Then it hit like an axe that it was not just because this was the last time he was going see or feel or think those things again, but because he wasn't going to be here to think or see or feel anything ever again.

He was about to become Nothing. He was not going to exist any longer than the dragon decreed.

His legs barely worked as they led him from the boat and walked him across the grass to stand in front of a high wooden platform.

High above him on the platform, Tog thought he could see Dragon, Merthen, Kradok and Jenna. He stood behind a wall of guards, attended by three others, one on each side and another behind. They checked his bonds and settled back on to their heels, as soldiers do when they have to stand and wait.

Things are gathering, Tog thought. Last night the sky was so full of heat and rain and clouds it had to explode. Today it is the earth's turn, concentrated here in this bowl of turf. The amphitheatre was ant-black with people. In the flat stage between his arms, he could see jugglers, pigs roasting, people drinking. The sound came to him in waves, sometimes deafening, sometimes faint.

Behind him lay the lake and on the edge of the lake stood the Greenmother, lit up by the setting sun that blazed through her wicker mesh like fire. She was supported by guy ropes that were guarded by Wickwicks. They screamed at anyone who got too close to the ropes, the piles of firewood stacked around the stumpy legs or the miserable prisoners, hobbled like sheep at the market. The crowd, milling around in front of the platform or sitting on the terraces, seemed happy to wait.

Tog's three guards were joined by half a dozen cloaked and hooded armed children. 'Are those Little Swords?' he asked his guard.

The guard, blank and bloody-faced from being scraped clean of hair, grunted. Tog craned forward to try and look under the hoods at the same time as one of the Little

Swords leaned forward and looked at him. He jerked back revolted. The creature had a grey wrinkled face, and he pulled his thin lips back in a smile to reveal rotten, sharpened teeth.

'That's right,' he said. 'I saw you break in.'

'And you're the ones that stole the queen,' Tog said. His defeat seemed total.

'And you're the prat who lost her.'

'Yes.'

'More fool you.'

He was aware that the others were looking at him: a redhead, a snotty girl, a mumbling idiot, a tall one with gangling limbs and a small one who gave him a shy, radiant smile before the tall one cuffed him on the side of the head.

'Why am I standing here?' Tog asked

'So the people can see you. You're an example of what happens when someone stands in the way of Dragon. You'll be last into the Greenmother, so you'll hear everyone else cooking before you do.'

Then the drums started: a series of high, hoarse violent yaps that settled into a throbbing cough. In front of Tog, the other side of the line of soldiers, he could see people dancing, stiff-legged, loose-armed, heads rolling, as they leapt and rolled and kicked the ashes from the fire pits into clouds of dust. They shouted, they screamed, they started to roll towards the cordon of soldiers, were pushed back, rolled forwards. The drums grew louder until the sound was in Tog's body, in his head until he was a drum and the Wickwicks were playing him.

When the drums stopped, the world stopped. Tog felt himself teeter as if he were on the edge of a very high cliff, staring down into the darkness.

Then Dragon started to speak.

'People, my people, Dragon speaks.' His voice was unexpectedly deep and carried into the horseshoe bowl of the amphitheatre. 'Listen to the dragon. The time of seeking is over. The time of finding has begun. The world will be reborn.'

In the front of the crowd, people groaned, picked up his words and repeated them so they sounded like echoes. Speaks . . . seeking . . . finding . . . reborn.

The voice rolled on. 'In the beginning was the dragon and in the dragon was the beginning. He was old when the Druids came to Britain and older when the Romans came to Britain and older still when the Christman came to him in Britain to sit at his feet and learn.

'People, you have followed me and I love you because you know the truth. You know that when you submit to the dragon's will, you are reborn. But the dragon you see before you now is only a shadow of the new dragon of new Britain: the Pendragon, the Great Dragon, who is the beginning of all things.'

He took Jenna by the shoulders and held her in front of him.

'My people, here is the secret that was hidden for hundreds of years. The Romans searched for it but never found it but the dragon has found it. He will make it his and he will make it yours. In the light of the Greenmother he will make it yours. Fill the Greenmother!'

Between the snaps of a single drum, Tog heard the prisoners begin to wail quietly as they were marched forwards. He looked upwards. Merthen was looking down at him, one eyebrow raised quizzically. Then it was his turn.

'NO!' He heard Jenna scream. 'You promised! Not Tog!'

This isn't happening to me, he thought, as the Little Swords surrounded him and led him away. He couldn't see the top of the platform so he couldn't say goodbye to Jenna. He couldn't see the crowds gathered on the amphitheatre's terrace. All he could see was the vast shape of the Greenmother, the ladder propped up against her, and the line of prisoners being beaten into it.

'They're drugged. You're not,' the Little Sword with the pointed teeth whispered. 'Keep sharp.'

The dazed prisoners were being shoved into the Greenmother's belly as fast as they reached the top of the ladder. Soon their faces stared out – sideways, upside down, pressed up against the lattice of branches, one even bursting through, a thin face with a ragged beard.

'You now.'

Tog was at the foot of the ladder. He put his hand on the rung, felt the rough lashings. Took a step.

''Ere, brother. I know you.'

The voice came from the press of faces staring out of the Greenmother's belly. Tog recognized the wrinkled face of Nm the boatman, who had carried them for the first part of their journey. He was grinning idiotically.

'You remember me now?' he bawled against the clattering drums. 'You was in my boat before it got wrecked. Thought I recognized you, then I thought I must be dreaming. I was picked up and sold upriver. How about you? What? Don't be proud, matey. What d'you make of this lark? Bit of a pickle, eh?'

Tog didn't know what to say so he climbed, his bound hands gripping the rungs. The drums rolled louder and Nm bellowed, 'Tell you what, mate, I saw another of your friends earlier, hanging around having a good look at us poor prisoners, and another all dressed up as a soldier. You've got friends all over.'

The drums stopped. Nm's voice rang through the silence. From the platform the wizard called out, 'Get him in! Burn him!'

The Greenmother creaked as the captives shifted. Beyond the guards, Tog saw a stretcher held high so the sick person could see the burning. A Little Sword at the foot of the ladder jerked his weapon at Tog. Someone lit the brushwood at the Greenmother's feet and, impossibly quickly, the flames leapt up its leg.

Tog saw the stretcher-bearers lift the patient up higher and tilt him over the heads of the guards. He landed, drew a sword and suddenly there was a pocket of violence as he attacked the guards from behind, just as his companions attacked from the front.

Below him the Little Sword was beckoning him, his mouth working, repeating one word: jump.

JUMP! Tog leapt forward, away from the ladder, jarring his shoulder as he fell. Seconds later Little Sword was on him sawing through his bonds.

'Get up to the platform,' he hissed. 'We'll cover you.' When Tog hesitated he hissed more urgently, 'We're her bodyguard! Who do you think drew the guards from you when you were breaking into the tower?'

Tog shook the blood back into his hands. 'You're …'

'With you. Have this.'

He handed Tog a sword and pushed him towards the platform steps. The guard thrust downwards with a spear but he knocked it to one side, then grabbed it so the guard toppled forward and past him down the stairs.

'PEOPLE! SEEKERS!' Tog could just hear the dragon's voice above the hissing roar of the flames. They flared up with horrible speed, moving from the brushwood to the thicker branches.

Smoke billowed across the lake. The screams from the prisoners inside rose to a horrid babble. Tog had only one thought: to get to Jenna, but now the choking smoke was blowing across the platform so thickly he could hardly see. He crawled up the last few steps on his hands and knees when the smoke parted. In that instant, Tog saw Merthen on his back and Kradok tearing at his throat with bared teeth. Jenna was clawing at the dragon's mask, the dragon knocking her away, punching her so hard she was lifted off her feet.

'Leave her!' Tog's voice carried over the roar of the flames and the dragon froze, then spun round, in a swirl of green. His black eyes glittered through his mask, blinked. Smoke curtained them from the crowd. Jenna lay still.

'Fight me,' Tog said.

The dragon attacked. He was stronger than Tog, bigger than Tog, faster and better balanced than Tog. Unlike Tog he had not been beaten, imprisoned, half starved. He had not survived an iron mine, rowed halfway through the country and climbed a tower.

I hope Jenna has the sense to wake up and run away, Tog thought. I've got the strength for one good move, maybe two. No more.

The dragon's first thrust was a feint. Tog ignored it and was ready for the slashing stoke that followed. He swayed back, just got his sword up in time, felt the blade jar agonizingly and remembered that most fights were over in seconds. Another slashing strike. He jumped back and cut at the dragon, who swatted his blade away with contempt and in the same fluid movement went for Tog's head.

He's elegant, Tog thought, and had a proper teacher. Good.

He made two clearly signalled stabs in the dragon's general direction, and as he felt his opponent's confidence swell, threw himself face down, stabbed at the booted foot, heard the dragon shout, rolled away, felt the wood shake as his enemy's sword slammed into the wood. He got to his feet in front of Jenna, his back to the crowd, facing the horror of the burning Greenmother. Off to one side, another horror. The wizard, rolling from side to side and clutching his throat, blood pumping from his fingers. He thought he heard Jenna groan.

Ignore her. Don't split your focus, Tog thought. He heard a strange, hollow snap and something long and dark whipped past him. The Greenmother lurched as one her guy ropes parted. Tog felt the dragon's attention move from him for a split second, and attacked in earnest.

He got lucky and managed to slice his enemy's sword arm and then went mad, as he had always been told he must not, except this time it worked. The dragon made one lunge and Tog sliced down, then stabbed at his belly, then his leg, his belly again, three sharp stabs with the little blade. He didn't feel the cut on his own arm, just stepped forward and hacked and cut and stabbed until he felt a hand on his arm and realized it was Jenna, half holding him, half holding herself up, the bruise on her face already showing.

The dragon lay at his feet. 'I've killed him,' he said.

'Many times over,' Jenna answered.

Tog felt stupid, heavy-armed and breathless. He coughed and looked at the fire. The Greenmother had fallen backwards into the shallows of the lake and split open. Heat made the sky shimmer as the flames ate the smoke and Tog ran to the edge of the platform.

Kai, Allanza and Ordan, along with the Little Swords

who had escorted him to the Greenmother, had formed a ring around the steps to the platform and were holding back the guards pressing in on them.

'I've got to go down and fight,' Tog gasped.

Jenna coughed, grabbed him and pulled him down.

'Dragon,' she said, and coughed again.

'He's dead.' Tog felt a spurt of irritation. She'd seen it. To reassure her at such a time was too much.

'Reborn,' Jenna gasped. 'Reborn!'

'No, that's what he wanted.'

'You. Dragon. Reborn.'

'Me? But I'm not—'

'The Chi Ro is about rebirth. This is the start.'

'But—'

'No choice. Look!'

She pointed down to the foot of the platform. She was right. It would take seconds for the guards to finish off his friends.

Dragon. Rebirth. Do it!

He tore the silver mask off the dragon's head. Jenna wrestled the body over and stripped off the heavy green cloak. As Tog put the mask on, the world seemed a different place. More distant. The heavy cloak fell over his shoulders and a sort of cold heat that ran up his spine. Dragon's strength.

'I'm ready,' he said. 'I'm ready.'

He took two steps up to the edge of the platform and raised his arms. Someone cried out, 'The dragon!'

A sudden flare from the bonfire and he shook his robe.

'The old world is fallen!' Tog shouted. 'The Pendragon is reborn!'

Now he heard a cheer grow at his feet and it spread like fire in dry grass and was answered by a louder cheer from the people gathered in the amphitheatre. But it wasn't enough, he thought. I've got to give more.

'What's the sign?' a voice called out.

The crowd picked up the word. 'A sign, a sign,' it shouted.

Tog raised his arms again. Suddenly he felt exhausted. A sign. What possible sign could he offer them? He looked beyond the crowd and saw that the rim of the amphitheatre was spiked with spears that had not been there before. Spears and soldiers.

So that was it. He closed his eyes, gathered the last of his strength and tore off the mask.

'This the sign!' he shouted. 'This is the sign and this is the truth! Dragon is a man. He has been reborn as a man!'

He let the green robe drop from his shoulders and stood, bedraggled, small and human but more alive than he had ever felt before. 'This the truth! This is the secret. The age of the dragon is over. You do not have to worship him. Go from here, go east and west and south and north and carry with you the knowledge of life. Be people. Be alive. Be free!'

And this time he did hear a cheer. But it did not come from the people standing in the amphitheatre but from the army ranged above it as its soldiers started to pour down the slopes, scattering the Seekers. He let the mask drop from his hand. Dimly registered Jenna standing by him, her arm firmly linked through.

'This is it then,' he said. 'We tried. At least we stopped the dragon.'

'That's up to the dragon,' Jenna said. 'Can't you hear what the army's shouting?'

Tog wrenched his eyes away from her. The soldiers massing against the platform were putting their weapons down. The army that was streaming down the grassed slope of the amphitheatre now stopped its onward surge and all soldiers were facing him with swords and spears raised, and some were roaring ARTOGNU and some were roaring DRAGON.

'Your army,' Jenna said. 'We're saved.'

'Saved?'

'Saved.'

And with his bloody sword raised, Tog roared his names back at his army.

40

Chi Ro: Luck, sacrifice

A month after midsummer, a traveller stood on a dusty hillside outside the ruined Roman spa town of Hot Baths and watched an army approach down the West Way. It smoked like a dragon, he noted, and within the smoke, he caught the glint of sunlight on metal.

His name was Melanius, he came from Constantinople but right now he was not missing his own home one bit. Next to him his bodyguard, a thuggish Englishman called Borth, was flossing his teeth with a grass stem. Borth had all the usual English vices – beer, sloth, arguing and telling tall stories – but Melanius liked to think he had civilized him to an extent. Borth now could apply himself to a task for more than half an hour, had learned to think logically and tolerated most people who didn't actually want to kill him.

'You think the high king will be changed?' Borth said. 'Now he's killed the dragon?'

'We still don't know which dragon the high king is,' Melanius said.

'It's Tog,' Borth said.

'We can't know that,' Melanius said.

'Yes, we can,' Borth said. 'And I do. The story. Remember?'

'That rambling account told to us by a drunken maniac? I remember. But may I remind you that it was, and shall remain, A STORY.'

'You weren't listening properly,' Borth said. 'I'll run over what you call the salient points. One: he said there are a couple of dragons, one bad and one good – well, that's obviously Tog and the other guy.

'Two: he said the bad dragon sends fairies to steal the good dragon's wife and take her back to his enchanted castle under a lake. That sounds true enough, especially the bit about the enchanted castle.

'Three: the good dragon follows him and on the journey is drowned, buried alive and burned, and only escapes by turning himself into a god. I've heard madder stories in my time, so we can accept that.

'Four: when the good dragon gets close to the bad dragon's castle, he's caught by the dragon's wizard and only rescued by a female centaur, who still pines for him, and guides him to the lake with the enchanted castle in it. Again, no problems. Tog's a good-looking boy and any centaur would go for him.

'Five: he dives into the lake to fight the bad dragon for his wife but there's a terrible fight, so terrible that both dragons are killed and his poor wife is blinded, but a crow who's flying past hears her crying (that's not convincing: Jenna would never cry) and asks her what the matter is. When she tells him, the crow says, "I can grant one of two wishes. Either I tell you which one of these two dragons is your poor husband, or I bring you a magic cup. All you have to do is brush the dragon's lips with it and it will come back to life. But, because both dragons look the same, you won't know which one you're saving until he's reborn. So what are you going to do?"

'Bring me the cup, the wife says. So the crow flies off to the land of the Picture People, brings the cup back and hands it to the queen, but instead of just bringing one dragon back to life, she brings them both back to life and asks them, "Which of you is the real dragon and my husband?" Of course they both say, "I am." Then she says, "Unless you tell me the truth, I'm going to kill myself.

Now, which of you is the real dragon and my husband?" and this time one of them says, "I am," and the other says, "He is." So she kills the one that says "I am" because he obviously didn't care whether she lived or died but the one who said "He is" obviously did. And she was right and she and the good dragon—'

'But suppose the one that said "he is" wasn't the queen's husband, just really clever, and the one that said "I am" wasn't too clever but very honest,' Melanius interrupted.

'Because that's not the way stories work,' Borth said.

'But this isn't meant to be a story, you English dunderhead!' Melanius exploded. 'We're trying to work out if the dragon who is leading that army is Tog or not.'

'It's Tog. It's just the way his mind would work, to think of Jenna first. Only a twisted mind like yours would think up the other version.'

'I give up,' Melanius said. 'We'll just have to watch and wait.'

For two weeks now, Melanius had been sifting river stories. He had bought more jugs of wine than he could count as word got round the docks that a mad foreigner with more money than sense was willing to pay you to get drunk and make up stupid stories. For his part, Melanius discounted most of the rubbish he was told: every boatman had rowed the high king to hell and back, been given gold, been cured of every form of sickness, been promised untold riches and so could he please have another pitcher of wine.

Melanius knew one thing: if Tog had been saved, it was by a combination of his courage and the common sense of soldiers. Just the other day a traveller had claimed that the two armies – the dragon's and Tog's – had met at High Cross, where the two great Roman roads met, and come to a sensible, soldierly arrangement. Stability and power were everything, so rather than fight each other, they would wait to see what happened at the Midsummer Festival and whatever the outcome, they would follow the winner. A king was a king. The dragon was the dragon. They were just soldiers and should throw combined weight behind the winner to make sure the victory lasted and they had expended as little energy as possible.

But now Melanius noticed that people were gathering by the roadside below them and the dry summer ground was beginning to tremble under the weight of the advancing army. He and Borth set off down the hillside as children were hoicked on to shoulders and flowers were hastily picked: chamomile and vetch; buttercups, daisies, clover and willowherb.

First came a line of marching soldiers, then two mounted soldiers, then a solitary figure, dressed in a green robe, wearing a silver mask.

Melanius stepped off the verge, Borth following. The figure glanced down at him and Melanius realized something that killed the elegant Latin speech he had been rehearsing for days. The dragon wasn't Tog but a fully grown man, and a big man at that, who dipped the blank, glittering mask at Melanius and then rode on.

What had happened? What had gone wrong? In spite of everything he had told Borth, he was certain Tog had won and was on his way south. He knew it in his bones . . .

A tap on the shoulder. He shook his head.

Another, more insistent.

'Not now, Borth,' he snapped.

'It's not Borth.'

He turned. A young man stood in front of him, whippet thin, burned dark by the sun, and recovering from a black eye.

'What it is?' he snapped, then a huge rush of hope engulfed him. 'Tog? Is it? It is. Borth! Look! It is!'

He fell to his knees.

'It is, and get up, please. Please.' Tog held out a hand to help the older man to his feet. Melanius held on to it, then folded Tog in a hug, pushed him away, held him again. 'But . . . I don't understand.' He glanced at the column of soldiers again and the hunched, green-cloaked, receding back. 'The dragon?'

'That's Ordan, the bard,' Tog said. 'We take turns. It was driving me mad just sitting up there all day long having flowers chucked at me. The mask can be useful. No one knows who's behind it.'

'But you are the high king? The real dragon?'

'So far,' Tog said.

'You've grown. And you've changed. But the queen? Where is the queen?' Melanius's quick eyes darted around. 'Kai, Allanza, delighted to see them but—'

'With us but not with us,' Tog said. 'Driving me mad. She's got a mission.'

'A mission?'

'Wait. Admire my enormous army. She'll be along in a second.'

Melanius watched soldiers, soldiers, more soldiers, carts, carts, more soldiers and finally, a sort of desperate, slouching, jaunty rabble of children. They were surrounded by guards and although they were unarmed, they looked strangely lethal. As Melanius watched, one tripped up the child in front of it and started a fight. A guard stepped in, snapping a knotted rope. All the other children jeered and walked on, sharp eyes staring out of faces pancaked in dust, scabs, snot and a lot of spitting.

'Who are they?' he asked.

'The Little Swords – child soldiers. Jenna wants to save

them; everyone else wants them dead. The thing is, she has actually managed to change some of them and that's given her hope. Here she comes.'

Melanius peered through the dust and at last saw the queen on horseback. She had wound a scarf around her mouth, and was surrounded by half a dozen or so children who were marching in some sort of order around her horse. A brown cat trotted alongside and, as he watched, one of the children picked it up and handed it to Jenna.

'The call themselves The Queen's Own Men,' Tog said.

'And they're safe?'

'Just about. Look, we've got to stop for the night soon. You will join us, won't you?'

'For the night?'

'I mean properly. Again. More properly than before, even.'

'Gladly,' Melanius said. 'I mean, with every scrap of gladness that is in my heart.'

'And you probably want to hear all about the map as well.'

They stopped above a river on a bank of thick, lush grass. Horses drank, soldiers washed, cooks cooked, the sun set.

'This is the problem,' Tog said. 'The Little Swords were trained to do the most terrible things from an early age.

They were changed from children into killers, and everything they did they did for the dragon. It didn't matter what: if he told them to do it, it was good. Obviously, looking at it one way, they deserve to die. Look at it another, it wasn't their fault.'

'Mmmph,' Melanius said.

'Train them properly,' Borth said. 'Turn them into real soldiers.'

'They have nightmares,' Jenna said. 'Terrible nightmares. They've done all the killing they can stand.'

'So you're saying they're broken,' Borth said. 'Because in my experience, there's not much you can do with broken—'

'I have nightmares but they're getting better,' Tog said quickly and Jenna shot him a grateful look.

No one spoke for a while, just listened to the crackle of the fire and the beehive murmur of the camp. Melanius pressed his hand to the ground, flicked the dew off it and said, 'To change the subject, I want to know about this map. Ordan, in all your travels, did you ever hear of anything like it?'

Tog looked around. Ordan had been sitting close to the circle the friends had made, but not quite in it.

'Ah, the map. It is a wonder,' he said. 'A wonder of the world.'

'And the dragon really thought it pointed to where the last of the Christman's blood was hidden and that would allow him to be reborn?'

'He seemed pretty certain.'

'And can someone tell me where?'

There was a general shuffling in the twilight. 'Not exactly,' Tog said. 'We haven't really looked at it again.'

'The secret of eternal life, the promise of rebirth and you haven't looked at it again?' Melanius's voice rose in exasperation.

Ordan cleared his throat. 'Perhaps you forget the . . . associations. The king was almost killed . . . and the queen . . . there was talk of . . .' His words were mild but his voice was unexpectedly steely.

'Skinning me alive,' Jenna said with a certain relish. 'In public.'

'I beg your pardon. I beg everyone's pardon,' Melanius said.

'And it's almost certainly just a scam,' Kai said.

'But we can explain how it works,' Tog said. 'Or perhaps Ordan should. He put it all together for us.'

Ordan made a modest murmur. 'My lord is too kind . . .'

'Get on with it,' Kai said. 'As far as I'm concerned, you're on probation. You came to Britain to steal our secret. Be grateful the king doesn't flog you. He's a member of a secret society,' he explained to Melanius. 'Wandering minstrels. No loyalty to anyone except their order.'

'Not so,' Ordan said. 'There are a few men, a very few in this world, who reveal truth through their actions, and our loyalty to them is the greatest. But enough of the secrets of my order, and on with the story. As far as I have been able to tell, there have always been stories connecting the Christman with Britain, unlikely as it seems. The first legend is that he was brought here by his godfather, Yusuf of Arimathea, a trader in precious metals. The Christman and his godfather landed in Cornwall and made their way to the island, where miracles occurred. The first was when the Christman met a dying man and cured him with the waters of a magical spring he created. When the Christman died, the spring turned the colour of his blood. The second story concerned the blackthorn staff of this Yusuf, which he stuck in the ground one evening. Returning the next day to retrieve it, he found it had turned back overnight into blackthorn tree. From death to life, you see. From death to life.

'The Romans killed the Christman, of course, and he too came back to life. Soon after, rumours started spreading that his followers had saved his blood in a cup, and that this blood had magical properties. Anyone who drank from it would be transformed but there was a catch: this would happen only to those who truly believed it would work. Even with this provision, such a cup was a treasure without price, the greatest treasure the world had ever known, and before long the Romans, the very men who had executed the Christman, started looking for it. They sent spies east and west and south and north, and before too long they came back with stories about the Christman's visit to Britain and more than that, there were rumours that his followers had brought the cup here, after the Christman's death, and hidden it.'

Kai said, 'Seems a lot for a bard to know.'

'Bards travel. Bards talk to other bards. More importantly, bards listen,' Melanius said with feeling.

'Like spies?' Kai asked, sounding innocent.

Melanius acknowledged the remark with a quick smile and Ordan continued. 'Rome now wanted the cup, but how to find it? Any normal race would have sent philosophers or lunatics or mystics on the quest. Rome sent her legions. First Claudius gained a foothold in Britain and then the armies spread north. Hadrian built his wall, Antoninus built another and lastly young Constantine, then just an ambitious general, sent his armies into the land of the Picts on his quest. Some say he found it and was so impressed that he became a Christian there and then and within a few years had converted the whole of the Roman Empire. Others say that the treasure had already gone and the Emperor sent his mother to the Holy Land to see if it had been returned to its place of origin. The truth is, we don't know. All we do know for certain is that the Picture People were made guardians of the treasure. They had the foresight to record the secret but then forgot what they had done and all that remained was a nonsense rhyme, some marks on a back and an old map that mouldered in a chest.'

'A rhyme? Marks on a back?' Melanius asked.

'The secret was carried by the women of the Picture People with marks, taken from the parchment and inked into the Crow Queen's back. Originally the bearer of the secret was called the Chi Ro Queen. Then this was corrupted to the Crow Queen and half remembered in sayings, such as "the queen is the cure", corrupted to "the queen is the key".'

'And how did the Emperor's name come to be on the parchment?' Melanius asked.

'Perhaps it was a Pictish document the Romans put their map on to or a Roman document the Picture People decorated with their marks. I think it was a Roman map that Constantine left with the Picture People – left it with them to stop other Romans finding it. There is much still to learn and I suspect it will be not learned through force. There is a thread that links the legend of the Old King, the Little Dancing Man, the Christman and maybe others in the far corners of the world, and that thread is sacrifice. The dragon did not understand this, but you, my lord,' here he nodded to Tog, 'I thought you might understand it all too well. That is why I refused to tell you what I knew that night in the forest when the pigseys came to visit.'

'You thought I might sacrifice myself?'

'Whether you sacrifice yourself or not is your choice but I did not want you to be influenced by what I knew. Would you have jumped from the Greenmother if you thought you were meant to be a sacrifice? Would you have fought like a king and killed the old dragon if you believed it was your destiny to die?'

'But the old dragon's the sacrifice now,' Tog said. 'Does that mean he's . . . like the Old King and the Christman? I can just imagine what people are saying: once there was a great king who ruled a great land in the very heart of the country. People flocked to him from miles around: the rich and the poor, the sick and lame and he promised all of them the chance of rebirth, or hope, of glory. But others were jealous and plotted against him … and so on.'

'Then we must remember and we must tell a better story so no one forgets the truth of the heartless dark that spread out from the dragon like a bloodstain.'

Melanius cleared his throat. 'All well and good,' he said, 'but back to the matter in hand. Two questions remain: where is this treasure hidden and what are you going to do about it?'

There was a pause.

'This is what we know,' Tog said. 'On the map, there are all these symbols. If you draw lines between them in the right order, you make an invisible Chi Ro. We think that tells you where the cup is – maybe where the lines meet in the middle; maybe in the loop of the Ro.'

'It would help if I could see it,' Melanius said.

'Perhaps now is the time,' Tog answered. 'Jenna's looking after it. Where is she? She was here just a minute ago.' He checked the circle, then outside it. 'Has anyone seen the queen?' he asked. 'HAS ANYONE SEEN THE QUEEN?'

Tog's panic was studiously ignored as everyone got up to look for the queen with great, unnatural calmness. They found her after a short while. She said she had not felt she could add much to the conversation and so had gone to find the cat. Tog, deliriously happy that she had not been kidnapped, missed the sarcastic edge to her voice. To be fair, when Jenna saw the state he was in, she said she was sorry, led him to their tent, took him in her arms and murmured, 'I'm here, I'm here' in his ear until he stopped trembling.

Later that night he sat bolt upright in bed and said, 'After all that, I never showed Melanius the map. I wonder if he's still up.'

He stood. The tent was as big as a house and was just one of the many wonderful things they had taken from the dragon's castle. It even had a flap in the roof so you could lie on your back and look at the sky.

This is what Jenna was doing and the stars were glittering in her eyes.

'I said—'

'I know what you said, my lord.'

At last Tog realized something was wrong. 'What is it?' he said. 'What have I done?'

'Who does the map belong to?' Jenna asked.

'What?'

'Who does the map belong to? Me? Not me? Who?'

'Well, you in one sense. In another, when you take into account everyone who's ever thought about it, who's got an interest in it, there are quite a lot of people . . .'

'How many? Two? Five? Five thousand?'

'Well, um. You. Me, I hope. Melanius could help us find out more, I'm sure, with his contacts.'

'And Kai, and Allanza and Ordan?'

'I suppose so.'

'And General Mailgwin?'

'I suppose it has security implications.'

'Why stop there?'

'If you're going to be sarcastic—'

'I'm not. I'm being . . . the opposite. If Mailgwin, why not someone else? What does he want from it?'

Tog had a vivid memory of Talar the horsewoman saying, 'It's all about power. The map is all about power.'

'Power?' he asked.

'Too much power for one man. Much too much for twenty. And for a whole country? Disastrous.'

'If they're bad, like the dragon,' Tog said. 'But suppose he's good.'

'Meaning you? If bad people can become good, then good people can become bad.'

Tog blinked and said nothing.

'Why do you think the Crow Queen mystery was entrusted to women?' Jenna pressed him.

Tog opened his mouth, then closed it guiltily.

'What were you going to say?'

'It was rude.'

'Tell me!'

'I was going to say, the secret was told to women because

they'd forget it but that's just soldier talk. I'm sorry.'

'No, no. Soldiers talk sense.'

'You're better than any of them and know more . . .'

'You're missing the point. You were right. The secret was given to the women *because* they would forget about it. Because they . . . I don't like to generalize . . . but because we're perhaps more inclined to deal with what's in front of us, rather than kill half the world to find the secret of eternal life. Which is what the Romans would have done. No man could keep that secret.'

'You think men are so bad that—'

'No, I think some of them deserve a second chance.'

'Thanks.'

'Not you. You're still on your first. Or last. It doesn't matter. You have lots of chances.'

Tog got out of bed and walked around the tent once, twice, three times.

'Some of them deserve a second chance,' he began, then his mouth gaped, as it always did when he understood something. 'The cat. You said you'd gone to find it. Not look for it, find it. So where is it? And the map.' He began to rummage through the chest they kept it in. 'It was here. That means you must have taken it earlier, when we were talking about it. You left us and . . . what? You hid it?'

Outside, there was a clatter of a sword hilt on a shield, the only way to knock at a tent's door.

'Please let them go,' Jenna said desperately, putting a finger across Tog's lips.

'Let them go? Who?' The banging was more insistent now. 'WAIT!' he shouted at the tent door.

'Trust me,' Jenna said. 'It's the last part of the story and it's my story. Please.'

Kai burst in looking flushed. 'Disaster!' he said. 'Traitors in the camp! All the Little Swords have escaped. I've roused the cavalry, got people searching but they'll be a distance away. God knows when they slipped out. They must have had help. I'm sorry to say it's looking like the queen's bodyguard were behind it. They've gone as well.'

'They didn't kill anyone?'

'That's the least of your problems. No disrespect, Jenna, but you were asking for trouble.' He paused. 'Well?'

Tog took a deep breath, Jenna's words still fresh in his mind: *Please let them go. It's the last part of the story and it's my story. Please.*

He thought of the pigsey telling him that Jenna could only work out her story with the dragon. Well, he was the dragon now.

'Tell the cavalry to stand down,' he said.

'But they're monsters,' Kai said. 'They'll tear the

countryside apart. They eat babies raw. They boil old people. They—'

'They're kids,' Tog said. 'They were doing what they were told to do. Now they've got a different task.'

Kai screwed up his face and mouthed the word 'what' disbelievingly.

Tog went to stand by Jenna. She had lain back down and he knew she was waiting for him to say the right thing.

Her ideas, his decision. Not a bad way of doing business.

He looked up at the night sky, thick with stars because the moon was down, and thought the simplest thought: that he would go to bed and wake up and there would be a new day and if he chose, he could be reborn into it because, really, if you had friends, food, shelter and love, you were free to do what you wanted. On the other hand, if you were in darkness like the Little Swords, you were trapped and needed help to escape.

'I . . . I sent them on a mission with the queen's blessing,' he said. 'I've told them to look for the Christman's cup – well, it was Jenna's idea really, but they're going after this . . . thing, whatever it is, and I believe, I believe they're going to be all the better for looking for it.'

'I don't believe it,' Kai said. 'They've got the map,

haven't they? They've got the bloody map. Have you any idea what that's worth? It's like the sacred sword all over again. You chucked that away and now the map! Are you mad or out to deliberately mess things up again?'

'The map is either Jenna's or everyone's,' Tog answered. 'I don't know where it's going to lead them. I just hope they'll end up in a better place. It'll be like being reborn.'

'You hope?'

Tog felt Jenna's eyes swivel towards him.

'Hope is a good thing,' he said.

And he saw Jenna smile and suddenly, quite suddenly, he saw that stories about the Christman and his cup and his uncle and the spring and the thornbush and the Romans were fine, but only as far as they went.

Right now, in the flash of Jenna's smile, his world was remade and he felt reborn. And that seemed good enough to him.

Acknowledgements

Jenna's tattoos were inspired by the wonderful book *Tattooed Mountain Women and Spoon Boxes of Daghestan* by Robert Chenciner, Gabib Ismailov and Magomedkhan Magomed Khanov (Bennet and Bloom, 2006).

In no way should my liberal interpretation of their meaning be confused with their scholarly, pioneering research.